The Wishing Stone

Madelaine & Mocha

Vivian Munnoch

This book is a work of fiction. Names, characters, places, and events are products of the author's imagination or are used fictitiously. Any resemblance to actual events, locales, or persons, living or dead, is entirely coincidental.

Front cover photo by Sereja Ris on Unsplash
Back cover photo by Rosie Fraser on Unsplash

Discover other titles
by Vivian Munnoch:

<u>The Latchkey Kids Series:</u>
The Latchkey Kids

The Latchkey Kids 2:
The Disappearance of
Willie Gordon

<u>The Wishing Stone Series:</u>
Madelaine & Mocha

My life is over.
I might as well just die right now.
Disappear.
Vanish.

Table of Contents

1   Mocha Runs Away

My life is over. I might as well die right now. Disappear. Vanish. I lost the only thing in the world that matters and I have no one to blame but myself. She is probably lying dead and torn apart somewhere in the forest right now, alone in the darkness. Is she suffering? In pain? Is she scared? Is she already dead? These are the thoughts tearing Madelaine apart as she moves through the darkness.

What started as a regular boring, no electronics and thank you very much for ruining my life, camping trip is about to change Madelaine and her life forever.

A pair of flashlights bob in the dark, shining their lights on the ground of a narrow dirt trail in a depressing dance that does not do enough to light the night. Two footsteps, one lighter the other heaver, plod along behind the dancing lights. Trees pressing in on the path block out most of the world.

The stillness of the night looms all around, filled with the haunting night noises of the forest. The moon and stars above give little light in the darkness.

Madelaine is devastated. Her little dog Mocha is gone.

"I should have tied her up."

She looks up at the dark sky. It is only slightly less black than the trees and bushes surrounding them. She feels like the darkness is pressing in, trying to swallow up the world.

The figure walking next to her in the darkness is taller, thicker, and more solid than her slight frame. His presence is a beacon of safety in the dark night. He is her dad.

"Stop beating yourself up about it." Clive moves closer to her and puts an arm around her shoulders, giving her a small comforting squeeze.

Madelaine pushes down the urge to push him off. Usually she doesn't like anyone to touch her at all. Not even the casual familiar contact of her family. It makes her feel hemmed in, overcrowded, caged by their proximity.

"Those few times I ever had to tie her up, Mocha hated it," she thinks hollowly. "She cried and yelped and lunged at the end of the rope. She kept whimpering and trying to follow me. She would spin and get herself all tangled up, then thrash around on the ground yelping and crying as if the touch of the rope was somehow hurting her."

Madelaine is filled with a fresh wave of the same guilt she felt then; guilt over tying Mocha up and guilt for not doing it this time.

"It's my fault Mocha is lost." She swallows, still keeping her thoughts to herself.

It usually is never necessary. The dog follows her everywhere, never straying far.

"To make things worse, we are camping in a strange place far from home. Mocha is lost somewhere in the forest and it's dark out. Stupid camping! I never even wanted to go camping. I hate camping."

Madelaine glances at her father as if worried he might have heard her thoughts. Her mind goes on, running through the list of dangers once more.

"There are bears, wolves, coyotes, and all kinds of other dangerous wild animals in the forest. There could be deep holes Mocha could have fallen into, too deep for her to get out of. Cars come and go from the campground and on the highway. She could have been run over. What if someone stole her? I'm never going to see my Mocha again."

The rush of loneliness and despair fills Madelaine like a hollow sickness. Alternating waves of loss and remorse pulse through her like waves of nausea.

Most of the time Madelaine feels like Mocha is her only friend. She always felt nervous in large groups and has trouble making friends at school. Mostly the other kids don't want to hang around with her because they are busy with their other friends. They all have their little groups and she isn't in any of them. She is always the outsider looking in and lonely.

"Mocha, you are my only real friend," she thinks miserably. "Now you are gone, maybe forever, and it's my fault. I should have tied you up like Mom told me to."

"Oh Mocha," Madelaine whimpers under her breath in despair, afraid for the little dog. The desolation and exhaustion is weighing her body down, pulling it to the ground with its great weight as though trying to stop her searching.

Hearing her whimper, Clive tightens his arm around her shoulder, trying to give her some comfort.

"I am so tired," Madelaine thinks. "I just want to stop, to give up looking for Mocha and quit, to lie down and rest. It feels so hopeless. We will never find Mocha in the dark."

"Don't you dare give up on her, Madelaine," she chastises herself silently. "Mocha would never give up on you, so you do not give up on her. Got it?"

She nods to herself, pushing on with her resolve to find Mocha before anything bad happens to the little dog.

"What if something bad already happened to her?"

The doubt creeps back in like an insidious claw, reaching and grasping, about to snatch Mocha away from her forever.

The thought of little Mocha coming face to face with a bear, wolf, or coyote fills Madelaine with an icy cold dread. She can almost feel the sharp teeth ripping through her own flesh, the bear claws tearing at her and leaving large ugly bloody gashes behind.

She swallows hard, trying to swallow the lump of tears pushing up her throat.

"Come on Madelaine," she tells herself, "you can do this. Be strong for Mocha."

Chilled by her thoughts and fears, she pulls her jacket tighter around her and keeps plodding on through the dark, the light of her flashlight wobbling on the ground ahead of her leading the way. The heavier footsteps of her father beside her give her little comfort.

She keeps going despite the feelings of hopelessness and the urge to give up. It feels like they have been walking and calling forever, looking for Mocha. Her throat is sore and her voice hoarse.

Madelaine hears a sound and pauses, swinging the flashlight around to see.

"What is it?" Clive asks.

"I heard something."

Clive shines his light up and down the path. The light splashes through the darkness, pushing it away momentarily and moving on. The trees and bushes seem to dance away from the light, pressing in after it's gone, the path narrowing again with the returning darkness.

Madelaine has the image suddenly of the forest closing together, swallowing up both them and the path cutting through the trees.

Clive listens to the forest. He shines his light through the trees surrounding them.

The night is silent except for the sound of the breeze in the trees. Even the nocturnal forest animals are quiet, as if they too heard it and are listening.

"Mocha!" he calls, cupping his hands to his mouth in an effort to make the sound carry further. He moves his flashlight beam steadily, sweeping a path of light through the trees. "Mocha! Here girl!"

He stops calling and listens for the sound of the dog, for any sound.

They are met with silence.

"Probably just a raccoon," he says, referring to whatever it is Madelaine thought she heard. He didn't hear anything. "Let's keep going."

They move on, their flashlights cutting through the dark ahead, the darkness closing in again behind them.

Mocha is hiding in the bushes. She shivers and whimpers quietly. She isn't cold, she is afraid. Her nose twitches as she sniffs the air.

It is still there, the smell that sent her running and hiding. It is an earthy smell, like old compost, but polluted and older than ancient bones. It is bad in the way a bear smells bad.

It is the smell of something dangerous.

She looks up.

Lights flicker through the canopy of leaves in the dark. A cloud passing allows the moon and stars to be briefly seen where the looming trees allow a view of the sky before they close again, casting the night back into deeper darkness.

Two beams of light flash and bob close to the ground in the darkness, swinging and bobbing as people walk with flashlights.

The little dog huddles beneath the thick bushes, watching the lights through the leaves. She can smell them. They are calling her name.

They are her family.

"Mocha! Mochaaa! Here girl!"

Mocha wants to go to them so badly. She does not want to be alone in the dark forest, but something holds her back. Fear of what is out there, whatever has that evil smell, keeps her in her hiding spot.

The dog's tail thumps the ground with her pleasure at having her people so near.

Mocha is an American cocker spaniel and young. Not really a puppy anymore, but not quite grown up either.

Her long hair is white and dark brown with some brown speckles. Her muzzle is short and soft, and her ears long with long hair. Her tail is not docked in the way considered fashionable for the breed and the long hairs of her tail are tangled with twigs and bits of old dried leaves from last year's fall. Her brown eyes are always watery and expressive.

Mocha lays her muzzle down, resting it on her front paws. A little tremor of fear goes through her again, making her shiver. She whimpers quietly.

She senses they are all in danger. Something is very wrong. She smells it; something evil and dangerous lurking nearby. Something she cannot identify.

It started following them on their hike this afternoon. Her people yelled at her when she barked and growled, trying to warn them of the danger.

It followed them back to the campsite and lingered there, watching them, unseen, somewhere in the bushes. Mocha knew it was there because she could still smell it. She felt its stare like putrid oil coating her.

That was when she ran away. Her fear became too much to bear and before Mocha knew what she was doing she was running. Now she is here huddled under the leaves in the dark. Alone. Almost alone.

Mocha's eyes follow them, sadly watching the feet walking nearby.

Madelaine walks by not far from Mocha's hiding spot, calling the little dog; her father walking close behind.

Madelaine thought she is so grown up, but she doesn't feel very grown up right now. Right now she feels very small and helpless.

She looks around, peering into the dark, tears in her eyes and sorrow catching in her voice as she calls Mocha.

Mocha can hear the tears in Madelaine's voice.

The little dog trembles harder, wanting so badly to go running to Madelaine, tail wagging and tongue lolling and full of kisses. She wants to make her sadness and fear go away. But fear has her frozen in place in her hiding spot.

Mocha watches Clive take Madelaine's hand.

"Come on Madelaine, we will look again in the morning," he says gently.

Madelaine turns her tear-streaked face to him. "We can't stop," she thinks, feeling like his words are meant to be cruel. "My puppy is lost somewhere in the dark, in the forest. What if something bad happens to her? What if she's hurt? What if something eats her by morning?"

Madelaine's throat constricts with grief and fear for Mocha.

"We can't stop looking for Mocha," she sobs, the words catching in her throat. "It's dark and she's alone."

Clive is not going to take "no" for an answer.

"Madelaine," he says, "it is late and it's dark. We won't find her in the dark. The dog will be fine. She will come back on her own."

"But what if something happened to her?" Madelaine sobs.

"She probably chased a squirrel or rabbit or something. She will find her way back."

Mocha watches Clive lead Madelaine away.

Madelaine drags her feet, trying to make them walk as slowly as she can without being obvious about it.

"I'm not ready to give up searching for Mocha," she thinks. "I don't want to give up until we find her safe and sound. If we don't-."

"If anything happened to Mocha, I will never be able to forgive myself," Madelaine thinks miserably.

Clive turns and gives the woods behind them one last look.

"The odds of finding the dog are stacked against us," he thinks. "I don't want Madelaine to know. It would break her heart."

He feels the pain and loss emanating off the girl. If they don't find the dog it will mean he failed her again.

"We need a miracle right now," Clive thinks, wishing he is the kind of guy who believes in miracles.

"We will find her in the morning," he says again, trying to reassure Madelaine.

Mocha stays huddled under the bushes, shivering, and watching them go with sad eyes.

Minutes later Madelaine's mother and younger sister, Zoe, pass Mocha's hiding spot.

Zoe turns and looks back behind her, her mother pulling her on.

"I heard something," Zoe thinks. "A rustle in the bushes, but I'm not sure. We should check it out. But, I'm scared of the dark. I don't want to go back and find out."

"Come on Zoe," Caroline urges. "It's getting late. Madelaine and your father are probably already back at the campsite by now."

Mocha's ears perk up and she stiffens. She pulls her lips back, showing sharp little teeth.

She heard the rustle too. It is the bad thing. She wants to run out barking and warn them, but she is too scared to move.

Caroline and Zoe keep walking, unaware that something is following them in the trees.

Zoe looks back, regretting letting her fear silence her, but saying nothing. She walks a little closer to her mother, feeling the darkness pressing in around them like an aura of danger.

"I'm sorry Mocha," she thinks. "If that is you I heard. I'm so sorry I didn't say anything and make us go back to look. But what if it wasn't you? What if it's a bear? I wish Dad was with us."

They leave the path and the sky seems to open up marginally brighter with the trees pushed back to make room for the narrow road running through the campground.

Guilt clings to Zoe. She has to force herself to not keep looking back. She can't stop thinking about the sound she heard. "If it was Mocha, she'd come running to us, wouldn't she?" she thinks.

Gravel crunches softly under their feet, but it sounds loud in the quiet stillness of night.

The family is camping in a campground located on the edge of a small town. Their closest camping neighbors are close enough to literally throw a stick at if the trees were not in the way.

Just around the bend in the road and only four campsites away from theirs are the stinky old outhouses. It's a bit of a hike to the big bathrooms inside a large building with flushing toilets, running water, and showers.

Mocha watches Caroline and Zoe walk away, the distance between them growing. She trembles and a low whimper escapes her throat. Her eyes dart back and forth. She is torn between staying hidden where she is and being with her family; torn between following them, and the bad thing that is following them, or getting as far away from it as she can.

Urgency fills her and her whole body trembles with it.

Skulking, her ears back and her tail tucked fearfully between her legs, Mocha follows Caroline and Zoe at a distance. Staying low, she darts across the road behind them to follow in the bushes on the other side, keeping them in sight as they walk back to their campsite. The bad thing still follows somewhere in the trees on the other side of the road.

Zoe and Caroline walk quietly past the dark campsites of other campers, arriving at their own.

Caroline looks at the coolers of food still sitting out. The fire pit with folding chairs set up around it sits cold, garbage tossed on top of the remnants of last night's fire. An unwashed pan still sits on the little portable cooking stove. The picnic table is cluttered with their paper supper plates and a large water jug.

A lantern sitting on the picnic table creates a ball of light that partially lights the table, fading quickly and does not reach much past the table.

Mocha huddles down in the bushes. Madelaine and her father are already there and her tail thumps the ground at the sight of Madelaine.

"Any luck?" Clive asks.

Madelaine looks up anxiously, hoping for good news. She looks for something good in their expressions, looking past them for Mocha.

Caroline shakes her head unhappily and Zoe looks at the ground with a lost look.

It hits Madelaine with a new wave of loss. She turns away, staring into the darkness in despair.

"No, nothing," Caroline says, her voice full of worry, looking carefully at Madelaine.

"Madelaine will take the loss of her dog hard," she thinks.

"Let's get a good night sleep," Clive says. "Mocha might come back during the night. If not-." The pause hangs heavily in the air between them.

He exchanges a look with his wife. A look the girls are not meant to see.

Madelaine is intent only on the darkness surrounding the campsite, but Zoe sees and understands. Zoe understands more than anyone realizes.

"They assume because I'm younger I don't understand most things," Zoe thinks. "That look means they don't think we will find Mocha."

"If not," Zoe finishes Clive's sentence in her head, "Mocha is bear meat."

Clive finishes his sentence, "We will look again in the morning." His voice is tired. Not only from the long day they had, but also from the long day he knows they will have tomorrow dealing with an inconsolable Madelaine if they do not find the dog alive and well.

Zoe is filled with guilt over her silence again.

"I should have said something when I thought I heard a noise," she thinks. "What if it was Mocha?"

She moves to Madelaine's side, putting an arm around her to comfort her sister.

With an annoyed motion, Madelaine shrugs her off and moves away, turning her back to her.

Zoe looks unhappily at Madelaine.

"I only want to make her feel a little better," she thinks unhappily, feeling the sharp burn of rejection. "I can't make her pain and worry go away, but I just wanted to help."

"Go in and get ready for bed girls," Caroline says. She turns to the table, her shoulders heavy with exhaustion, and starts gathering up the dirty paper plates and plastic glasses and cutlery. Her hands fumble with them and she almost drops the first items she picks up.

"Leave those." Clive comes and takes them away from her. "It's late. We will clean it up in the morning."

Caroline looks at the mess anxiously, wanting only to crawl into her sleeping bag with the warmth of Clive at her back and slip into blissful sleep. She looks at him, the lines in her face showing how haggard she is and her eyes full of stress.

"But, the bears-."

"They can come back tomorrow." He smiles, tossing the paper plates in the fire pit.

"At least put the coolers in the car."

"Okay." He moves to put them away, closing the trunk and car door softly to not disturb any neighbors.

Zoe is still standing there watching them and Madelaine is unhappily staring off into the darkness.

"Come on girls," Clive says, "let's all get a good sleep. We'll look again tomorrow."

Mocha watches as one by one her family crawls into their tent.

Zoe and Caroline are the first to go in.

A lantern turns on inside the tent, making it glow from within, shadows splashing and dancing on the walls from the shapes moving around inside.

Although they got there first, Madelaine and her father are the last to go in.

"Please Dad," Madelaine sobs, looking at him plaintively. "We have to keep looking for Mocha. She's my only real friend. I can't just leave Mocha lost in the forest to get eaten by a bear or coyote or something."

"It's too dark." Clive shakes his head. "Go to bed. We'll look again in the morning. She will probably be back on her own before then."

Madelaine's shoulders slump in defeat and, with one last look at the dark forest, she crawls into the tent, her father following.

From her hiding spot in the bushes Mocha watches the shadows of the family, grotesquely warped caricatures of their real shapes, dance on the tent walls from the lantern inside. They finally settle into their sleeping bags and the lantern turns off.

With a little whimper Mocha tries to make herself comfortable, digging a little bed into the ground beneath the bushes. She turns around three times the way dogs do, like it's some kind of magic ritual to ward off evil spirits or bad dreams. Or, maybe they are trying to find the most comfortable spot.

Mocha looks back up at the tent and trembles, wanting to go running to it barking to announce her return and snuggling into the warmth of Madelaine's sleeping bag.

She sniffs the air. The danger smell is still there. She can't tell where the bad thing is and still does not know what it is. She only knows that it is very close. She is shivering with fear.

Mocha stays hiding, watching the tent until sleep takes her off to dreamland.

2 Bad Night and a Dreary Day

The wind hisses through the trees and the night insects sullenly make their noises, seeming more hushed than they should be. After some shifting and restlessness, the four finally settle quietly into their sleeping bags. Clive and Caroline are soon breathing the slow deep breaths of sleep. Neither girl can sleep. Each is trapped in her own thoughts.

Madelaine feels hollow inside and her stomach is sick with worry for her missing dog. She imagines all the bad things her mind can think of that might have happened to Mocha. She cries silently until, after a few hours, she finally cries herself to sleep.

Zoe watches her motionless sister. She can barely see her. Everything is obscure forms in the darkness of the tent.

She can feel the night outside pressing in on the tent and it gives her a sick feeling, like something bad is out there trying to get in with the darkness. The soft sound of her parents breathing gives Zoe only a little comfort.

Unable to sleep, Zoe has nothing but time to think.

"Sometimes it feels like Madelaine thinks we are a lot further apart in age than we are. She treats me like I'm the way younger sister, instead of just a little younger. When she does that, it makes me feel so frustrated and angry.

Today was one of those days. Madelaine only wanted to play with her dog when we got here. She always just wants to play with Mocha. I tried to play with her and talk to her, but Madelaine didn't want anything to do with me. Sometimes I feel like she hates me."

Finally Zoe ended up stomping off with angry tears to sit by herself. Zoe was filled with jealousy that Madelaine cared about a dog more than she does her own sister.

She swallows her misery in the darkness.

"I was so mad that I wished Mocha would go away. I wished Madelaine never had a puppy. I don't even know why she got a puppy all for herself. Mom and Dad said it was because of something that happened, but nobody would say what. They were just all quiet and cryptic when I asked. When I asked Madelaine, she only shrugged and walked away.

Whatever the big secret is, it's not fair. Mocha should have been for both of us. She always rubs it in my face that Mocha is only hers."

Zoe swallows through her tears, making an effort to not make a sound in the dark tent. Outside, she can hear the wind and insects.

"I- I thought that if Mocha was gone, then Madelaine would have nobody to play with on this camping trip but me. Without Mocha, maybe Madelaine would talk to me again. She never wants anything to do with me anymore."

Tears roll down her cheek in the dark.

"I feel so bad for ever thinking those horrible things. I don't like to see Madelaine hurt or sad, even when I cause it in a rash moment of anger. And I never wanted anything bad to happen to Mocha. Not really. I didn't think it through when I wished she was gone."

Zoe feels hollow with her own empty ache.

"Even though Madelaine almost never lets me play with her dog, and Mocha seems to only love Madelaine best, I still love that little dog too. It's just hard to get past my jealousy sometimes."

The pain of her guilt and the worry over Mocha and Madelaine fills Zoe up like she is stretched out and filled with a pain that is too big to fit inside her.

"It's my fault Mocha is gone," Zoe thinks. "I wished it so hard and then it happened."

She reaches her hand under her pillow and finds the small lump. She rubs her fingers on it, trying to take comfort in it. It is a small smooth stone, round and kind of flat. It is polished so smooth that it almost seems to have a warmth of its own.

"Wishes don't come true. Not like that. But, this one did. Maybe if I wish really hard Mocha will come back," Zoe thinks. "No. That's dumb. I was only playing. When wishes come true it's only a coincidence. But, if it could be, if wishes could come true, then maybe if I wished hard enough for Mocha to come back

Madelaine will forgive me and not hate me for wishing her dog would go away."

She chokes back a sound, her throat catching.

"If only I could believe that and it could be true. I want Madelaine to forgive me. But, unless I tell her what I did, Madelaine will never forgive me. She doesn't know I wished Mocha was gone and I can't tell her because she would hate me more.

Madelaine blames herself for losing Mocha. Mom told her she should tie Mocha up, but Madelaine didn't. She thought that would be mean. Mocha always gives her such a sad look when she leaves her and panics when she is tied up. And Madelaine never wants to be without Mocha."

"But how can I let Madelaine keep tearing herself up with guilt over it when I feel like it's my fault?" Zoe thinks.

Zoe lays there in the darkness feeling sorry until she finally drifts off to sleep.

Bad dreams torment Mocha's sleep; monsters chasing her, her little legs pumping desperately as she runs from them. She can't see the monsters but she can feel them, deeper shadows looming in the darkness. She knows they are twisted and ugly, as ugly as pure evil. She dreams her family is in danger. The bad thing is coming and she is helpless to help them.

Now Mocha is running through the woods, terrified. Something she cannot see and can only smell is after her family. She has to get to them in time. Mocha turns in every direction, but cannot find the danger. Suddenly she cannot find her family either. She howls and cries desperately in her dream, trying to warn them they are in great danger.

Mocha twitches and whimpers in her sleep, her eyes scrunching as if she is closing them tight in her dreams. She wakes up with a start to a sound nearby. The night is dark and silent. Even the crickets are quiet, as if scared to make a sound.

Something is lurking very close. A dark shape looms outside the tent. The smell of danger fills the air with its unpleasant stink; old and nasty. It is the smell of the bad thing.

Mocha wants to bark a warning to her family inside the tent, but is too scared to make a sound. She huddles in her hiding place, watching the shape outside the tent, trembling with fear.

A crack of a branch snapping echoes dully on the night air.

The shape outside the tent goes still. It turns and fades away into the night.

The soft tread of something moving through the trees moves past the campsite.

Mocha lifts her nose, sniffing the air. Whatever it is, it is downwind and she can't catch its scent.

She huddles into a tighter ball, trembling, and stares into the dark waiting for morning.

Madelaine's eyes crack open and she reaches for the soft warm bundle of fur.

Outside, the leaves hiss with the breeze rubbing them together, insects call, and a bird chirrups sporadically. The shadows of leaves dance on the tent in the morning sunshine.

"Mocha," she murmurs sleepily, still groping for the dog. "Mocha?"

It hits her like a wall of pain. Images run through her mind of Mocha, torn, ruined, mauled and eaten by some unknown animal. Mocha injured and scared, shivering and cold in some deep dark hole somewhere, whimpering piteously. She turns over, pressing her face into her pillow to muffle her sobs.

The sound of muffled crying wakes up Zoe. She blinks as her eyes adjust to the morning light, feeling disoriented. It takes her a moment to remember where she is. It takes another moment for the sound that woke her to register.

Zoe looks around, wondering where the sound is coming from.

"Who is crying," she thinks. "Oh. Yeah." She feels foolish. "Of course, who else would it be? But why is-."

Zoe frowns. "Oh yeah. Mocha."

A fresh swell of guilt fills her along with shame at having thought such betraying thoughts towards Madelaine and Mocha.

"How could I have ever wished Mocha away?" she thinks. "Poor Mocha. Poor Madelaine."

She slides out of her sleeping bag, crawling over closer to Madelaine.

"Madelaine," Zoe whispers, moving to put a comforting arm on her. "I'm sorry Maddie."

Madelaine shakes her off, moving further away stiffly. She does not turn to look at her.

"Leave me alone."

Hurt, Zoe backs up and returns to her own space. She lies down and turns away, facing the tent wall. She feels miserable.

Caroline mumbles and murmurs, waking up. The sleeping bag hisses softly with the sound of her movement.

"Madelaine? Are you up?"

Madelaine doesn't respond.

Caroline is struck with the irrational fear that Madelaine is gone. She sits up, stretching and rubbing her eyes, looking around the tent for Madelaine. Beside her, Clive rolls over, trying to stay asleep.

Relieved everyone is safely accounted for; Caroline surrenders to the warmth of the sleeping bag.

"It's too early, go back to sleep," she murmurs.

The tension between Madelaine and Zoe hangs heavy and cold in the tent. As cold as the chill early morning air.

Madelaine wants only to get out of there and Zoe feels too twisted in her own feelings of hurt and guilt to sleep any more.

Madelaine sits up and rummages in her clothes bag next to her. She pulls a change of clothes into the sleeping bag with her, struggling to change in the tight confines of the sleeping bag. It is the only privacy she has in the tent.

She crawls out of her sleeping bag, putting on her jacket and shoes.

"Where are you going?" Caroline asks sleepily.

"Just outside," Madelaine says coldly, unzipping the tent and crawling out without looking back. She looks away as she zips it closed. She does not want to look at any of them right now.

"They don't understand my pain," she thinks miserably. "Mocha is just a dog, but she is a lot more than that to me."

Madelaine looks around, half hoping to see Mocha there wagging her tail and half dreading not seeing her. There is no Mocha. The loss is like a fist clenching her chest tight.

Dark clouds fill one end of the sky, moving swiftly towards the campground. In a few hours they will block out the sun.

Madelaine pulls her unzipped jacket tighter around her against the cool morning air. The wind above the trees picks up, the tops of the trees swaying and their leaves hissing more loudly in the gusting winds. It has little effect on the ground.

"It suits my mood," she thinks, looking up at the sky with a possible storm rolling in.

Madelaine stares up at the dark clouds in the distance. They fill her with dread.

"No," she says softly. "It can't storm. We haven't found Mocha."

She wanders the campsite aimlessly; feeling lost, and finally plunks down in a folding chair in front of the cold fire pit. She can't help the rising anxiety the clouds bring.

Huddled under the bushes, Mocha watches her family with sad eyes.

The little dog almost runs to Madelaine when she crawls out of the tent, but Mocha hesitates, sniffing the air. The scent of the bad thing lingers. She is not sure if it moved on or not.

Trembling, she lets out a whimper so quietly she almost makes no sound.

Mocha settles in to watch from her hiding place.

Caroline comes out of the tent, stretching stiffly. She gives Madelaine a sympathetic look.

"She didn't come back last night."

"No." Madelaine's voice cracks.

"We will look again after breakfast."

Madelaine does not respond.

Feeling bad for her, Caroline turns her attention to making coffee and breakfast. She gets bacon and eggs from the cooler in the car trunk and the potatoes from the box next to it. She looks at the sky.

"If we leave the cooler in the car all day, it will heat up too much and won't keep the food cool. Clive, I need you to pull the cooler out of the trunk and start the stove," she calls.

Inside the tent, Clive mumbles and groans, turning over in the sleeping bag. He decides he has no choice about getting up and sits up, wishing he could keep sleeping.

"Come on Zoe, time to get up." He crawls out of the tent, stretching and scratching.

Clive looks around, sees Madelaine sitting moodily staring at the empty fire pit, and no Mocha.

"We will look again after we eat."

"Mom already said that," Madelaine mumbles, an edge of anger in her voice.

Clive goes to the car to get the cooler. He feels helpless to ease the pain he knows she feels.

Zoe finally crawls out of the tent, staying away from Madelaine and not looking at her. She is still hurt over Madelaine's rejection.

Caroline starts cutting the potatoes while Clive starts pumping the little canister on the portable gas stove and trying to light it.

After an awkward breakfast eaten in silence they start out searching for the little dog. Zoe goes with Clive and Madelaine goes with Caroline, splitting up to cover more ground.

Madelaine ate little, her appetite ruined by her misery.

Mocha watches them go anxiously, undecided if she should stay or go. After they are out of sight and their footsteps fading, she scurries across the campsite to vanish in the bushes on the other side, following them at a distance but staying hidden in the bushes. She keeps testing the air for the scent of the bad thing.

3   Searching for Mocha

Gravel crunches under their feet as Madelaine and Caroline walk along the road running through the campground, calling Mocha. They pass by smaller roads that trail off with sporadically occupied campsites.

With each road they pass, Madelaine's already low hopes of finding Mocha fade more and she becomes more angry with herself and despondent.

"We will find her," Caroline says. She keeps looking at Madelaine with worry as they walk along. "She's a smart dog. She will find her way back. And we can put up posters."

Madelaine walks on, not responding or looking at her. Her body language is stiff and angry. It is taking everything she has to not cry.

"Don't cry," Madelaine tells herself. "Don't look stupid. If you cry, you will just get everyone's pity worse than you are now."

She can feel her mother's pity-filled looks and they are making her self-conscious. Finally, she turns on her angrily.

"Stop looking at me like that!"

"Like what?" But Caroline knows. It's her worried look.

"With pity," Madelaine snaps. "Stop looking at me like you feel sorry for me. I know what you all think. Yes, she is only a dog, so you don't have to keep looking at me like I just lost the only thing in the world that matters."

She speeds up, her feet crunching quickly on the gravel, leaving her mother behind.

"I did just lose the only thing that matters," Madelaine thinks unhappily. "And their constant pity looks are a constant reminder we will probably never find Mocha."

Caroline stares after her, feeling hurt and lost. She is helpless to ease her daughter's pain.

"I have to go after her," she thinks and is about to call after Madelaine to come back.

"Let her go," Clive says from behind her.

Caroline turns, startled.

Clive sees the pain and helplessness in her eyes. It makes him feel more helpless himself.

Zoe is following him mutely, her expression moody.

"All my girls are hurting and there is nothing I can do about it," Clive thinks.

"Let Madelaine go," he says again gently. "She needs some time alone."

"But-," Caroline starts.

"She will be fine. She's strong. She needs to sort out some of these things on her own."

Caroline's expression is disappointed and hurt. She needs to make things better, but can't.

Zoe watches her sister walk angrily away, ignoring them. She still feels hurt over their morning encounter.

"If Mocha wasn't just Madelaine's this wouldn't have happened," she thinks. "I could have tied Mocha up. Then she wouldn't have run away. But she is Madelaine's and she would have got mad at me for tying up her stupid precious dog."

Despite her anger and jealousy she can't help but be worried too that something bad happened to poor little happy Mocha. Zoe keeps looking at the dark clouds rolling in.

The three continue walking together, calling for Mocha.

Madelaine can hear them behind her and she speeds up more, the fast pace and the sound of their voices fueling her anger.

"Stupid camping. If we didn't have to come camping Mocha would be safe. She would be with me right now instead of lost in this stupid forest. Even the drive out here was torture."

For Madelaine the car ride was an endless misery of watching trees, rocks, and fields through the window to the steady drone of the tires on pavement.

For the whole drive she thought about how much she did not want to go camping.

"Why did they even insist on this stupid camping trip?" Her feet continue crunching angrily on the gravel road.

Madelaine tried to read her book on the drive, but Zoe kept trying to talk to her. Then Zoe started singing and that only grated on her nerves more. Even Mocha was restless and started squirming and nosing at her for constant pets until Madelaine got angry and yelled at her. After that Mocha slumped on the floor and curled up with an unhappy sigh and went to sleep. By the time they got to the campground it felt like they were driving days instead of hours.

Madelaine can't stop thinking now about how unhappy the little dog was after she yelled at her in the car.

"I wish I could take that moment back. If we could go back I wouldn't have yelled at her. I would have given her all the pets and rubs she wanted and hugged her instead."

Madelaine spots an empty picnic table against the bushes in a cleared area with horseshoe pits. Looking around to make sure no one sees her; she goes over and sits on the table with her feet on the seat. She glances back at the road to see how visible she is.

"Good, anyone passing by might not see me."

She doesn't want anyone to find her.

Madelaine rests her elbows on her knees and sits hunched over with her cheeks in her palms, staring angrily at nothing. Her thoughts are still on the drive out the day before.

They were all so stiff and grumpy after the long ride that they were all angry and yelling at each other.

"It was such a relief to get out of that car and put a little space between me and Zoe. She drove me crazy the whole time."

"Hey, are you the girl who lost the dog?"

Madelaine starts, straightening up quickly and looking around for the source of the voice, startled. She is angry at the intrusion and surprised to see a boy who looks her age.

He walks over and stands in front of her, looking at her. He notes her angry look and decides to ignore it.

"So, are you her?"

Madelaine almost asks who. It is an automatic response. She stops herself because she thinks it will make her sound dumb.

"Yeah," she says instead.

"That sucks. You haven't found the dog yet?"

"No."

"What's its name?"

"Her. Mocha."

"It's a girl? A small dog, right? Long hair, brown and white?"

"Yes."

"Can you say more than one word?"

Madelaine gives him an annoyed look and rolls her eyes.

"Of course I can."

"Can I sit with you?" He doesn't wait for an answer and climbs up to sit beside her.

"I guess you can," Madelaine says, her tone a bit sarcastic.

"You look pretty miserable. I guess you're worried about your dog."

Madelaine's eyes burn and feel like they are swelling up and going to pop out of her head with the building pressure of the tears behind them. She tries to fight the tears, but they come anyway. She swallows a lump forming in her throat, but it doesn't go down. She can't speak. She can only nod.

She feels stupid crying in front of this strange boy on top of her desolation over losing Mocha. She wipes at her tears angrily.

"You lost her yesterday? That's what I heard. There are some other campers looking for her too now."

Madelaine smiles a small smile, grateful that someone is helping, but also feeling weird about having strangers helping look for her dog. She feels the need to talk. Just to talk. It doesn't matter if the boy is there or not.

"I wish he would leave. I don't want anyone to hear me talking," she thinks.

She almost doesn't talk because he is there, feeling self-conscious. But once she starts, she starts feeling better for it. Madelaine sniffles and her voice cracks when she starts talking.

"Mom and Dad made us come camping and now Mocha is lost. I hate this place."

"I think it's pretty nice here," the boy says.

"Nice?"

"It's beautiful. And peaceful."

"Not with Zoe for a sister."

The boy smiles and lets out a small laugh. It makes Madelaine smile too, although she doesn't feel like she should be smiling about anything right now.

"So she's a handful then?"

"After driving me crazy Zoe took off."

"No one knew where she went?"

Madelaine nods. "Mom was upset. She was worried Zoe would get lost. Dad had to go looking for her. He was pretty mad. He wanted to get the campsite set up."

"Did he find her?"

"Yeah. I guess she was as hyper as Mocha from the long drive. When he came back, Dad decided we should leave the stuff to set up later and go for a hike."

"A hike, nice. There are some pretty nice trails here."

Madelaine shrugs and rolls her eyes.

"What?" he asks.

"It was awful. Mom and Dad were grumpy. Mocha kept racing ahead and coming back and that was making Mom madder. She kept telling me to put her on a leash. Zoe kept bugging me about some dumb stones she found and trying to get me to play with them with her. And then Mocha started barking and wouldn't stop and everybody was yelling at her."

The more Madelaine talks, the more she feels a little better.

"I could never talk to anyone in my family or at school like this," she thinks. "I think it's easier to talk to someone you don't know and you will never see again."

"Is that when she ran away?" the boy asks.

Madelaine shakes her head. "After. We got back to the campsite and Mom told me to tie her up and I didn't. Everybody was busy. Mom and Dad were setting up the tent and everything and Zoe was exploring the bushes around the edges of the campsite.

Then I realized Mocha was gone. I looked around and called her, but she didn't come."

A tear slides down her cheek and Madelaine's eyes redden. They feel like they are swelling up again and her sinuses are closing up and plugging like she has a cold, putting pressure on her nose.

"What were you busy doing?"

Madelaine's voice catches in her throat.

"I- I was feeling sorry for myself and I was mad at everyone. I was thinking only about how horrible this week is going to be."

Two more tears roll down her cheeks and she rubs them away self consciously.

"That's pretty rough," he says. "Hey, you didn't know your dog would take off."

His words don't make Madelaine feel any better.

"She probably chased a squirrel or something," he says. "You know, dogs are pretty smart. Did you know that even when they are lost they can find their way home by following their own trail?"

He touches his nose. "They smell it. Dogs have even crossed the country on their own to find their way home."

Madelaine looks at him skeptically.

"It's true," he says. "She will find her way back."

"Mocha can't even find a piece of food on the floor in front of her. We're only here for a week. What if she doesn't? It was a four hour drive. She can't follow that trail."

"Dogs do that, don't they?" He almost laughs and catches himself. "They get so excited, they forget they can smell or something."

He shrugs. "Someone will find her. Put up posters. They can call you if they find her."

Madelaine looks down again.

"The campground is closing for winter soon. There won't be anyone here to find her. If Mocha comes back, she'll be wandering around the campground, but there won't be anyone here."

"I'll be here."

Madelaine looks at him.

"I live here," he says.

Madelaine blinks in surprise. "You live here, in the campground?"

"I live on the edge of town. I come here all the time. I help out the park rangers in the summer, kind of a part time job. I come here to hike and bike around on the trails too."

"Even in the winter?"

"All year round. The trails here are great for snowshoeing and cross country skiing. If you don't find your dog by the time you leave, I'll keep coming to look for her."

The corners of Madelaine's mouth twitch almost into a smile.

He smiles. He almost made her smile.

Madelaine frowns again.

"It's a long drive. I don't think my parents would want to drive all this way for a dog."

"I'll look after her until we find a way to get her back to you."

The corners of Madelaine's mouth creep back up into almost a small hopeful smile.

"What's your name?" he asks.

"Madelaine."

"Well Madelaine," he climbs down, standing in front of her, "let's go look for your dog."

This time she manages a small smile.

"What's your name?" Madelaine asks, climbing off the table to join him.

"Geoffrey."

He pulls out his phone.

"If we give each other our numbers or follow each other on Snap or Instagram, I can let you know if I find her. I mean, if we don't find her before you go home." He pauses. "Or, if I find her and we're not together."

Madelaine frowns at his phone. Geoffrey is looking at her expectantly.

"I don't have my phone. My parents made me leave it back home. They decided this is a stupid 'no electronics' camping trip."

"Harsh. Well, give me yours and I can message you when you get home if we haven't found her before you leave."

Madelaine gives him her information and he gives her his.

"I'm never going to remember that." Madelaine gives him a look over his weird user name.

"I'll message you. When you get home, you will have it," Geoffrey says.

Madelaine nods uncertainly.

"I hope it doesn't come to that. I have to find Mocha before we go home," she says unhappily.

They walk away together, searching for Mocha.

Caroline, Clive, and Zoe step out of a trail onto the gravel road just in time to see Madelaine and a strange boy turning up one of the campground bays up ahead.

Caroline's pulse quickens at the sight and her stomach tightens with a knot of worry.

"Who is that boy she's with? Did you see him around earlier? I haven't seen him before."

Jealousy tugs at Zoe. "Madelaine already found a friend to hang out with? I'm going to have nobody to hang out with at all now."

Caroline starts to walk faster and Clive puts a restraining hand on her arm. She turns to him.

"We should get up there," Caroline says. "She's with some strange boy."

Clive can see the worry on her face and hear it in her voice.

"She's fine," he says. "Let them be."

"But after-." She stops, glancing quickly at Zoe, worried about saying too much in front of her. "What if-."

"You have to give her a chance and stop being so overprotective. Madelaine needs to move on and so do we. She needs to work through things in her own way. Maybe this will help. Come on, let's search this way."

Caroline goes along unhappily, not liking it but realizing he's right.

"So what do you do when you aren't here looking for lost dogs?" Geoffrey asks as they continue walking.

Madelaine gives him a cold hard look out of the corner of her eye.

Geoffrey does not pick up on it, but realizes his mistake as he is saying it.

"Sorry. I didn't think." He looks down guiltily. "What I mean is what do you do, normally, when you aren't camping?"

Madelaine shrugs. "Nothing."

"Nothing?" Geoffrey gets a mischievous glint in his eye. "You don't even go to school?"

Madelaine rolls her eyes at him again. She has an urge to hit him in the arm.

"Of course I go to school."

"Okay, so you go camping and you go to school. What else?"

"I hate camping. Nothing. I don't really do anything else, just school."

"That sounds pretty boring."

Madelaine glances at him and turns her attention back to the road ahead.

"Hey, I meant what I said." Geoffrey looks at her. "We will find your dog. She'll be fine."

Tears burn at Madelaine's eyes.

"My parents don't think so."

"Forget what they say. They don't know this forest like I do. I know this forest as good as the rangers do. Ranger Davis Morgan knows it even better than I do. We'll find her. Come, this way."

He leads her off the road and down a trail she didn't notice.

"Where are we going?"

"You will see."

They push through the narrow trail. The ground is mossy and overgrown.

"Is this even a path?" Madelaine asks.

"It's a deer trail."

Geoffrey stops puts an arm out in front of Madelaine, stopping her.

"What?"

"The path ended. Take my hand and take two steps forward."

Geoffrey is holding his hand out to her and she looks at it, deciding whether or not to do it.

Finally, Madelaine reaches out and takes his hand. He grips hers firmly, urging her forward.

Madelaine takes two steps and tightens her grip on his hand with a sudden rush of fear she is falling, feeling the spin of vertigo.

"Beautiful, isn't it?" Geoffrey says.

Madelaine gasps at the view.

The world has dropped away below her in a jumble of fallen rocks where the cliff face had broken off and dropped to the ground far below a few times over the decades or even centuries.

The broken rocks below are grown over with moss and lichens; bushes, trees, and wild flowers sprouting among them wherever their roots can grab purchase. Beyond is a rolling hilly sea of tree tops and open sky. The mountains in the distance rise from the trees like a hazy island in a sea of green. A pair of birds dives past them, soaring into the sky chasing each other in a game of cat and mouse.

Madelaine turns slowly to look at him and sees a butterfly with black veins on its white wings and a smudge of black pattern at the tips of its front wings sunning itself on the leaf of tree a right behind her, its wings flapping in slow motion as though to dry them.

Thinking how pretty it is, she reaches towards it with one finger extended to see if it will climb on and the butterfly takes wing, fluttering around her head and up over the edge and down towards the trees below.

"That's a Pine White," Geoffrey says.

Madelaine does not see him waving a shooing motion towards it with his free hand.

She wobbles on the edge of the precipice and Geoffrey gently pulls her back from the edge, releasing her hand.

Madelaine looks at him. "Wow. I never knew something like that was here."

"There is a lot here to see that most people have no idea about," Geoffrey says, staring out beyond the edge.

"We should get back to the road." Madelaine feels guilty for enjoying the moment when Mocha is lost and possibly injured or dead. Thinking about the dog sends a new wave of loss and fear through her.

The moment gone, Geoffrey leads the way back to the road.

After a long day of searching for Mocha with no success, Caroline, Clive, and Zoe return to the campsite for supper.

Caroline keeps looking at the campsite entrance with a worried frown as she prepares hamburger patties and Clive lights a fire in the fire pit.

"We have to wait for the fire to burn down to coals to cook the burgers," Clive says, poking the fire with a long thick stick.

"Maybe you should look for Madelaine. She should have come back by now." Caroline looks at Clive to see if he is going to go.

Madelaine and Geoffrey are getting close to the campsite.

"I guess I'll see you around," Madelaine says, dismissing him.

"Maybe tomorrow?" Geoffrey asks.

"Sure, I guess."

"Go away," Madelaine thinks, trying to will him to leave. When he doesn't, she stops in the road. Geoffrey stops too.

"Um, this is my campsite," Madelaine says.

"Good to know." Geoffrey nods.

"Okay so I guess I'll see you tomorrow."

"Tomorrow." Geoffrey nods again.

Madelaine starts walking again. She hears the crunch of his footsteps on the gravel too.

He is still walking with her.

Madelaine stops again, turning to him.

"So, you um, go the same way to go home?"

He is looking at her curiously, like he isn't sure what she means and thinks she hasn't finished talking.

"What I mean is," Madelaine continues awkwardly, "you have to go past our campsite?"

"No, I go that way." He indicates the other way up the road.

Madelaine bristles.

"So, why are you still following me?"

"I'm walking you to your campsite."

She blinks at him.

"That really isn't necessary."

"I want to."

Madelaine growls on the inside, clenching her teeth. "I don't want you to follow me to my campsite," she thinks.

"I'm good. I can walk there by myself," she says and starts walking.

He walks too and Madelaine stops again.

"Really, you don't need to walk me to my campsite."

"That's okay," he says.

"This is going to be so embarrassing," Madelaine thinks. "Oh my gawd, I don't want you to walk me to my campsite."

Instead of saying what she is thinking, Madelaine wrinkles her nose at him to show her annoyance, wondering why he isn't getting it.

Geoffrey only waits patiently, smiling at her.

"Ugh," Madelaine groans inwardly. She wants to tell him she doesn't want him coming to the campsite. Not now and not ever.

"Fine," she says, not feeling it is fine at all, and starts walking gain.

"Please go away," Madelaine pleads silently. "Please go away so they won't embarrass me in front of you."

Geoffrey does not go away. He cheerfully walks alongside her while Madelaine feels his presence without looking at him.

Madelaine rolls her eyes and purposely ignores him, hoping it will make him get the hint and leave. His cheerfulness is annoying her now.

Clive looks up when Madelaine walks into the campsite with Geoffrey.

Caroline tries to hide her worried frown at the sight of them.

Zoe turns away, pouting and feeling miserable. "I wish there was someone I can hang around with," she thinks. She fights the urge to get in there and talk to Madelaine's new friend. She wouldn't think twice any other time, but she can see that Madelaine is still very unhappy over Mocha.

"Hello there," Clive says, directing his greeting to Geoffrey. He turns his attention to Madelaine. "You are just in time for supper. Who is your friend?"

Madelaine blushes.

"Don't blush, stupid," she thinks, the blush adding to the embarrassment she already feels from her family's reaction to her walking in with Geoffrey. She looks at each of them, seeing her mother's frown, Zoe's crushed eagerness to take over her new friend, and her father trying too hard to be friendly and pleasant.

"Geoffrey," he introduces himself, stepping forward and putting his hand out to shake Clive's hand.

The moment makes Madelaine feel weird and awkward, watching the exchange between Geoffrey, who she hardly knows, and her dad.

Clive steps forward and shakes his hand, noting the boy's strong handshake.

"I'm Clive, Caroline," he indicates Caroline, "and her sister-."

"Zoe," Geoffrey finishes for him, giving Zoe a small wink that sends a rush of pleasure through her at realizing he knows her name.

"Maybe Madelaine's friend isn't so bad," she thinks.

"Are you staying for supper?" Clive asks.

This brings another frown from Caroline, unsure how she is going to feed the extra mouth. With limited space, they only packed the minimum. She keeps her silence, mashing the patties harder with a small flare of irritation.

"Clive knows we only have enough for us," Caroline thinks. "They are going to be very small patties if I have to make the meat into five. We don't even have an extra bun."

"Sorry, I can't," Geoffrey says. "I have to get home. Bye Madelaine. Goodbye Zoe." He gives Zoe a good natured wink and Madelaine rolls her eyes.

Ignoring her eye roll, Geoffrey walks away with a grin, leaving the campsite.

"Where is this boy from?" Caroline asks before he is out of earshot. "Is he a camper?"

"Mom!" Madelaine wants to say with an angry look to let her know that she is being too pushy and is embarrassing her. She holds back.

"He lives nearby," she mumbles instead. "He works here helping the rangers."

Caroline is about to say something else, not liking Madelaine hanging around with this boy they don't know, but Clive gives her a warning look and she stays quiet.

Madelaine flops down into a folding chair in front of the fire pit, staring miserably into the crackling flames. She feels cold despite the warmth coming from the fire. She huddles into herself.

"We will look for Mocha again after supper," Clive says.

"I can't even think about eating when Mocha is out there somewhere hungry and alone," Madelaine mutters quietly, "or maybe worse." She stops herself, not wanting to say the word. Dead.

Geoffrey stops in the road a few campsites up. He turns and looks back.

"Her mom really does not like me."

His smile falters.

"I feel bad for her. Madelaine seems really upset about her dog."

He looks up at the sky.

"I think I can give it a little more time." He shrugs. "So I'll be a little late. Getting in trouble will be worth it if I find the dog. The forest is not a good place for a little dog."

Geoffrey walks on up the road and down another to collect his bike where he left it out of sight in the bush earlier.

"I'll be able to cover more ground looking for the dog on my bike."

He starts riding, heading for the hiking trails. Geoffrey keeps his eyes on the ground and lower branches, watching for any signs of a dog. It could be anything, a paw print or tuft of hair.

Madelaine suffers through supper, picking at her food and barely eating while Caroline keeps giving her worried looks.

Zoe eats stiffly. She keeps looking at the edges of the campsite where the trees and bushes block out the rest of the world in the hope Mocha will suddenly appear.

She glances at Madelaine, feeling the sting of guilt, keeping her thoughts to herself.

"If Mocha would just come out of the bush right now," she thinks, "if she would just come back-. Is she even okay? Did something eat her during the night? I shouldn't have wished Mocha would go away."

After supper is cleaned up they leave the fire to burn out and head out with flashlights to search again for Mocha with the sun hanging low in the sky already warning of the darkness that will soon close in.

More campsites have filled with campers taking advantage of one of the last nice weekends of the season. They walk along the road and the paths between them, quietly calling for Mocha, taking different trails through the campground.

Mocha slinks through the bushes following them at a distance but wanting to stay close. She pauses and looks back. There is a cracking noise behind her, a dead branch on the ground snapping under the weight of something.

She shivers and bares her teeth. The wind changes, blowing the scent to her, the foul stink of something that should not be.

Mocha scurries faster, almost bursting from the trees to go charging to the safety of her family. But the changing wind turns again. She freezes. The scent is coming from ahead now. They are heading directly for the bad thing.

She trembles and growls a very low growl.

Zoe pauses, looking back.

"Did you hear something?"

Clive stops, listening.

"I don't hear anything. It's late and getting dark. We will have to try again tomorrow. Let's go back to the campsite."

"No, we have to keep looking for Mocha." Madelaine insists.

Caroline almost agrees, feeling bad for Madelaine. But it is late. "We can't see enough in the dark. Let's go back," she says.

"No," Madelaine insists. "We can't leave her out here for another night."

"If she could hear us, she would have come. She would have barked. Something," Clive says gently. "Madelaine, you need to start to understand, she might be gone."

Tears well in Madelaine's eyes and her chest feels like it is tightening to the point she will not be able to breathe and will die. She wishes she will die.

"If Mocha is dead because of me, then I deserve to die," she thinks miserably. But really, she feels like death would come as a welcome embrace. It would be an end to the pain.

"Come on, let's go back. We need a good night sleep. Maybe we will find some sign of her tomorrow," Clive says.

Zoe looks at him and then at Madelaine. The look of abject misery on Madelaine's face breaks her heart and fills her with remorse. The guilt of wishing Mocha gone is eating away at her, tormenting her. She feels the need to confess.

"Madelaine," Zoe starts.

"Leave me alone!" Madelaine snaps, angrily walking faster so they don't see her tears.

The sting of Madelaine's response brings tears burning to Zoe's eyes. "Why does Madelaine have to hate me so much?" she thinks miserably. "She always hates me."

Clive moves closer to Caroline, whispering so neither girl will hear, "Maybe we should get Madelaine another dog when we get back."

"Really?" Caroline whispers back, her voice harsh. She is torn between anger at his suggestion and the helplessness filling her. Helpless to do anything to take away Madelaine's pain. "Do you really think you can just replace her dog? This isn't like when her fish died, or when you accidentally sucked up her hamster with the vacuum. You can't just go find a look-a-like and think everything is going to be okay. She is too attached to that dog."

"But, the whole reason we got the dog," Clive pauses, glancing at Zoe who seems to be oblivious to their conversation. He lowers his voice further. "We got her the dog because of what happened. To help her deal with-." He ends it there; worried Zoe might overhear after all. "We should get her another dog."

"You are getting Madelaine another dog?" Zoe interrupts, saying it too loudly. She turns to stare at them in angry shock.

Walking ahead of them, Madelaine hears and it only makes the pain filling her worse.

"They think Mocha is dead," Madelaine thinks. The knowledge is like a knife slicing through her. "I don't want another dog. Mocha can't be replaced."

"We're not getting Madelaine another dog," Caroline whispers, trying to shush Zoe.

"But Dad said-."

"Forget what I said," Clive says, glancing at his wife and cringing inwardly at the cold anger he sees in her eyes.

Zoe clamps up and walks on, silent in her unhappiness.

"They are getting Madelaine another dog. Another stupid Madelaine only dog and don't touch it Zoe because it's mine not yours. And I get nothing," she thinks, her anger building.

Zoe is torn between her jealousy of Madelaine, anger at her and their parents, worry over Mocha, and the guilt plaguing her.

Her parents' other words click with the realization of their meaning.

"I knew it," she thinks. "Madelaine knew it too. The fish, the hamster, they were different. We both suspected they died and Dad replaced them." She feels a small burn of betrayal. Not too much, neither of them was really attached to the fish or hamster.

Zoe's thoughts turn to last night's search for Mocha and the sound she thought she heard. The rustle.

"What if it was Mocha?" she thinks. The guilt filling her again over her silence and worry over Mocha intensifies. She looks at Madelaine's angry back ahead and at her parents behind her.

She slows to let them catch up and moves closer to her parents, looking at them hopefully, her face filled with regret.

"I heard something last night."

They both look at her.

"It was probably nothing," Clive says, "the wind or something."

"If anything was outside the tent, if it was Mocha, she would have barked or whined or tried to get in," Caroline adds.

"No," Zoe says. "When we were out searching for Mocha I thought I heard a noise, a rustle in the bushes. What if it was Mocha?"

"Why didn't you say anything?" Caroline's voice goes up an octave indicating she is stressed and shocked.

Zoe looks away guiltily.

"I- it was dark and I didn't want to go back," she says quietly, realizing how much worse and more selfish it sounds than she felt.

Madelaine stops in the road, turning to stare at them, her mouth open and eyes wide.

"Zoe! How could you?" Her voice is filled with the pain twisting her face. "You left Mocha out there! It was her, we could have found her, and now she's gone! I hate you!"

She turns on her heel and starts angrily walking faster to put distance between them.

"I- I didn't mean it," Zoe says quietly, filled with the misery of failing Mocha and the pain of Madelaine's words.

"You should have said something," Caroline says. "What if it was Mocha?"

Zoe looks at her.

"Don't you think I know that? Don't you think I feel miserable enough already?"

She turns away, walking faster too, keeping distance between herself and both Madelaine and her parents.

"It probably wasn't Mocha," Clive says, trying to help. She would have come. If she couldn't come, she would have barked or cried."

Caroline only walks beside him without responding, lost in her own unhappy thoughts.

Frowning and feeling useless, Clive walks along.

Madelaine keeps herself ahead of her family all the way back to the campsite, but not too far ahead. She does not want to be alone in the dark woods.

"Let's all get settled in for bed," Caroline says as they reach the campsite.

Madelaine gives Zoe a hate-filled glare and turns to give one last desolate look at the dark trees and bushes before crawling into the tent.

Zoe holds back, not wanting to go in the tent at all. She definitely does not want to be alone in there with Madelaine right now.

"Come on Zoe, let's go," Caroline says. She crawls into the tent and Zoe follows hesitantly.

Inside, the tension is so thick Zoe swears she can taste it like a foul smell. She smells the air discretely.

"If I didn't know better, I'd swear I can smell Madelaine's hatred for me," she thinks miserably.

Madelaine is changing for bed with angry motions, almost tearing her nightgown.

Zoe turns her back to them both and changes with stiff motions, crawling into her sleeping bag.

"They are changed," Caroline says so Clive can hear.

His head appears at the opening and he looks at his three unhappy women. For a moment he almost decides against entering the tent, the tension a palpable force he does not want to face. He crawls in, sliding into his and Caroline's shared sleeping bag, using the bag to cover himself as he slips his pants off and his pajama pants on.

Mocha scurries up the path. The scent of the bad thing had driven her off. But now she realizes her family is gone.

The putrid odor of bad is still strong on the air, but panic tingles at her and she wants only the safety of being with her family and her Madelaine.

Mocha follows the lingering scent of her family, running full speed.

She is about to charge into the campsite, but a dark movement in the bushes on the other side makes her pause. She trembles, sniffing the air, and almost flees the other way.

The bad thing moves off quietly through the trees, moving away from the campsite.

Mocha slinks into the bushes, creeping closer to the campsite and hides in the bushes bordering it.

Hungry, unhappy, and scared, she turns three times and settles in. Her stomach feels sick from that toad she ate. Mocha shivers, staring at the now dark tent in the campsite and glancing around the dark bushes for the bad thing that is there somewhere.

Eventually, Mocha falls asleep.

Inside the tent, Madelaine lays in her sleeping bag staring into the darkness listening to the night sounds outside. She thinks she heard something out there.

"If it's Mocha she will bark and scratch at the tent. If it's not-. Please be Mocha, please be Mocha," she thinks unhappily, but not feeling the hope the words suggest. All hope is gone. Her parents believe Mocha is dead.

Zoe watches Madelaine's back under the cover of darkness, still feeling the sting of her sister's hatred and the pain of guilt for wishing her dog gone.

"I'm a bad person and a horrible sister," Zoe thinks. "It's no wonder Madelaine hates me. Please Mocha, be okay. Please come back, for Madelaine," The first tear slips from her eye and rolls down to wet her pillow.

Caroline feels the numbness of trying to cope with her feelings of failing her kids.

"A mother is supposed to protect her kids, no matter what," she thinks. "And all they feel now is pain and loss over that dog. We never should have gotten the dog."

Clive's warmth next to her gives her some comfort against the cold reality that she failed them.

Clive lays there with his eyes closed. His nose starts snoring as he drifts off, escaping from his misery at failing his family and not finding Madelaine's dog in sleep.

A few hours later they are all sleeping.

4 Dark Dreams

Bad dreams torment Mocha's sleep again, the monsters returning to chase her. Her little legs pump desperately as she runs from them. They are there, their presence strong in all her senses. Their scent is strong. They are loud, the pounding of their feet on the ground making the earth shudder, the slathering gnashing of teeth and snarling, the cracking of trees and bushes being torn apart to reach her, and their panted breaths. She can feel their presence.

Yet she cannot find them. They are insubstantial shadows looming in the darkness.

Mocha's senses tell her they are twisted and ugly; as ugly as pure evil.

Her family is in danger. The badness is coming for them and she is helpless to stop it. She can't help them.

She tries to run faster, to reach her family in time, but they are always just as far away. She turns one way and then another in her dream but cannot find the danger.

Suddenly her family is gone. Mocha looks around frantically, smelling the air and the ground. There is no sign of them and no scent trail to follow. Only the memory of their scent is left hanging on the air and it is fading as if they were never there.

She howls and cries desperately in her dream, trying to warn them of the danger.

Mocha twitches and whimpers in her sleep.

A quiet noise wakes Mocha up. She raises her head to look around, sniffing the air.

The earthy stench of forgotten decay hangs on the air; the odor of a place where moss had grown, died, and rotted into sludge before drying up to feed a new cycle. A cycle of poisonous life and death that happened millenniums ago in a place that hides deep within the earth's history. The sickening stink of the bad thing.

Something is lurking very close to the tent, a dark shape looming in the night. It moves silently around to the front of the tent, nothing more than a darker shape against the darkness of the night with no moon or stars lighting the sky.

Mocha is scared. She is on the verge of barking a warning to her family, but is too afraid. She huddles in her hiding place, watching the tall figure outside the tent, trembling with fear.

The shape outside the tent goes still.

Mocha backs up, putting distance and the shelter of more bushes between her and the bad thing, turning and ready to bolt.

Mocha pricks her ears at the sound of the tent zipper going up, some rustling, and then the zipper going down. She stares intently at the tent.

She focuses intently on the tent to see who is coming out. She hopes it is Clive, but also hopes no one comes out. The father is big and strong and could maybe scare away the bad thing. But Mocha is scared the bad thing might hurt him.

Nobody comes out of the tent.

Mocha creeps closer again, fighting the urge to flee.

The dark shape is standing there before the tent like it is waiting. It lumbers off into the darkness. It appears to be carrying something, but Mocha cannot be sure in the darkness.

The unfamiliar smell suggests it is a human. But the smell is all wrong. It is not a normal person smell. That smell does not seem to belong with the other smells of the bad thing. Whatever that thing is, the old smell of decay and old bones hangs off it. The smell of the family is also strong around the tent.

Mocha half rises to follow, sniffing at the air, trying to sort all the smells out. She thinks better of it, and settles back into her hiding space, shivering with fear.

Hopefully it will not come back.

After a while she dozes off and does not wake up again until the light of morning brightens the world.

Terrifying dreams fill Mocha's sleep again.

Zoe also tosses and turns in her sleep. In her dream something looms over her. The world swings and sways and, for a moment, she thinks it is tumbling over and she is going to fall off. She opens her eyes a crack, closing them again as the nightmares hold her in their grip.

The sensation of falling shocks Zoe awake.

Tired and disoriented by the nightmare, she does not know where she is. Everything is unfamiliar. She rubs her tired eyes, looking for the familiarity of her bedroom at home, then for her parents, and for Madelaine. The memory comes sluggishly. They are in a tent. Camping.

"Madelaine!" Zoe cries out. "Mommy! Daddy! Madelaine, where are you?"

5   Madelaine Is Missing!

"Zoe, what is it?" Clive mumbles sleepily.

Caroline moans, tempted to bury her head and go back to sleep, but the edge of fear in Zoe's voice jarred her awake.

"What's wrong Zoe?" she asks, her voice shrill from the fear in her daughter's voice.

The fuzziness and fear from the nightmares still cling to Zoe's mind, making everything strange. She is shaken by the quickly fading memories of the nightmare she had. They leave a cold dread behind.

"Madelaine," Zoe manages, unsure if she is still dreaming or finally awake.

Caroline shifts, craning to look at Madelaine's sleeping bag. She looks confused.

"Madelaine?"

Mocha is woken up by the family making a lot of noise.

The sun is in the sky but it is still early in the morning and it sits low to the East where it rises.

Mocha watches the family from her hiding place. The night terrors left shivers clinging to her little body. Her stomach is hollow and empty with hunger and it makes her feel more stressed. The anxiety she smells from her family compounds it.

Caroline is frantic, searching places she already looked and calling Madelaine. Her face is etched with worry and her eyes and voice are scared.

"Her jacket and shoes are here, her clothes. Her nightgown is missing. She didn't even get dressed. Clive, we have to find her. Where would she go without even shoes?"

Clive seems angry and scared all at once.

"She probably went to the bathroom."

He wanders out of the campsite, stopping to look around in the road, and up the road then back up the road the other way. He bellows Madelaine's name.

"MADELAINE!"

Zoe seems oblivious, sitting and holding her doll on her sleeping bag inside the tent, visible because the tent flap was left flipped open onto the tent roof.

Mocha sniffs the air from her hiding place, trying to catch any smells that might tell her what is going on. Only one thing seems to be clear. Madelaine is missing.

Mocha remembers the bad thing that came in the night. It must have taken Madelaine. The knowledge fills her with sadness and worry.

"I'm going to check the bathrooms," Clive says.

"They won't let you in," Zoe says softly to her doll.

Caroline glances at Zoe and looks at Clive.

"Take Zoe with you. You can send her in."

"Right. Zoe, come on. We're going looking for your sister."

Zoe puts her doll down, puts her shoes on, and crawls out of the tent.

The gravel in the road crunches softly under their shoes as they make the walk to the building with the bathrooms with flushable toilets, running water, and showers.

Spotting an outhouse closer to the campsite, Clive stops there and tests the door. It opens to release the stronger stench inside and a pair of buzzing flies swirling in their stinking prison. The flies seem grateful to be freed, but one swoops back in as he closes the door. The outhouse is unoccupied.

They walk on to the concrete building with bathrooms. When they reach them, Clive stops outside. He nods to Zoe.

"Go in and check if she's there. Make sure you check every stall and the showers."

"I know how to search a bathroom Dad." Zoe pushes the door open and enters the bathroom.

She wrinkles her nose at the smell. It doesn't smell like body waste like the outhouse, but it is not pleasant smelling. She walks the length of the building looking into every bathroom stall and the two showers at the far end. She is alone with only the slow drip of a tap staining one sink yellow for company.

Zoe leaves the bathroom.

"She's not in there," she says.

"Are you sure?"

"Dad."

"Yes, you're right. I checked the laundry room while I was waiting. She's not there. Let's go back."

They start walking back to the campsite.

"Can you think of anyplace Madelaine would have gone?" Clive asks.

Zoe shrugs. "Except the bathroom and looking for her dog, I don't think she'd go anywhere."

When they arrive at the campsite Zoe crawls back inside the tent, taking her spot on her sleeping bag and her doll.

Clive stands in front of the tent looking worried.

He shakes his head. "Not a sign of her."

"Where could she have gone?" Caroline asks.

"She must have gone looking for the dog."

Mocha watches Clive. He wanders back into the road and looks up and down it like he is lost, and finally comes back the campsite, turns in circles, then starts walking out again.

A couple of curious campers come into their campsite.

"We heard you calling," the woman says. "Have you lost a dog or something?"

"Yes," Clive says, turning to them, his face full of worry. "We lost the dog the other night and now one of the girls is missing. We think she snuck out to look for the dog."

"We have to find her," Caroline says anxiously.

More campers are starting to come. Some of them were woken up by the commotion and others are drawn by their interest in finding out what is happening.

News of a missing child is whispered quickly from one camper to the next, the word spreading fast through the immediate area of the campground.

"Don't worry," the woman says to Caroline, "we will find her."

"I hope so," Caroline says. "She could be lost in these woods."

"Yiip!" Mocha lets out a startled yelp when something suddenly grabs her from behind.

"Bad thing!" Mocha thinks, yelping and crying. She squirms and fights to break free.

Two hands hold her now, gripping her firmly so she cannot get away. They drag her backwards out of the bush.

Mocha squirms and struggles to break free. She turns her head to see what is attacking her, sharp little teeth bared to fight back, and stops fighting immediately. She lowers her head sheepishly, refusing to look at him.

It is a man and she is sure it is not the bad thing that came in the night. This one smells like normal human smell. His smell is strong from not bathing for a few days, but normal.

He carries the little dog into the campsite with a grin.

"Is this what you're looking for?" He proudly shows off the dog he captured.

"Mocha!" Caroline says with only a little relief in her worried voice. "You found her. Madelaine is out there somewhere looking for her."

"Thank you for finding her," she says to the man, taking the little dog from him.

"Now we just have to find Madelaine," Clive says.

Mocha whimpers. If only dogs could talk.

She squirms in Caroline's arms, trying to get down.

She has to find some way to tell the people, but she doesn't know how. The thought going through Mocha's head is, "Madelaine, Madelaine, find Madelaine, find Madelaine."

With the dog squirming, Caroline holds her tighter. She carries Mocha to a tree where she ties her up with a rope before releasing her.

Mocha is running as soon as her feet touch the ground.

"Madelaine, Madelaine," Mocha yips, "Find Madelaine."

She reaches the end of her rope and the force of the rope holding her back meeting the momentum of her run flips her over in the air with a hard jolt to her neck, landing on her back.

Mocha gets up; feeling a little bit dazed, her neck sore, and shakes her head to clear it.

She looks back at the rope with resentment. It is keeping her from going to her Madelaine.

Looking up at Clive imploringly, she lets out a little yip. The look is clear. She is begging him to untie her.

Clive looks amused, but only for a second, and the look does not reach his eyes. His face is etched with worry over Madelaine.

"You aren't going anywhere," Clive says, trying to smile. If he can hide how afraid he is, maybe Caroline and Zoe will feel a little better. He can't let them know how worried he is.

He turns his back on the little dog and walks to the group of campers talking to Caroline.

They are making plans to search the campground for Madelaine.

"We should take the dog," Caroline says.

"Walk the dog later," someone says. "You need to focus on finding your daughter."

"Yeah, the dog will just be in the way," someone else says.

Irritation at these strangers telling her how to find her own daughter flashes through Caroline. She looks at Clive.

"Mocha will find her," she says. "She'll follow her scent. She will probably lead us right to Madelaine."

Clive looks back at her unhappily.

"I wish she could, but she's a lapdog. Mocha isn't trained to track anything. She can't even find a piece of food on the floor in front of her. No, they're right. She'll just slow us down."

"I'll go to the park rangers and alert them," one of the men offers.

Clive nods to him appreciatively. "Thank you, but I'm not sure that's necessary yet. She hasn't been gone that long."

"How long has she been gone?"

Clive frowns.

"She was gone when we got up." He nods. "You're right. We don't know when she slipped out. She could have been gone most of the night."

"Right." The man heads off for the ranger station.

Mocha watches the people unhappily.

As they prepare to head out searching, Clive turns to Caroline. "You and Zoe are staying here, right?"

Caroline blinks at him in surprise, at a loss for words.

"But-," she starts.

"He's right," one of the other campers butts in. "You should stay here."

Caroline pushes down the angry glare, stiffening and working to keep her voice calm. "We need everybody out there that we can get looking for Madelaine."

"Someone should be here if she comes back," Clive says. The butting in camper nods her head in agreement. Other campers nod or make sounds of agreement. The looks of pity towards Caroline burn resentfully in her stomach.

She doesn't like it, but sees the sense in it.

"Fine," she says woodenly and watches them all go in small groups without her.

Clive pauses, looking at her and trying to look hopeful.

"Madelaine will probably wander in at any time with no idea so many people are out looking for her. Won't she be embarrassed?"

Caroline does not smile at his attempt to make her feel better.

"Go. They're waiting for you."

She watches him go, seeing the heaviness in his heart reflected in his eyes as he looks away.

Soon everyone except Zoe and Caroline are gone, searching and calling for Madelaine.

Caroline sits in a folding camp chair by the cold fire pit, putting her head in her hands. She looks very sad. Despite her best efforts to hide it from Zoe, she is scared and it shows in her face.

"I have to be strong," she thinks. "I can't cry in front of Zoe. It will make Zoe scared too."

Caroline feels completely helpless. She doesn't want to stay at the campsite. It feels like she is doing nothing to find Madelaine. She wants more than anything in the world to go charging out there into the forest and find her daughter.

She resents her husband and the others, strangers who don't know her, for insisting she stay behind as if she is some child who might get lost too.

"I know they mean well and only want to help," she thinks miserably, "and why I have to stay. But it doesn't make me feel any better about it."

And so Caroline stays for Madelaine. It is the hardest thing she has ever had to do, but she has to stay here in case Madelaine comes back.

She mentally runs through all the reasons why she has to stay and do nothing to help Madelaine.

"Somebody has to be here. Otherwise, finding an empty campsite, Madelaine might decide to go searching for us and go missing again. If she does come back, someone has to put the word out to all the people looking for her that she is back. Someone has to be here when the park rangers show up."

Caroline swallows the tears threatening to come and takes a slow deep breath, trying to control her fear.

"Why, Madelaine?" she whispers. "Mocha came back. You should have waited for morning when we could have looked together again if Mocha was still missing."

Mocha pulls and tugs against the rope, trying to break it, and then trying to slip her collar over her head, and finally resorts to chewing the rope.

"Mocha. Stop." Caroline says sternly, her voice cracking with strain at the end.

Mocha stops chewing and lies down with a big unhappy sigh.

Zoe goes and sits with Mocha, petting her slowly. "Madelaine isn't looking for you, is she?" she asks quietly.

Mocha looks up at her without moving anything but her eyes. Her tail thumps on the ground in a slow wag, happy that someone seems to finally understand, even if it is Zoe, who probably cannot help.

But, sometimes it is the smallest people who can be the biggest help.

Zoe rubs Mocha's ears, glances at her mother to make sure she is not watching, and unties the rope knotted to Mocha's collar.

She leans in close to Mocha.

"I'm worried about her too," she whispers. "Go find her Mocha, go find Madelaine."

Zoe gets up and goes to her mother, climbing in her lap. She puts her arms around her mother's neck and rests her head on her shoulder, watching Mocha.

"It's ok Mommy," Zoe says softly in her mother's ear, "Madelaine will be ok."

Mocha sneaks away, disappearing into the bushes. She pauses at the edge of the campsite, looking back through the leaves at Zoe and Caroline taking comfort in each other.

Caroline's eyes fill with tears that threaten to spill over. It is not lost on her that little Zoe is the one trying to comfort her.

She pulls Zoe away into a sitting position so she can look her in the eyes.

"That's right Zoe," she says, trying to keep her voice light. "Madelaine is out searching for Mocha. Your dad is right. Madelaine could walk into this campsite any minute."

They both glance at the entrance as if to see if it is true. The entrance has only their car.

"She probably doesn't know we are looking for her," Caroline says. "I bet she isn't far."

"Maybe if we call her," Zoe says. "If we keep calling and calling, maybe she will hear."

Caroline nods. "That's a good idea. Let's call."

They both raise their heads, looking up to the sky, and start calling together.

"MADELAINE!!! MAAADELAINNNE!!!"

Over and over.

A noise breaks into Madelaine's sleep; very quiet and very far away.

She shivers. So cold. She tries to snuggle down deeper into her warm sleeping bag, but there is no warmth, no softness of the down-filled bag.

Groggy with the need to sleep more, she slowly opens her eyes.

6   Madelaine in the Dark

It is dark. Pitch black.

"It must still be night," Madelaine thinks.

She shivers. She is cold and immediately misses the furry warmth of Mocha. She tries to snuggle deeper into her sleeping bag, sleepily calling her dog to come curl up with her.

"Mocha," Madelaine calls softly.

Sorrow fills her with a dull ache as reality returns to her sleep-groggy mind. Mocha is gone, lost in the woods. Then she realizes something does not feel right.

"My sleeping bag; I'm not in it. No wonder I'm so cold." Madelaine blinks her eyes, trying to see, but it is so dark.

"Did I crawl out of the sleeping bag in my sleep?"

She feels around, but cannot feel her sleeping bag. She cannot feel any sleeping bags at all.

"Where is my sleeping bag? Where is everybody?"

Her questing fingers push on, feeling around her. The first jolt of fear runs through her.

"There are no air mattresses. This doesn't feel like tent fabric."

Madelaine spreads her palm flat on the surface beneath her, exploring it by touch in the pitch black darkness. The floor is hard and cool like she is lying on the stone patio outside in the backyard at home. She sits up in the dark.

"Mom? Dad? Zoe?" she tries whispering, but there is no answer. Not even the soft fabric rustle of someone moving.

"Mommy? Daddy?" Her voice trembles, sounding small with her fear.

The absolute silence presses in on her like the blackness it fills.

"Where am I?" Madelaine whimpers. "This isn't the tent. The last thing I remember is falling asleep in the tent."

She forces her voice to come louder.

"Mom? Dad? Zoe?" Her voice is shaky.

Again, silence responds.

A stronger surge of fear courses through her.

She blinks again, willing her eyes to adjust to the darkness. She sees only blackness.

"Do I see something?" she thinks. "It's so dark it could be a trick of my eyes."

She blinks, trying to make her eyes work.

"Straining to see is making my eyes hurt."

Madelaine lets out a little whimper.

"Get yourself together girl," she thinks, afraid to make any sound. She feels anything but together.

Madelaine sits there trying to feel out her surroundings, afraid to move from her position with no idea what might be around her.

"Okay, where do I think I am? There is no wind. Not even the slightest breeze. It smells old and musty and closed in. So, I can't be outside."

She holds her breath and listens intently, and is met only by her own breathing coming too raggedly as she tries to breathe slowly and softly through her nose.

"No sound. No insects or cars. No people. Nothing."

Madelaine tries to work up some courage.

"Okay, I can't just sit here. Stop acting like a little kid scared of the dark and move."

Getting to her feet and feeling around in the darkness, Madelaine feels like terror is swallowing her up. She feels numb. It takes a moment to get past that terror and feel her own body. She is stiff and sore from spending hours sleeping on a cold hard surface. She feels like the chill has seeped into her bones.

Madelaine steps forward cautiously, feeling the floor with each step before putting her weight down, her hands ahead of her reaching and feeling. The ground beneath her continues to be cool and flat against her bare feet.

A few steps forward her fingers brush something cool and hard. She inches closer, sliding her palms over it. It is a flat surface, smooth yet a slightly rough, like the floor. Madelaine follows it, running her hands up and down and side to side carefully, aware there could be something to hurt her that she cannot see in the dark.

"It's a wall," she realizes. Her heart is racing in her chest, and she feels her chest tighten further with fear.

She swallows hard. A cold fear fills her.

Trying to keep her bearings and counting her steps, Madelaine blindly follows the wall, sliding her hands along it as she goes.

"Hopefully I will find something, a doorway or window."

It does not take very many steps to reach the corner. She stops, feeling the wall stop. Turning with it, she follows the second wall until she reaches the corner at the end, and then continues again along the third wall to its end.

Moving along the fourth wall, the endlessly rough-flat surface of cool stone finally changes.

Madelaine feels it out carefully.

"It's a door," she whispers. She does not know why, but she senses she should be very quiet.

She forces herself to move past the door despite the irrational fear it will vanish if she stops touching it. Continuing her slow cautious exploration, she comes to the corner again.

"I'm in some kind of small room."

Going back, she follows the wall to the door. It is taking too long. Panic surges up from Madelaine's stomach and she clenches her teeth to keep them from chattering.

"It's gone. The door is gone. I shouldn't have taken my hands off it," she thinks.

Her throat is swelling up with fear and she swallows; her fingers feeling uncertainly along the cool wall in the dark as she keeps shuffling her feet along.

"I've gone past it," she whispers softly, her voice choked with emotion. "It really is gone."

Another sideways shuffling step and her fingers brush something sticking out a little from the wall, a change in the texture.

Relief washes through her with a sick feeling.

"The door is still there. How stupid am I? I thought it could vanish like it was never there; as if there could be a room with just walls and no door."

Tears burn her eyes and mounting pressure presses against them. She tries to swallow, but it feels like a lump has swelled up to fill her throat.

Madelaine rubs at her eyes, trying to swallow again. She feels sick and a cold fear sweat breaks out, chilling her.

"How did I get here?" she whimpers.

All Madelaine can be sure of right now is that she is in a little room with no light. She has no idea how she got there or where her family is.

She tries to open the door. It holds firm. Not even a rattle when she shakes the handle. The door is locked.

"Why would someone lock me in here? Who would have done this to me?"

Madelaine's mind turns to another dark moment in her life, making her stomach churn with nausea and her head swim, lightheaded and weak. Any moment the room will tilt and spin, causing her to fall.

She suddenly feels like she is going to vomit. Her mind wants to shut down, to retreat into the safety of nothing.

It takes everything she has to push the memory away, the edge of it teasing at her thoughts with cold fingers of fear and faint whispers of terrible things.

"I won't think about that. This is not that. It can't be."

Madelaine reaches out again, feeling the door handle and anything that might be a lock or key, a way to open the locked door.

"It's an unusual handle. Is it some kind of shed?" The thought is in the back of her mind, an idle thought, while the rest of her is busy trying not to freak out.

Madelaine's heart is pounding so fast in her chest that she thinks this must be what it feels like when someone is having a heart attack.

Her chest fills with a tight pain. It is agonizing. She wants to cry out.

Madelaine bites her lip to keep herself from making any noise.

"I'm dying, I'm having a heart attack," she thinks, panicking more. Madelaine has moved from fear to terror. The urge to mindlessly rattle, kick, and pound the door fills her.

She makes herself move, shuffling to what she thinks is the center of the room. She sits down on the floor, pulling her knees in to her chest; head down to rest her chin on her knees and wrapping her arms around her legs.

"Where am I?" she whispers quietly. The urge to scream wells up in her and she fights it.

She huddles into herself rocking slightly in the pitch black. Her eyes strain to see in the dark despite the hopelessness of it. She starts shivering uncontrollably from shock, her teeth chattering. Tears run down her cheeks.

Madeleine sits like that for a very long time in the dark. She has no sense of time and no idea how long she sits there.

7   Madelaine's Captor

With the sound of Zoe's and Caroline's calls echoing off the sky, Mocha slinks away from the campsite, staying hidden in the bushes.

As soon as Mocha is sure she won't be seen she starts running. She circles the campsite, staying in the bushes, sniffing the air and trying to find the smell of Madelaine.

It is no use; her smell is everywhere because Madelaine has been everywhere.

Then Mocha remembers; the bad thing. She tries to remember the bad thing's smell.

Sniffing the air, she runs around trying to find the smell. Her nose is overwhelmed with all the strange new smells out here.

Madelaine is sitting on the floor in the middle of the small room feeling absolutely wretched and hopeless. She has given up.

"I've been waiting in the dark for so long." Her words are choked and rough, her voice hoarse. She sniffs, rubbing her eyes and nose.

"I have no idea how long I've been here. It feels like time is rushing forward at breakneck speed and yet dragging endlessly slowly. I lost count of how many times I explored this stupid prison, feeling my way shuffling sideways around it looking for some way out."

Madelaine opens her eyes. She was keeping them closed. It feels easier than trying to see in the dark. Her eyes are sore from straining to see. She blinks and looks ahead. Something there catches her attention and she stares harder.

She realizes now, after staring for long hours at the door, that the faintest of light is leaking in through the cracks around the door. Now that she sees it, it seems so obvious. It makes no difference on the absolute darkness.

"Why didn't I see it before?"

Madelaine feels she can almost sense the vague shapes of the floor and walls in the darkness now.

"This must be what it's like to be blind. Oh, hello, don't mind me. I'm just the blind girl who somehow got herself lost in her tent with her family and locked in some weird room somewhere."

Madelaine shifts, her legs feeling a combination of numbness and pins and needles spreading through them from sitting in that position for too long.

"I can't sit here any longer."

She gets to her feet, arms out and feeling for the wall ahead of her, and shuffles forward. When she feels the wall, she slides her hands until they find the edge of the door.

Madelaine puts her ear to the door, listening. She pulls away, staring through the darkness to where the door is.

"Hello?" Her voice is a hoarse whisper from her repeated bouts of screaming for help.

"There is no one out there." Her voice chokes with fear and her tears. "Nobody can help you if they can't hear you. What if whoever locked me in here is the only one out there to hear me? What if they locked me in here and left? Left me to die here? They could be long gone.

If anyone else comes along, they would have to leave so they don't get caught. What if someone came along and scared off whoever locked me in here? And then they left not knowing I was in here?

Or, if I scream for help again, whoever locked me in here might hear if they are still around. They might be mad that I'm making noise."

Madelaine blinks away the dry red itchiness of her dried tears.

"The only thing I know is I woke up here, locked in the dark, and nobody came to my calls for help. I can't stay locked in here forever and I can't get out. I have to get someone's attention. It's the only way out of here."

The conversation with herself does not make Madelaine feel any better.

"I have to try again. What's the worst that can happen? Whoever locked me in here will hurt me anyway if that's their plan."

"H-hello," she calls out nervously and not very loud.

Her fear catches in her throat. She clears her throat and tries again. Her heart is pounding furiously in her chest, making her feel dizzy.

"Hello," she calls, a little louder. "Somebody? Is anybody there?"

Madelaine listens. She does not hear anything. She tries the door again.

"Still locked."

Bracing herself for something bad to happen, she tries calling out again, louder this time.

"Hello, is anyone out there? The door is stuck. I can't get out."

She bangs on the door then stops and listens again. This time she hears quiet muffled sounds she thinks might be someone moving around.

Madelaine freezes, her eyes wide. This is the first time she has actually heard any sound outside of herself. She holds her breath, listening.

"I think someone is out there."

She is filled with doubts.

"Should I be quiet or should I call louder and hope they rescue me?"

Waking up in the strange place with no idea how she got here has her feeling very confused.

"Did I sleepwalk or was I kidnapped? Who would kidnap me and why? I never walked in my sleep before, but how could they kidnap me without waking up anyone, even me?"

The growing pressure verging on pain in her full bladder makes up her mind.

Madelaine pounds on the door.

"Hello," she calls again louder, "I'm stuck in here. Can you let me out?"

She listens, hearing the sounds again.

"Someone is definitely out there."

She bangs on the door harder.

"Help me! I'm trapped in here! I have to pee!" she yells through the door.

She puts her ear to the door, listening.

It sounds like the person moved right up to the door. She is sure she can hear them on the other side.

"Use the bucket," a man's raspy voice says through the door after a too long pause. The voice sounds low and rough, like the man's voice is hoarse.

"Bucket?" Madelaine screws up her face.

"What?" Madelaine yells through the door.

"I can't have heard that right. He could not have just told me to pee in a bucket."

"Use the bucket," the man's voice comes again. "In the corner."

Madelaine looks around the darkness, seeing nothing. She imagines the shape of a bucket in a corner of the tiny room.

She moves carefully around the room with her hands stretched out before her trailing along the wall as she explores the room again, swinging a foot side to side in front of her when she reaches the corner, then moves on to do the same at the next corner.

Her foot connects with something cool, making it move with a scrape and a dull clang when one side lifts and falls back to hit the stone floor.

The bucket is tucked right into the corner. Her foot missed it each time she went around the room before.

"He can't be serious," she mutters.

The idea of baring herself to pee in a bucket in this strange place makes her feel exposed.

"I can't pee in the bucket. What if he is some perv and is watching me?" The idea sends a new chill of dread through her. Her head swims and her stomach feels sick with it.

"Be strong Madelaine, think this through. I am probably safer here with a locked door between him and me. But if I can convince him to let me out, maybe to use a real bathroom, I can see what kind of building I am in. I can see if there is any way to escape or call for help.

But if I don't do what he says and he gets mad-."

"No," she tries to steel herself with determined resolve. "I have to be strong. I have to at least try."

Madelaine moves back to the door.

"I can't pee in the bucket!" she yells through the door. "Let me out! I have to pee!"

"No," the voice comes gruffly. "Can not."

"What if the door really is stuck and he does not know how to get me out in time so I don't pee myself?" Madelaine wonders. "But how does he know there is a bucket and why is the bucket the only thing in the room?"

"Now I am definitely scared," Madelaine says quietly.

She thinks about that nasty metal bucket in the corner. The urgency in her bladder is a painful pressure.

"I don't like it, but I have no choice. I can't hold it any longer," she whimpers.

Madelaine goes to the corner and pulls the bucket out a little, loathe to touch it. Watching the blackness anxiously, she adjusts her clothes, trying her best to cover herself while pulling her nightgown up and her panties down, and squats over the bucket to pee.

Tears burn at her eyes. She wants to cry. Shame burns her face with a hot flush.

"I wish I was back at the tent with Mom and Dad and Zoe," she sobs.

Finished peeing, Madelaine stands up and steps away from the bucket, careful not to tip it, and straightens her panties and nightgown.

She moves closer to the door, listening. "I should hear some kind of sounds if he is trying to get me out." She hears nothing.

"What are you doing out there?" she yells through the door. "Looking for tools or something?"

Madelaine listens. There is nothing. She bangs on the door.

"Are you still there? Hello!"

She is met by silence.

"At least somebody knows I'm here."

Now Madelaine is cold, alone again, scared, and the small dark room smells like urine.

"Maybe he went to get help? How long will that take? What if he is not going to get help? I can't wait."

She grabs the door handle again, pushing and pulling, trying to rattle it. The door is solid. She throws her weight against it, trying to force it open, and finally kicks it and only manages to hurt her toes.

Madelaine cannot hold back the tears any longer.

"Someone, please, get me out of here," she cries and leans against the door, sobbing helplessly.

8   Ranger Davis Morgan

Mocha sniffs the air, running back and forth in the road outside the campsite, trying to find the bad thing's smell. With all the strange new smells filling her nose and overwhelming her, it is hard to identify one she is unsure of.

Suddenly Mocha has it. She finds the trail. She sniffs at the air and ground, trying to figure out which way the scent trail goes.

It makes her sneeze and wrinkle her lips, baring her sharp little teeth. It is a very bad smell. It smells older than rocks and like something that died and dried up a very long time ago. It smells like danger.

Mocha makes chewing motions and sticks her tongue out repeatedly with a look of disgust, wanting to get the smell out of her nose. She has to put up with it to find Madelaine. She goes back to sniffing the ground to follow the trail.

Mocha has just found it and is about to leap forward with a happy yip when she is suddenly grabbed from behind.

She yelps in surprise, squirming and trying to break loose.

"Your dog got loose again," the man says as he picks her up, carrying her back into the campsite.

Mocha turns to glare at him sullenly. It is the same man who caught her the first time. She huffs with frustration.

"Oh Mocha," Caroline says, jogging over to take the dog as he walks in carrying her.

"Thank you so much," Caroline says.

"You might want to keep this one tied up," he says as he leaves.

Caroline brings Mocha back and ties her up again, double-checking her knot.

She gives Zoe a reproachful look.

"You didn't untie her, did you?"

"Nuh-uh," Zoe shakes her head.

"I hope not," Caroline says, not believing her. "We don't need to lose her again."

She does not say it, but the haunted look on her face says it for her. They don't need to lose the dog when they have already lost Madelaine.

Mocha lies down, resigned. She puts her head down, resting it on her front paws, and stares sadly in the direction the smell of Madelaine's abductor leads.

Caroline paces the campsite.

"I hate just waiting here, not knowing what is happening," she thinks unhappily, "but I can't drag Zoe through the woods all day looking for Madelaine. Besides, someone still has to be at the campsite in case Madelaine comes back."

Caroline stops pacing when a pickup truck stops in front of the campsite. A rush of alarm and hope pulses through her.

"Why are they here?" It could be good news or bad. She stares at it anxiously. The truck is old and battered and has the logo for the park rangers on the door.

A middle-aged man in a park ranger uniform gets out of the truck.

"Good morning ma-am," the man says, tilting his hat respectfully.

His face is tanned and lined from spending a lot of time outside in the sun, and his brown hair is beginning to turn salt and pepper with grey hairs. Everything about him seems friendly.

"My name is Davis," the ranger says as he approaches, "Davis Morgan."

He holds his hand out for Caroline to shake.

She takes it a little nervously. His hand is calloused and grip strong, a man accustomed to hard labor.

"Hello," she says as they shake hands. "I'm Caroline." Caroline tends to be shy around people she does not know and shaking this man's hand makes her feel awkward.

"I understand you are missing a child," Ranger Davis says. "Your daughter is lost in the campground?" He is relaxed, giving off a calming feeling of authority that comes with strength of character.

Davis glances at Zoe, hoping she is the lost child that was reported.

"Yes," Caroline says, her voice almost cracking with emotion.

He can see it in her eyes; the pain and worry that tells him the child in the campsite is not the missing child.

"Our dog ran off the other day," Caroline says. "We couldn't find the dog and Madelaine was very upset. It's her dog and she was very worried."

Caroline sniffles and wipes a tear away from her eye.

"When we woke up this morning Madelaine was gone. We think she snuck out last night to look for Mocha."

"Mocha, that's the dog?" Ranger Davis asks, taking note of the small dog tied to a tree.

"Yes," Caroline says. "Mocha was found this morning, but we can't find Madelaine."

"You don't know when she left?"

Caroline looks confused.

"Was it shortly after going to bed? Middle of the night? Early morning?"

Caroline shakes her head, her watering eyes threatening tears. She fights them off, her voice choking despite her effort to control it.

"No," she manages. "She was here when we went to sleep. When we woke up she was gone.

"Hmm," Ranger Davis rubs his chin, thinking. "You checked everywhere in the campground? The outhouses and bathroom?"

Caroline nods yes.

"You checked the hiking trails and beach?"

"They're searching right now."

"There are a lot of places a child can hide in this campground," Ranger Davis says. "The kids have little forts and hideouts all over the place. I'd say it is a pretty good bet she hasn't gone far. She could be playing in one of the forts."

Zoe slips from her seat and goes to sit on the ground with Mocha. She starts slowly stroking the little dog's head, watching the adults covertly.

"Madelaine isn't the kind of girl who will go looking for forts to play in," Caroline says. "She never has been. Besides, she is too old for that. What if she's not in the campground anymore?"

She looks at him imploringly.

"What if she got lost in the forest and kept going? She might not even know she left the campground. Who knows how far she might have gone, or which way."

"Let's hope not," Ranger Davis says. "If she left the campground, well, the forest is pretty big."

Caroline is even more frightened now.

"What was she wearing?" Davis asks.

"That's the odd part. We don't think she got dressed and her shoes and jacket are still here. We think she's in her nightgown and barefoot."

Davis tries to conceal the alarm he feels.

He looks at Zoe. She seems completely unaware of the adults talking.

"Keep an eye on that one," he says, pointing at Zoe, "in case she gets any ideas about going looking for her sister. We don't want another child lost in this park."

"We might never find them," he thinks, keeping that part to himself. He does not want to lie to the woman about the chances of finding her daughter if she did leave the campground. He also doesn't want to upset her more than she already is.

Caroline stiffens, tired of people telling her to keep a watch over her kids and their dog like she is one of those parents who do not watch them.

"I guess I am one of those parents now, aren't I?" she thinks miserably. The pain of it cuts her deep. She has always been so cautious about keeping the girls safe and always knowing where they are and who they are with.

"And I still failed them." The unwanted thought comes and she has to push it away.

Caroline almost starts crying. She is scared.

"The ranger is right," she thinks. "The forest is huge. If Madelaine is lost out there we may never find her."

"You will find Madelaine, won't you Mocha?" Zoe whispers to the little dog. She heard every word of their conversation. Zoe is worried too, although she is not really showing it. She tends to not show a reaction to things at first, keeping it all inside. When she does finally let it out, it is a big reaction.

"I'm going to call in reinforcements," Davis says. "We will bring in more rangers and I have to contact the police too. We will organize a detailed search to methodically cover as much ground as we can. I will make sure someone comes back to update you on the situation."

He levels his gaze at her as if he is about to say something, then changes his mind.

"We will keep you posted," he says instead.

He gets back into his truck, starts the engine, and drives away.

Caroline watches the truck go with an emptiness that can never be filled; except by the safe return of her daughter.

"He never reassured me. Don't they reassure distraught mothers whose child is lost?"

There is only one reason in her mind why you would not reassure the mother. You do not want to get her hopes up for nothing.

Caroline is even more worried now.

Mocha watches the truck drive away with sad eyes. She whimpers, staring off in the direction the bad thing's scent trail leads.

Her soft whimper draws Caroline's attention.

She looks at Zoe and the little dog and a thought comes to her. "Mocha follows Madelaine everywhere. I know she's our best chance to find her. But she's not a tracking dog. She wouldn't know what to do."

Caroline holds back an unhappy sigh.

"Spaniels are a kind of hunting dog, aren't they? All dogs have good noses, don't they? If she wanted to find Madelaine, Mocha could probably follow her scent."

She is torn with misgivings.

"No, I can't. Madelaine will be devastated if anything happens to Mocha. She is just a little dog. Who knows what is out there; bears, coyotes, wolves, cougars. But, I have to do anything it takes to find Madelaine. I have to. I have to do something." She is full of indecision, a need to do something, and the overwhelming feeling of complete helplessness.

Caroline feels it in the very heart of her soul that her daughter is in trouble. Madelaine is in very big danger. She looks at Mocha again, watching Zoe pet the little dog slowly.

"It's like nothing is going on to Zoe," she thinks. "She's not upset at all. Does nothing affect that child? Does she even understand how serious this is?"

Her thoughts turn back to Madelaine and Mocha.

"They are inseparable. That dog probably wants nothing more right now than to go find Madelaine."

Mocha turns her head to stare at Caroline as if reading her thoughts. The little dog is trembling.

They stare into each other's eyes.

"Whatever it takes," Caroline whispers.

Mocha's ears perk up and she turns her head to look towards the scent trail and back at Caroline as if to say, "Let me do this."

Ranger Davis Morgan mulls it over as he drives away.

"Every year at least one kid goes missing in this campground. So do countless pets. Many of the pets are found or make their way back to the campsites, following their own smell or the smell of food. The kids don't have that advantage.

The kids don't usually go far, don't even leave the park, and are found quickly. But every now and then a kid is not found and it has to be assumed they left the park and are lost in the forest. My gut tells me this could be one of those times. These first hours are crucial to finding a missing person." He feels sick over it.

"It's a large park. Odds are she is still in it somewhere. But if she isn't, if she does make her way out of the park-."

He shakes his head at the thought.

"The forest stretches for hundreds of square miles; that's more than a hundred thousand acres, tens of thousands of that old growth wilderness. She has to still be in the park. She is on foot, and barefoot, so she can't have gone far."

His hands clench the steering wheel, his mind going over a visual of the map of the park, planning his search strategy. An icy chill shivers down his spine, casting doubt on his determination that she will be found quickly.

"The forest is large, but not large enough. We will find her."

Davis is driving too fast, hurrying to the ranger station. The tires lose traction for a moment on a curve, kicking up plumes of dust, and he regains control. He reaches for the radio mounted on his dash, grabbing the mouthpiece and pressing the button as he brings it to his mouth.

"Station one, come in." He releases the button.

Seconds later the radio crackles to life and a voice comes out the speaker with an underlay of static.

"Station one, over."

"This is Davis. We have a missing bird, lost sometime last night. Looking for a runaway pet. Probably still in the park. We need to mount up. I'm on my way to the station now. Over."

"On it. Over."

He lets the radio go silent.

"The first thing I have to do is place the calls to get reinforcements on the way. The rangers will be geared up to head out on horseback by the time I get to the station. It's the only way. Even the jeep won't make it far out there.

The reinforcements can join us when they get here. We can't wait for them. The odds are stacked against us and growing with every hour the girl is missing."

Davis arrives at the ranger station, parking the truck haphazardly in front and hurrying in.

There is no one in sight.

He rushes into his office, quickly making the calls to alert the other stations and the police about the missing girl.

Davis steps out of his office to find Geoffrey standing in the station looking around awkwardly.

"Geoffrey, good," he says, stepping out of his office.

Geoffrey turns to him with a startled look.

"I heard a girl camping here is missing," Geoffrey says, looking to the ranger for help. "Madelaine. She was looking for her dog. Maybe she snuck off to keep looking."

He is worried. He likes her and the thought of what can happen to someone in the forest tugs at him. "What can I do to help?"

Davis smiles.

"The boy is such a go-getter," he thinks. "But he's too young to be out there searching after dark and it will be dark soon."

"That's what her parents think," Davis says. "Geoffrey, can you stay here for a while and watch the phone and the radio? Everyone is out searching for the girl. I called in reinforcements, but they'll take time to get here. There is no one here to man the phone and the radio right now."

"I can help search. I'm a good tracker," Geoffrey tries to plead his case. "I know the park inside and out of the campground pretty good."

Even as he says it, Geoffrey has the sinking feeling the ranger will keep him here or send him home. He feels more mature than most adults give him credit for being and hates being treated like a kid.

Ranger Davis Morgan is one of very few adults who don't treat him like some dumb kid. Until now. He feels it in Davis's words. He sees him as a kid he has to keep out of trouble.

"I've been all over these woods, all the trails and off them, and I can track and shoot," Geoffrey tries to press his case.

"I can do this," he thinks. "I don't want to stay back here like some kid. I want to find Madelaine and her dog."

Davis shakes his head. "I need you here. I need someone on that radio and to answer the phone. You would be doing me a huge favor."

"Okay," Geoffrey says sullenly.

"Thanks Scout," Davis says with a reassuring smile and hurries out.

Geoffrey stares after him, a slow burn of anger rising in his gut.

"Scout. That's what he calls the kids when he's patronizing them."

He angrily plops himself down in the chair by the radio to wait. He stares at the desk top. Both the phone and radio are in reach.

"Next time I go looking for Madelaine I won't be checking in with Ranger Davis," he mutters.

Madelaine is staring blankly into the blackness of her cell. She is huddled into herself, her arms wrapped around her legs with her knees pulled up to her chin. She is shivering and the coolness of the floor feels like it has seeped into her bones and she will never be warm again.

Her eyes are red and swollen from crying, if anyone were able to see them. The tears stopped hours ago, dried up. Madelaine cried so much these past hours she doesn't think she can physically cry ever again.

She stares at the door, afraid to move or make a sound, listening.

"I thought I heard a sound," she thinks, "a very faint one."

Hearing nothing more, Madelaine gets up slowly, her limbs stiff from cold and sitting still so long on the hard floor, and feels her way in the darkness to the door, hands outstretched and searching.

When she feels the solid wall ahead of her she runs her hands along it to the right and then back to the left until she finds the edge of the door.

Madelaine carefully lays her ear against the door. She thinks it is wood, but can't be certain in the darkness. She listens.

All she can hear is her own breathing. She holds her breath, listening again.

There. She hears it. The faint sound of what might be someone moving around out there.

Scared and uncertain, Madelaine swallows and steels herself.

"Hello?" she calls through the door, her voice choked and hoarse. "Mister? Are you back? Have you found help or something to get me out of here with?"

She listens at the door. Nothing.

"I feel him out there. I'm sure of it," she whispers, still listening at the door.

"Mister?" she calls louder through the door. "Hello? Mister?"

She listens again and is sure she hears him moving.

"I know you are out there. I can hear you. Why don't you answer?"

Madelaine pounds on the door and grabs the handle, trying to rattle it.

"Answer me, please," she sobs loudly through the door.

"Please answer me," she whispers, choking on her need to cry. She cries dryly, her eyes unable to produce more tears and feeling sore and achy and too dried out.

She bangs on the door again.

"Mister, please. Please get me out of here." Her voice is as cracked as her throat feels.

She listens at the door again; sure she either hears or senses him right on the other side.

His raspy voice comes quietly through the door. It is garbled and hard to understand.

"K—tt—en m–st –t–ay."

Madelaine swallows.

"Did- did he c-call me k-kitten?" She stutters the words out in her fear and shock. Madelaine feels wrapped in an icy blanket of unreality.

Davis arrives at the stables. He pulls up outside the fence and parks his truck, getting out and walking the short distance to the opening in the fence. The ground here is dried mud with some trampled grass and weeds.

The fence opening is just wide enough for a man and has a section of fence a few feet in front of it so that a gate is not required and the horses cannot get out.

Inside, he finds his crew saddling up for the search.

"Almost ready boss," one of them says, looking up when he enters the barn.

Davis nods, noting that they already saddled his horse and she is patiently waiting, flicking biting flies off her rump and back legs with her tail.

"We will start with the standard search grid," he says, taking her reins and mounting up.

He waits for the others and leads them out of the fenced yard outside the barn through the wide gate for the horses. They plod along in single file through the yard before he urges the horse to a faster pace. Davis keeps the pace easy, not wanting to tire the horses before they reach the difficult terrain.

Geoffrey is sitting in a false relaxed posture, leaning back in the chair, the seat tilted back and his feet on Davis's desk.

He can't sit still any longer. He gets up and paces the room impatiently.

"I have to do something."

He paces back and forth to the wall with a large map covering most of it and back to the desk. He paces to the door, where he quickly looks out and sees no sign of anyone arriving through the windows there, the same view of the front as the window in the office, and back to the other wall with worn metal lockers, cupboards and filing cabinets. He repeats the route again and again, pacing restlessly.

Geoffrey stops when his pacing brings him face to face with the large map covering one wall for the fifth time.

He stares at it, studying it. It is a terrain map of the park and surrounding forest.

Madelaine is sitting in the dark little room crying, huddled into herself and shivering. She has no idea how long she has sat there. It feels like a very long time. She feels sick with fear.

"I don't like sitting in the dark," she whispers hoarsely, barely audible. "I don't know where I am and I don't know how or why." Her voice chokes off.

Her stomach is an empty hollowness of long past hunger pain. Her lips are parched and her mouth feels dry and pasty with thirst.

By now she knows the door isn't stuck or locked accidentally. The man outside the door is holding her captive.

"Mommy, Daddy, please find me," she chokes out through her tears. Her voice is tiny with fear, like a very small child.

9   Hornsby

"How did I get here?" Madelaine asks herself, her voice thin and small with misery and fear. "Why? Why am I here? Why me?"

She jumps at the sound of a scrape at the door. She scuttles backwards on the floor, away from the door, staring at it in wide-eyed fear. Her back is pressed to the far wall, sending its coolness seeping into her chilled body. She can't stop shivering, not only from the cold.

There is the sound of the lock being unlocked and the door opens a crack, its hinges creaking loudly in the small room.

Madelaine's breath catches in her throat and she feels a fresh wave of panic pushing up through her, filling her chest and pressing out as if it can escape. She is numb from hours of mindless fear and not moving for so long. Her legs feel like they have lost circulation and the urge to scream swells up her throat.

She holds her breath, panting through her nose, trying to be silent, and stares at that crack of terrible light.

With another cry of the un-oiled hinges, the door swings open all the way, the light behind it filling the room with a brilliance that burns her eyes, making them water after hours of total blackness. It takes everything Madelaine has to not scream and try to scurry backwards through the cold stone wall pressing against her back.

Madelaine squints against the sudden onslaught of light. She is huddled against the wall, looking haggard and her hair wild. She is trembling so hard her teeth are chattering.

The air coming in is refreshing after smelling only the closed little room filled with her own fear and the soiled bucket.

Madelaine is so hungry that her stomach is a hollow ball of nothing and it feels like she is going to get sucked into it, but until this moment that discomfort was lost in her fear.

"Why am I even hungry?" she thinks, feeling irrational. "I've gone crazy. I'm about to be murdered and I'm thinking about how hungry I am."

She stares at the open door, trying to force her squinting eyes to open wide. Her burning wincing eyes win and she has to close them against the light and its pain.

"Oh gawd, it feels like the light is stabbing my eyes," she thinks.

Madelaine tries again, squinting so that she is looking through the thin slit between her eyelids, her eyelashes shading the world. It makes looking almost bearable.

At first she doesn't see anything.

The room beyond is a hazy image of shapes and muted colors. She blinks her eyes as they begin to adjust to the change in light, the world outside her small prison slowly coming into focus after so many hours in complete blackness.

Madelaine wants to run through the door, but she is scared.

"Maybe I can escape. But maybe he is out there waiting to grab me when I run out," she thinks.

Madelaine is startled when a dark shadow suddenly steps in front of the open doorway, blocking both the light and her escape. He is a dark shape draped in the shadows from the light behind his back.

"Come," the man says quietly in his low rough voice. The word comes out long, as though he has trouble pronouncing it.

He waves with his hand, motioning her to come out of the little room.

Madelaine hesitates. She wants to leave the dark little room, but is terrified of what he might be planning.

"What does he want with me?" she thinks, feeling sick with fear. "Whatever it is, it can't be good."

The man turns and moves away from the doorway, his movement more of a shuffle than a walk. He is wearing a long well worn drab brown robe covering him head to toe, the hem lightly touching the floor. A deep hood is pulled up to cover his head, leaving his face lost in its deep shadow.

Madelaine hesitates. Her heart pounding wildly, it feels like she stands there for a long time. She swallows hard and then steps cautiously to the open doorway. She peeks out, squinting, and sees the man waiting away from the door. Her eyes are becoming adjusted to the light now and it does not hurt her eyes as much.

He gestures to her again. His long-fingered hand is thin and bony. He repeats in that same slow way, "Come."

Madelaine steps out into the room and looks around. It is a small room, but not nearly as small as the one she was locked in. It is cluttered with bookcases, tables of various sizes from the size of a nightstand to a small kitchen table, small wooden chairs, and chests. Stacks of papers and very old looking books and other strange ancient looking artefacts cover every surface. The bookcases and chests are piled with stuff inside and out, so over-filled with papers and books and scrolls that the clutter seems to be growing from them like a wild bush. More piles have taken refuge in the corners, some taller than the tables next to them. Everything is coated with a layer of dust, its perfection ruined to show where things have been touched.

The room is lit by oil lamps. The flame in each lamp dances sinuously slowly behind its glass cage, barely moving as it burns the oil that soaks up the fabric wicks. The lamps give the room a soft orange-yellow glow, casting deep shadows in the corners of the poorly lit room.

"I can't believe it seemed so painfully bright," Madelaine thinks.

She studies her new surroundings, staring at the walls. They look like rock. Not the sort of wall made with stones and grout, but rather a single rough flat slab of stone complete with veins of minerals running through it.

"I've seen buildings with rough stone walls on the outside," she thinks, "and my school has inside walls made with large flat bricks painted the most ghastly puke orangey-yellow and white. I have never seen walls like this before. There are no seams. It must be fake rock."

The robed man grunts at Madelaine.

"Eat," he says in his rough low voice. Again, the word is drawn out longer than normal. He points at a worn out looking wooden table with two chairs. A space had been cleared on the table and a silver plate of food and a silver cup of water are there looking out of place.

Madelaine looks at it uncertainly. The plate and cup look like they came from another time, one that has vanished into the past at least a hundred years ago.

"I don't want to eat it," she thinks. "What if it's poisoned?"

The smell of the food is making her hungrier. The hunger is a gnawing pain filling her gut and making her head feel woozy.

She looks at him now, studying him. There is not much to see but his long very old and worn looking cloak with the hood leaving his face in shadow. He is taller than her, but maybe not taller than her dad, she isn't too sure. He seems stooped over, like he would be taller if he stood up straight.

"Like he thinks he's some kind of monk or something," she thinks. "Oh my gawd, he really is some kind of weird creeper guy." She almost says it out loud, pursing her lips in time to keep the thought only in her head.

The man grunts at her again, a little impatiently this time.

"Eat," he says again, the word drawn out like before, pointing at the table.

Madelaine steps to the table nervously, her movement stiff and wooden, and sits down. She stares at the plate of food. She can't figure out what it is.

The man points again at the plate of food, and then makes a motion towards his mouth. His movement reveals his mouth in the shadows beneath his cloak hood.

The sight of his open mouth beneath his hood disgusts Madelaine with his yellowed crooked teeth and pink gums, and open spaces where he is missing teeth.

Madelaine picks at the food, looks up at him, and back down at the plate unhappily.

"I could refuse to eat," she thinks. "I would be useless to him if I starved to death, whatever he kidnapped me for." Her stomach grumbles, reminding her how hungry she is. The hollow empty pain filling her stomach gurgles and rolls with the audible rumbling.

"If I'm too weak with hunger, I won't be able to escape," she thinks.

Finally, she tentatively picks up a piece of food and puts it in her mouth. Her starving feeling surges, making her sourly empty stomach lurch sickly, the annoying hunger swallowing her up in its eagerness to be fulfilled. That small piece of food does not taste bad either.

Madelaine tries the water, sniffing at it first before taking a small sip. It tastes off, different, nothing like water from the tap at home or bottled water, but she is thirsty enough to drink just about anything.

She eats another small piece of food and before Madelaine knows what she is doing, she is devouring the whole plate of food and thirstily drinking the whole glass of water.

When the food is gone Madelaine stares down at the empty plate. She still feels hungry, her parched mouth desperate for more water.

She also feels shame at having so greedily scarfed down food that came from her kidnapper. "What if it's poisoned?" she thinks again, chastising herself for her weakness.

Suddenly, Madelaine does not feel so good. Trying to ignore the nausea and hoping it goes away, a surge of panic that the food really is poisoned teasing at her thoughts, she looks around the room for her kidnapper.

He is puttering around the room, moving stuff around with no purpose like he is trying to look busy. His movements are slow, unhurried. He seems nervous.

Madelaine watches him for a few moments, building her courage.

At one point his hood shifts back on his head, not quite falling off but giving her a partial look at him. Her first impression was right.

"He is definitely kind of stooped over beneath that thing he's wearing," she thinks. His fingers are long and bony and what she can see of his face shadowed beneath the hood is wrinkled and old, the skin papery thin and mottled with age spots. The wispy bits of hair that shows is long, white, and thin looking. He looks very old, older than old.

"How could someone so old manage to take me without me waking up and get me here?" she thinks. It makes her feel a little more brave to think that she is up against a very old man. "He can't be that strong. If I can get a chance to run, this old man would have no chance at catching me."

She considers the possibilities. Her thoughts are all over the place in a panicked frenzy.

"What do I do in the meantime?" she thinks. "What if I'm underestimating him? He's so old. What if he couldn't do it? What if there is someone else, younger, who carried it out? Maybe if I get him to see me as a person not just a victim he will let me go. At least I might make him put off whatever he, or they, are planning to do with me. I might be able to buy myself a little more time to find a way to escape. Maybe get him to trust me, giving me a better chance to escape."

Madelaine scrapes together what little courage she can and forces herself to speak to him.

"W-what's your name?" Madelaine asks nervously, her voice small and stammering. The fear is making it nearly impossible for her to speak; impossible to speak normally.

"Hornsby," he says gruffly. Even saying his own name, it comes out slow and stilted, as if his mouth has trouble making the sounds of words.

"Hornsby? Is that it?" Madelaine wonders. "If I get his full name, when I escape they can arrest him."

"H-Hornsby what?" she asks, cursing her voice for trembling and stuttering. "You do have another name, don't you?"

"Only Hornsby," he says.

"Everyone has more than one name," Madelaine says, her curiosity pushing back the fear a little.

"Used to," Hornsby says gruffly, sounding annoyed by her questioning.

He motions towards the little room she has spent hours imprisoned in.

"Back."

Madelaine feels a surge of panic at the thought of going back into that dark little room. She blinks her eyes at him as if she does not understand.

He motions again.

"Back. Girl must go. In."

Madelaine shakes her head slowly in horror.

The old man sighs, his shoulders moving beneath his cloak in a motion that suggests irritation.

"What is problem?"

Madelaine's panicked mind can't think clearly. She tries to think fast, some reason why he should not lock her back in that room.

"I-it's dark," she stumbles the words out. "A-and the bucket," she wrinkles her nose, "the room smells bad."

Hornsby pauses for the smallest moment, but it gives her hope.

"Back." He motions to the room again, gruff and angry.

"Please, Hornsby, don't lock me in there again."

"Go," he says more forcefully, stepping forward as if to physically force her into the little room.

Fear surges through Madelaine, chilling her, and she scurries back to the room. The idea of him laying one of those old bony hands on her fills her with dread and disgust.

Hornsby follows at his slow shuffle, swinging the door closed with a screech of the un-oiled hinges, closing out the light to leave Madelaine in darkness.

Madelaine can only watch in wide eyed fear as the door swings closed, the light shrinking until it thuds closed and the light is gone. The lock engages with a dull sound that echoes with a menacing finality in the tiny room.

She is back in the pitch blackness of her prison. She wants to cover her face and cry, but can't see her hand in front of her face.

"I'll poke myself in the eye," she thinks miserably. The tears come.

"Seriously? Why am I thinking such stupid things?" she chokes out. "I should be thinking about how to get out. What that creepy old man is going to do to me."

A shiver of terror trembles down her spine.

"No, don't think about that. Think about how Mom and Dad must be looking for you; that they will find you. How you can escape. What was in that room that I might be able to use for a weapon?"

Madelaine tries to think about these things, but her mind is frozen with the sick dread of fear and won't cooperate.

She stands there in the dark, fighting the scream that is caught in her throat, making her throat ache with the need to shriek and cry hysterically. A chill seeps deep into her, making her shiver uncontrollably.

Madelaine wraps her arms around herself, rubbing them in the dark and trying to keep some small shred of control over her sanity.

"He didn't even empty the pee bucket," she whimpers desolately.

Finally, she carefully lowers herself to sit down on the cold stone floor. The coolness seeping through her nightgown chills her more.

"I'm still dressed for bed," she thinks miserably, unsure if she should be embarrassed by that or not. It's not like she has any choice.

Over the next endless hours Madelaine alternates pacing restlessly, sitting and rocking, and curling up lying on the floor in a little ball of misery. She wonders if it is still the same day, if he will ever come back or if she is going to die here alone in the dark, and what terrible thing she did to deserve this horrible fate. She reminds herself that she doesn't believe in fate, wonders what her parents and Zoe are doing, if they are still looking for her or if they gave up. Fresh tears of loss surge at the thought of Mocha, lost and probably eaten in the woods. She thinks about that boy, Geoffrey, and wonders if he will be able to find Mocha if she's still alive.

"Will he even try now that I'm gone?" she whispers hoarsely to the dark.

Unable to sleep and feeling ill with exhaustion, Madelaine jumps; startled at the sound of the lock being unbolted.

With a threatening squeal of the hinges, the door slowly swings open to splash a crack of light into the room.

Madelaine's mind races through terror to shaky hope. "What if someone came to save me?" she whispers breathlessly.

The door swings open further, the light widening to splash across Madelaine, and all hope is brutally dashed at the sight of Hornsby on the other side of the door.

He motions to her.

"Bucket."

"What?" Madelaine's mind cannot comprehend the word or what he wants.

"Bucket." He motions again.

He is holding out another bucket, his other hand pointing to the soiled bucket behind her. He waggles the fresh bucket at her.

Madelaine would not have thought it possible, but her already crushed hope just took a big heave downward.

"He plans to keep me locked in there," she thinks miserably.

Trembling so hard she can barely make her limbs work, Madelaine woodenly stumbles back to the bucket. It takes effort to pick it up and not drop or spill it with her shaking hands.

Bringing the bucket to the door, she hands it to him, taking the fresh one and gripping it awkwardly.

Being this close she can smell him and it is not pleasant. He smells stale, musty, old. There is something else to it too, an unpleasant sour earthy smell, but she can't identify it. Just smelling him unnerves her more.

"Old man smell," she thinks. "He smells like my grandfather, but worse." She swallows. "Try to keep him talking. Stall. I have to keep trying to make him see me as somebody, not a victim."

Swallowing her fear, Madelaine's voice quivers as she speaks.

"Hornsby, when I asked you about your other name, you said you don't have one anymore. Most people have two names, a first name and a last name. Some have a middle name. Why do you have only one?"

"Do not know," Hornsby says, turning and setting the soiled bucket on the floor out of the way.

"You don't know why you only have one name?" Madelaine can't believe this.

"Do not know."

Madelaine blinks at him.

"Everyone knows their own name."

"Do not know question."

Madelaine looks at him, perplexed.

"When I asked what your name is, you said you only have one."

The old man grunts. "Hmm. Hornsby."

"Yes, you said your name is Hornsby. But what about your other name? Everyone I know has at least two names, a first name and a last name. You said you don't have a second name anymore, so you must have gone by another name before. What was your other name?"

"I forgot," Hornsby says.

"How could you forget your own name?" Madelaine asks.

"Just old," Hornsby says. "This old; you forget. Does not matter."

"How could it not matter?" Madelaine is shocked. "It's your name. Names are important."

Hornsby shrugs.

"Still have one name," he says. "Another name," he shrugs, "not important."

He seems agitated now, like something is bothering him.

Madelaine wonders if he is upset about forgetting his other name, embarrassed maybe.

"Hornsby must go now." He starts turning away, reaching for the door to close it.

"Wait," Madelaine sobs.

He pauses, looking at her.

"I-it's so dark in here," Madelaine manages, "and cold." She rubs her arms for emphasis.

He stands motionlessly, breathing, and then turns away, leaving the door open.

"Little Kitten stay." He moves off, rummaging out of site.

Madelaine stares at the open door breathlessly, filled with the urge to bolt, but is too scared. She thinks about the odd way he speaks.

"Do you have trouble saying words?"

"Hornsby not usually speak."

"Are you telling me that you aren't used to speaking? Do you never speak to anyone?"

"No need. Only Hornsby. No need to talk to Hornsby." He steps half into view and points at his temple to put his point across, moving out of sight again.

"Yes, I guess if it is just you here alone you really don't need to talk, do you?"

Hornsby steps back into view, holding out a wool blanket to her.

The thought of touching it, and of having to move closer to the old man to do it, fills Madelaine with a sick feeling, but the chill that is still making her shiver involuntarily wins out and she steps forward and takes the blanket, quickly stepping back again.

He moves out of sight for a moment and returns carrying an oil lamp. He motions her to put down the blanket and take the lamp.

"Light."

Madelaine nods self-consciously, setting the blanket down and stepping forward to take the lamp. Her every movement is careful. The moment her hands grip the base of the lamp a thought flashes through her mind, her hands moving with a quick violent motion, splashing oil and fire over the old man, his arms coming up with a cry of surprise and pain to ward off the flames covering him. Another thought flashes through her mind on the heels of the first, her smashing the oil lamp on the floor at Hornsby's feet in an explosion of the glass cover shattering and clang of the metal bottom on stone, oil erupting to splash up. The oil splashing up covers the old man, the flame of the lamp freed from its own prison and engulfing him with a dull roaring whoosh.

Hornsby releases the lamp to her grip.

Numb with fear, Madelaine can only step back into the little room and carefully put the lamp down.

"Hornsby go now."

Something in the way he says it strikes a new chord of fear in Madelaine. There is a heaviness to his voice and manner. She has the unpleasant feeling that he does not mean he is just leaving the room.

"A-are you going somewhere?"

Hornsby nods and grunts. It tightens the knot in her stomach.

"How long will you be gone? When will you be back?"

"Do not know."

The door closes with that wretched screech of the un-oiled hinges and the lock thuds into place, and Madelaine almost loses her sanity.

She stares at the locked door; feeling like something she cannot control has swallowed her up. The world is closing in, the walls pressing in, and the air getting heavy and un-breathable.

"He-he's abandoning me here," she whimpers. "With no food or water."

Madelaine's breaths start coming heavier, rough and ragged. She looks around at her small prison, her eyes wild with panic.

"I can't breathe. I'm going to run out of air. I'm going to starve, die of thirst. No, he can't. He can't abandon me here."

She leaps forward, banging on the door with her palms, sobbing and screaming.

"Hornsby, don't leave me here! Please! Come back! HORNSBY, PLEASE!"

Madelaine pounds the door with her fists, kicking at it and viciously attacking the handle in a frenzy of panic, sobbing and screaming at Hornsby to come back.

The banging and hoarse screams echo through the still and dim corridors of the place where her prison resides. They continue on and on, her voice growing hoarser and more desperate, her hands and feet aching with the bruising attack on the locked door.

Finally, Madelaine wears herself out and exhaustion wins against her feeble continued attempts to call her kidnapper back.

Her voice almost gone now, her hands red from the abuse and her face twisted in despair and stained red with tears, Madelaine turns, leaning against the door, and slowly sinks to the floor.

She sits there against the door, sobbing, her weakened voice barely croaking out her tortured throat in a hoarse whisper, repeating the words over and over and over.

"Hornsby, don't leave me here. Please come back. Hornsby, please come back."

10   Geoffrey

Geoffrey's eyes open. He blinks. It is not dark in his room, but dark enough he could easily sleep until noon.

He forces himself to get up out of the comfortable warmth of his bed.

"Madelaine doesn't have a warm bed."

The thought makes him feel guilty for having that comfort.

He quickly pulls his pajama pants off and jeans on. Pulling a shirt over his sleep-tousled hair, he looks in the small mirror on the wall and tries to straighten his hair.

Failing, he goes down the hall to the bathroom and splashes water on his hair to tame it before combing it and quickly brushing his teeth.

In the kitchen, he slips on his boots and jacket. Grabbing an apple and a bagel, he starts heading out the door.

"Where are you going?"

Geoffrey stops, looking guilty. He turns to see his mom in the kitchen doorway.

He considers lying. It does no good. She always sees through the lies.

"I'm going out to look for Madelaine."

His mother frowns.

"You are spending too much time out there looking for this girl. I think you should stay home."

Geoffrey's look darkens. She can see he is getting his back up against her, but she pushes on.

"You are putting your own safety at risk for some girl you don't even know, out there day and night searching for her. If you haven't found her yet, you won't. Let the professionals deal with it."

"Mom."

"She is nothing to you. Why are you so obsessed with finding this girl? You don't even know her."

"Mom, I have to do this. She's out there alone in the forest. While I'm here safe and warm in my bed, she's probably huddled on the cold ground with nothing but her fear. She doesn't even have shoes and a jacket."

His mother's look softens.

"How did my son grow up to be such a caring person? Oh yeah, I must have done something right."

"Mostly, I feel like I failed him," she thinks.

"I still don't like this obsession," she says. "I understand why you feel you have to find her. I think. But I don't want you spending so much time out there alone. At least make sure you are with one of the rangers."

"Yes, Mom."

Geoffrey ducks out the door.

"And don't forget to eat!" his mother calls after him.

Geoffrey races down the campground road on his bike, skidding to a stop up the road from Madelaine's campsite. He stares down the road towards it, getting up his courage.

Riding on more slowly, he stops again outside the site and out of sight of anyone inside. He listens. There is the quiet sound of voices, female. He can't make out what they are saying.

A surge of hope fills him. Standing the bike up, he walks into the site hesitantly.

He sees only Caroline and Zoe.

Caroline looks terrible, like she hasn't slept or really eaten since Madelaine went missing. Geoffrey's hope slips.

Zoe looks no worse for wear, but angry and pouty. Her face brightens when she sees him.

"Geoffrey!" Zoe almost squeals it out, jumping up to rush to him and catching herself. She looks at her mother almost contritely, the smile quickly slipping off her face, and looking down. She gives him a quick shy smile, conscious of her mother's mood.

Caroline looks up from cleaning up from breakfast. Geoffrey's first impression of her was a weak mimic of what he sees now.

Her look is not welcoming. It's not exactly hostile either. Her disheveled hair is pulled back haphazardly in a ponytail and her face is waxy and pale with stress lines, making her look older. So does the rough complexion from exhaustion and insufficient food and water. Her eyes look like she has not stopped crying since yesterday and are dry now only because she is completely spent of all tears, emotions, and strength.

The breakfast she is cleaning was barely touched. Her hands have a slight tremble.

Caroline puts her focus back on her task.

"Hello Geoffrey," she says, keeping her eyes down as she packs up the uneaten food.

"Hi Mrs. Winslow. Zoe."

Geoffrey looks down uncertainly, swallows, and forces the words out. "I-I came to see if-." He stops, unsure what to say.

"You came to see if Madelaine is here," Caroline finishes for him. She still can't bring herself to look at him and keeps her hands busy so she doesn't have to, taking longer than necessary to arrange and seal the plastic bags with leftovers.

"She's not here." Caroline almost chokes on the words and has to work to control her voice. "We haven't found her yet."

Caroline almost breaks down with the admission. She has to force her legs to keep standing and her arms to not drop her hands uselessly at her sides.

Zoe and Geoffrey exchange a look of understanding, his holding sympathy.

"I'm very sorry Mrs. Winslow. I came here hoping for good news. I'll keep looking today."

Caroline looks at him with a flash of alarm.

"It's okay Mrs. Winslow. I know these woods like my own back yard. They kind of are, in a way. I won't get lost."

He pulls out a compass from his pocket to show her.

"Even if I get turned around, I can always find my way back. My bike moves pretty fast and is sturdy and I can ride these trails like nobody's business. I can cover a lot of ground."

"I appreciate it. I don't want you out there if your parents don't know you are doing it."

"It's just my mom and she knows."

Caroline nods, unsure how she feels about it.

"Mom won't let me go look for Madelaine," Zoe complains.

"We've been over this Zoe. Someone has to stay here in case she comes back."

"It doesn't take two of us."

"You are not going out there alone." Caroline's tone is firm with a strangled pain.

"She can go out with me for a bit," Geoffrey says. "I'll leave my bike here and we can walk. There are lots of trails and places the searchers probably didn't think of."

Zoe looks at her mother hopefully, giving her a pleading look. She needs this more than her mother can possibly guess.

"I guess," Caroline says hesitantly, already regretting it. "But stay together and don't go far. I can't have another daughter lost in the forest."

She gives Geoffrey a hard warning look.

"Look after her." There is a threat beneath the pain, worry, and exhaustion in her tone.

"She's safe with me," he says.

Eager to go, Zoe drags him out of the campsite before her mother changes her mind.

"How are you holding up?" Geoffrey asks after they are out of the campsite.

"Madelaine is still missing. How do you think I'm holding up?" Zoe seems unaffected, showing no real emotion.

Geoffrey feels like a jerk for asking.

"Sorry." He looks at her. "For the stupid question and for what you are going through."

"Yeah, I guess you were just trying to be nice. Sorry." Zoe feels bad for being rude.

"Your mom looks like she's having a really tough time," Geoffrey says.

"She is. She's so worried it's making her sick. They won't let her or me help look for Madelaine. Nobody seems to care how we feel or that we need to look for her too. It's like everyone only sees me as some stupid little kid who'll just get lost too. Even Mom feels like they all think she's helpless and has to be kept back."

"She said that? Because, really, someone should be there just in case, Madelaine does come back. It should be someone she knows."

"Why can't it be Dad sometimes? Why always Mom and me?" Zoe challenges him, feeing a rush of defiance and anger.

"You're right. You should take turns so everyone feels like they are helping find Madelaine. It can't be easy having to sit there all day and wait."

"It's not."

"At least you are searching with me now," Geoffrey smiles.

"Why?" Zoe looks at him curiously.

"I know the places none of these campers know about. This way."

He leads her up a trail Zoe didn't see when they were approaching it.

"Do you think wishes come true?" Zoe asks.

"Sometimes. Maybe. Usually I don't think they do." Geoffrey's expression is serious as he leads Zoe along the trail.

"But do you think you can make them come true?" Zoe presses.

"I wish we could," Geoffrey says. "Then we could wish Madelaine back safe."

"And Mocha." Zoe looks down, hesitant about whether she should continue.

"Usually wishes never come true," she continues. "But what if you find something so special that wishing on it hard enough could actually make wishes come true?"

Geoffrey looks at her, feeling a pain in his chest over what Zoe and her family are going through. The pain he feels himself worrying about Madelaine is a weak echo to what they must be suffering.

"It would be nice if that was true. What kind of special thing?"

"I don't know," Zoe shrugs. "Anything, like a rock."

"A rock." Geoffrey lets out a little snort.

Zoe feels defensive, like he's making fun. She fingers the small object in her pocket.

"I found a rock. I never saw one like this before. It was pretty and unusual, so I kept it."

She pulls it out, holding it in her palm for Geoffrey to see.

Geoffrey looks at the stone dutifully.

"It feels even smoother than it looks," Zoe says. "Feel it."

Geoffrey rubs it with a finger.

"It is smooth. Pretty too," he says.

"It feels warm. Do you feel it?" Zoe asks.

"I do. That's from being in your pocket."

Zoe nods. "I was just playing around. It seemed so special. I wished hard on it that Madelaine didn't have Mocha so she would play-," she cuts off quickly, changing her words, "hang out with me, and then Mocha got lost."

She looks at him and he stares back, seeing the pain in Zoe's eyes.

"It's not your fault," Geoffrey says.

"Then, when I saw how unhappy Madelaine was, I wished hard on the stone that Mocha came back. I wished that Madelaine was out looking for her. I-I guess I didn't really think the wishes through. They both came true. Now Madelaine is lost and Mocha was found."

Geoffrey shakes his head.

"It's only a stone, Zoe. You can't wish someone gone on a stone."

Tears slip free, rolling down Zoe's face. She sniffles.

"But I did and it did. I wished Madelaine could go look for Mocha and she did. They both went missing and I wished it."

Zoe feels more miserable than she has in her life and finally admitting her guilt to another person only makes her feel more wretched. At least keeping it to herself she could pretend to convince herself she isn't such a bad person.

"I'm a horrible person. No wonder Madelaine hates me."

"She doesn't hate you. She's your sister."

"No, she hates me. Madelaine is always angry and wants nothing to do with me. I think she wishes I was gone."

She looks at Geoffrey.

"What if Madelaine was the one who found the stone and wished me gone? Then I'd be the one lost in the forest."

She rubs the tears away angrily.

"But she didn't and I'm not. It was me."

"Hey, you can't blame yourself for this," Geoffrey says. "It's not your fault. You didn't really mean those wishes anyway. You were frustrated. You didn't make them go away."

"But I wished it."

"Not really." Geoffrey puts his hands on her shoulders, making her look him in the eye.

"We all say things we don't really mean, that we don't really want, sometimes when we are angry or frustrated. I don't want you blaming yourself any more. Got it? It's not your fault."

Zoe nods reluctantly, not feeling it.

"Okay. Let's keep looking."

They continue searching and talking, Geoffrey trying to make Zoe feel better, to give her hope, and Zoe feeling utterly miserable and scared for Madelaine and Mocha.

They return to the campsite after a few hours, Zoe not really feeling better but putting on a brave face.

Caroline looks up with relief when they walk into the site. She tries to hide the flash of irritation and distrust directed at this strange boy who was with Madelaine before she vanished.

"You can't blame him," she chastises herself silently. "She was with us. Madelaine snuck out of the tent to look for Mocha."

"Would you like to stay for supper?" Caroline asks because she feels obligated, hoping the boy declines.

"Thank you Mrs. Winslow, but my mom will be expecting me home," Geoffrey says.

They turn at a commotion outside the site.

A group of exhausted looking people walk by. Clive breaks off from the group, entering the campsite with the weary walk of the defeated.

Caroline's heart flutters and she almost dares to hope, but it is immediately quashed by the misery and defeat in his face and posture.

"No luck?" she asks unhappily.

Clive shakes his head.

"Nothing. Not a bloody sign of her."

He pushes back the tears, trying to be strong for his family.

Zoe cries for him. It is almost a relief to feel he doesn't have to because someone else is.

Feeling like an awkward extra wheel, Geoffrey slinks off home.

Geoffrey puts his bike away when he arrives home, slinking into the house quietly.

"Did they find her?" His mother's voice comes from the living room.

His shoulders sag. He was hoping to avoid this conversation.

Knowing it is expected Geoffrey takes off his shoes and goes to the living room.

His mother is looking at him from her chair. A single light glows softly and the book she was reading is resting cover up in her lap.

"No," Geoffrey sighs. "They didn't find her."

Her look is sympathetic, but without the understanding he is hoping for. The same goes for her words.

"I think you should leave this to Davis Morgan and his team. The rangers know what they are doing and don't need a boy running around the forest too."

Geoffrey bristles at this, but tries to hide it.

"It's fine, Mom. I know my way around the forest. I'm not going to get lost."

"Maybe not, but you could get yourself into trouble. I don't like you running around the forest and you know why. It isn't worth the risk for a girl you don't know."

"If I was lost you would want someone to look for me." He can't keep the edge of anger out of his voice.

"Someone is looking for her." His mother tries to look more sympathetic. "I can't lose you too Geoffrey."

Her words are a knife to his heart. Geoffrey looks down.

"You won't lose me," he mumbles. "I'm tired. I need to get some sleep."

He turns and leaves.

"I mean it," his mother's voice calls after him. "Stay out of the forest and leave finding this girl to the rangers."

11 Find My Madelaine

Mocha shivers and whimpers. She is still tied to the tree, powerless to go find Madelaine.

It is getting late and the stress is wearing down all three of them. After eating and a short rest, Clive rejoined the others to search again for Madelaine. Caroline has alternately paced the campsite anxiously, fidgeted with rearranging things, and sat forlornly in the chair before the cold dead fire pit.

Zoe mostly sat quietly and finally broke down crying inconsolably.

Mocha can hear Zoe's sobbing and smells her unhappiness and it makes her feel even more miserable.

Zoe, who has been so calm and quiet through all this, finally let her feelings get the best of her. Mocha smelt her sadness all day, despite Zoe seeming unaffected to the people around her.

Mocha sighs unhappily. The little dog looks back at the rope, weighing her options and tempted to chew through it.

Zoe can't stop crying.

"This is all wrong," she thinks miserably. "This is not how this trip was supposed to go."

"It's my fault Madelaine is gone, Mommy," she sobs.

Caroline sits her up to look into her eyes. Zoe's eyes are wide with the pain and remorse filling them.

"No, honey. You can't blame yourself. She went looking for Mocha. Why do you think it's your fault?"

"I was mad at Madelaine because she wouldn't have anything to do with me. I wished Mocha was gone and then she was gone."

"That wasn't your fault," Caroline tries to sooth her.

Zoe isn't having it. She shakes her head. She pulls a little round flattish stone out of her pocket and shows it to her mother.

"It's magic. It's a wishing stone. It made Mocha go away. When Madelaine was so unhappy in her sleeping bag, upset we had to stop searching for Mocha; I wished Madelaine was out there finding Mocha and Mocha was back. And then it all came true. Mocha came back and Madelaine was gone looking for Mocha. That's where everyone says she is. And now she is lost out there in the forest."

She stares teary-eyed, tears staining her cheeks, at her mother.

"Oh, honey, Zoe, it's not your fault. This rock, wishes on it coming true isn't real. It's only make-believe. You can't wish on a rock and make someone go away. It just happened and it's not your fault."

Zoe shakes her head.

"I was tired and worried. I wished so many things. I wished Madelaine would forgive me for making Mocha go away. I wished something would happen to make Madelaine like me better. But that didn't work. Madelaine still hates me."

"Madelaine doesn't hate you Zoe. She's angry at the world sometimes. She doesn't hate you."

"She does," Zoe sobs. "And wishing on this stupid stone didn't work. I was going to throw it away. I wanted to. But I wished on it again, just in case. I'm scared to throw it away. What if that means Madelaine never comes back? I don't know if Madelaine will ever forgive me, or even like me more, but the rest came true. It's all my fault Madelaine is gone."

"I want Madelaine," Zoe wails with tears streaming down her face. "Where's Madelaine?"

"Hush," her mother sooths, stroking her hair and rocking her in her lap, holding her tight as if she too might be somehow taken by the forest. "It's just a silly little rock and a silly little wishing game. The rock didn't make Madelaine go away and neither did you. We will find her. Madelaine will be ok."

But Caroline isn't sure herself if they will find Madelaine or if her daughter will be ok. She is terrified they will never find her, and if they do she will be already lost forever.

"The forest is so big, and she is just one small girl," she thinks. Knowing Zoe blames herself is a new pain twisting in Caroline's heart.

"Zoe is overtired and unhappy because she is worried and misses her sister," Caroline thinks.

Caroline and Zoe sit for a long while, Zoe mourning the loss of her sister and Caroline trying to sooth her and feeling useless and helpless while she herself needs soothing.

Zoe has nearly cried herself out. Her mind keeps going over everything, her wishes and her fight with Madelaine, her dreams and Madelaine lost in the woods.

"Madelaine must be so hungry and scared," she thinks. "My dream." Patchy memories of the dream keep insinuating themselves into her mind. "Of course, it was only a dream."

But she can't push it aside now. The dream keeps haunting her. Something she can't identify looming over her, nothing more than an indistinct shadow. She senses the presence of something and it leaves a soiled feeling that she cannot shake. Flashes of motion, the whole world swings and sways. She is flying, fleeing, urgency pounding in her chest and the sickness of- no, she is not flying; she is falling. She is falling with the sickness of the motion filling her stomach. For a moment she thinks the world is tumbling over and she is going to fall off. The dream flashes are disorganized and fuzzy.

"Was I falling or flying in the dream?" Zoe wonders. But then another thought worms its way into the confusing dream bits. "Or was it Madelaine?"

Zoe sits up in her mother's lap.

"Mommy, what if Madelaine did not run away to look for Mocha? What something took her? Like a bad man?"

"Only it wasn't a man," she thinks.

Caroline meets her eyes, staring into them. The steady gaze of the little girl sends a chill down her spine.

"Does she know something she isn't telling?" Caroline wonders. "What does she know?"

"Where is this coming from, Zoe," she asks. "Of course no bad man took Madelaine. She was with us in the tent. She snuck off to find Mocha."

Zoe leans against her mother, snuggling for comfort and warmth. She can't shake the cold gripping her at the thought of her nightmares.

Caroline looks at the sky. It is getting dark and the stars are starting to show. The growing darkness feels like it is seeping into her heart.

Zoe's words gnaw at her. The suggestion Madelaine did not go of her own choice sits cold and hard and empty inside her. It refuses to be ignored.

Clive and the others have not returned yet. She has had no word from Ranger Davis Morgan since he came buy that morning either. He promised to keep her posted.

Caroline feels as empty and alone as if it is she who is missing and everyone is looking for.

"I wish it was me instead of Madelaine," she thinks. "Then Madelaine would be safe."

The pressure of unshed tears presses against her eyes and she has to push down the thought of Madelaine alone and scared, hungry and cold, frightened and lost in a sea of trees. Caroline fights back the tears.

The growing darkness is pressing in on them in the fading light of the evening. She imagines it gobbling them up, her and Zoe and Mocha, never to be seen again.

"Just like it gobbled up Madelaine. Oh Madelaine, where are you?" she thinks desperately, fighting harder to push her tears away. Fear fills Caroline with a hollow despair.

"Mocha could find Madelaine," Zoe murmurs quietly. She is sure her mother couldn't have heard.

Mocha's ears perk at the sound of her name, the rest of her body motionless where she lays on her belly on the ground behind Caroline, still tied to the tree.

Caroline keeps rocking Zoe until she finally falls asleep in her arms.

She looks down at the sleeping girl.

"My little girl, who will always be my little girl despite not being so little anymore," she whispers into her hair.

Very gently, Caroline tries to lift and carry Zoe to the tent, but she is too heavy for her. She has to gently shake her awake.

Zoe responds groggily. "Uh?"

"It's time for you to go to bed."

With an unintelligible mumble, Zoe lets her mother help her to her feet, stumbling along and crawling into the tent and into her sleeping bag without fully waking up.

Caroline tucks her in and Zoe falls back into troubled sleep. Zoe moans and turns, her forehead wrinkling with worry.

Caroline goes back to sit in the chair before the cold fire pit. She does not feel like lighting a fire tonight. Campfires are cheerful.

The cool air chills her and Caroline shivers, wrapping her arms around herself both for comfort and warmth.

"I should put a jacket on."

That makes her think of Madelaine.

"Madelaine doesn't have a jacket. She's only in her nightgown and bare feet."

She feels dizzy with grief and worry.

"She must be so cold."

Caroline sniffles, wiping away tears.

"If Madelaine is out there cold and alone with no jacket or fire for warmth, then I won't have them either."

She blinks back the tears and rocks back and forth as if she is swooning on the verge of fainting.

"Oh Madelaine, my Madelaine, where are you?" she whispers sadly to the night.

Clive returns with a few of the other searchers.

Caroline jumps up from her chair and rushes to him hopefully.

"Did you find her?" she gasps, looking past them anxiously for her daughter. When she doesn't see Madelaine with him she feels broken. She lowers her head miserably.

"You didn't find her." Caroline says softly.

Clive looks very tired and sad. "No."

"You have to keep looking." She stares at him, begging him to find her daughter.

"Please, you have to keep looking," she cries softly, not wanting to wake Zoe. "It's night and it's cold. We haven't even heard from the ranger. Are they still out looking?"

"It's too dark. We have to stop and try again in the morning."

"But, the ranger-."

"We saw them coming back. The ranger, Davis Morgan, told us to call it a night and get some rest. His people are too. He said he will talk to us in the morning before they head out to search again."

Clive shakes his head, feeling helpless.

"It's too dark. Caroline, we will find her."

Caroline turns away from him in angry devastation. Her baby girl is going to be spending the night alone in the forest. She isn't angry just at him. She is angry at herself too. For being so helpless to find her daughter, for letting Madelaine's disappearance happen, for not doing enough to keep Madelaine safe. She is angry at the forest for taking her daughter away. She is angry at whatever happened to Madelaine, even though she does not know what that is.

A thought comes to her, unwanted and chilling. She almost turns to Clive, stopping halfway.

"You don't think-," Caroline doesn't look at him. She doesn't finish the sentence. She doesn't have to. He knows what she is saying.

"No," Clive says. "We came here to heal, to become a family again. He wouldn't even know where we are, even if he could come looking for her."

Clive tries to put his hands on her shoulders to comfort her. Caroline pulls away stiffly and walks away from him, not wanting to be touched, wanting only to be alone in her misery. She sits down and sobs into her hands.

Her refusal to accept his attempt to comfort her is a knife in Clive's heart.

Exhausted and not knowing what to do, he looks at his wife sadly and crawls into the tent and into their sleeping bag. He feels helpless and alone.

"I couldn't find Madelaine," he thinks, the pain filling him. It is filled with a heavy sense of déjà vu, the feelings of pain and helplessness, of loss and failure, and the thoughts. "I can't protect Madelaine from whatever danger she might be in. I can't even console Caroline and Zoe. They both turned away from me when I need comforting as much as they do."

Clive needs to be held, to be told everything is going to be all right, that they will find Madelaine and she will be safe.

"I'm supposed to be the strong one making everything all right for everyone else. I'm the dad, the husband," he thinks miserably. "I feel like Caroline and Zoe blame me for Madelaine's disappearance. I didn't find the dog when she went missing and I should have. I blame myself."

Clive lays there awake listening to Zoe's soft breathing and the night noises outside. He listens to Caroline's muffled sobs until they finally die away, leaving only the gentle hissing of leaves rubbing in the breeze above and the chirruping of insects.

He hears Caroline move around outside the tent, her soft murmurs, and thinks she must be talking to the dog. The last thought on his mind before sleep comes and his snores drown out the outside noises is, "She will take comfort from the dog but not from me."

Caroline sits there for a long time staring at the trees looming around the campsite as the darkness closes in completely around their little site, sobbing quietly.

Crickets chirp and somewhere an owl hoots sleepily.

There isn't even the crackle or light of a single campfire in the campground, as if the other campers too are going without in deference to the girl lost alone and cold somewhere in the dark forest night. Everyone is too exhausted from searching for the missing girl and just crawled into their beds.

At last Caroline stops crying. She rubs the tears from her eyes. Her eyes and face are stained red from weeping. She gets up and goes to crouch in front of Mocha.

The little dog looks up at her with watery sad brown eyes.

"You're worried too, aren't you?" Caroline asks, keeping her voice very quiet so Zoe and Clive won't hear.

The little dog thumps her tail on the ground a few times in a half-hearted wag.

Caroline rubs Mocha's ears.

Mocha sits up, rising up and trying to lick the tears from her face, but Caroline stops her. She pushes Mocha back down gently.

"She's out there alone in the dark; alone and cold and scared. They can't find her, not with only their eyes. Maybe you can with your nose."

She cups the little dog's face in her hand, looking into her watery eyes.

"I won't forgive myself for this. If we find her, Madelaine will never forgive me for this. If anything happens to you-. You are all I have, Mocha, my best hope at finding Madelaine. They wouldn't listen to me. They won't. They wouldn't even take you."

Caroline closes her eyes against the pain.

Geoffrey pedals hard, his tires spinning and bike flying through the darkness. He breaks free from the trail to the narrow ribbon of paved road and follows it.

He rides to the houses on the edge of town, slowing as he coasts into the driveway of one. He is hopping off while the bike is still in motion, leaning it against the house and going quickly to the back door.

Making a conscious effort to slow and trying to control his racing heart and panting breath, he opens the door quietly and walks in.

"You're late Geoffrey," a woman's voice says from somewhere inside the house.

"Sorry Mom. I was out looking for Madelaine."

Taking his shoes off; Geoffrey steps from the back landing into the kitchen.

His mother appears in the kitchen doorway, coming from the living room.

"We've been over this too many times. Leave that to the rangers and police."

She looks at him sharply.

"You don't know this girl. You don't know her people. It's too dark out to be running around the forest at night. They'll be looking for you too soon."

"I met her. She's nice. I know my way around," he says.

"You haven't eaten. Your dinner is on the table. You'll have to heat it up."

"Thanks, Mom."

"You are spending too much time alone out there," she complains. "It's not good. You should be around people more, your friends."

Geoffrey gives her a look, one corner of his lip curling up with a hint of sarcasm.

"Yeah, my friends."

"You have to forgive people. They say things without thinking it through and they don't know about us. I'm sure they didn't mean it. If they just knew-."

He cuts her off. "They know enough. They don't need to know anything else. I can't tell them anything about us anyway."

"No, but you can let them get to know you otherwise. You need to open up to somebody. You need to trust somebody. Geoffrey, you can't keep on like this."

He shrugs, turning his back on her as he puts his dinner in the microwave.

"I have you, Mom."

She frowns at his back, wishing she could make him open up to people and make friends.

"I'm just saying it's not good for a boy your age to spend all his time alone."

"I'm not alone," Geoffrey counters, turning to look at her. "I'm helping the park rangers."

"That's not the same. They are adults, not people your age."

"Summer is over. I'm back at school. There's lots of people my age there."

"You have to talk to them. Are you going to do that this year? Make some friends?"

Geoffrey shrugs. The microwave beeps and he retrieves his plate, sitting down to devour it and put an end to the conversation.

Giving up, his mother slips out of the room, leaving him to his aloneness.

Geoffrey pictures the moment he first saw Madelaine walking the trail with her family, the little dog racing ahead and coming back to them.

"She had a sadness about her even then," he thinks. "I almost didn't bother going to look for her when I heard the dog was lost.

They were stupid to let the dog run loose like that. It would only take one rabbit and the dog would be lost in the forest.

I went looking for her, but I wasn't going to get involved. Not over a little dog they should have kept on a leash.

Then I saw her sitting on a picnic table, alone with her misery as if that was her natural state. Like she could somehow know me. What I am inside."

"I'll find you Madelaine. They will give up. They always do eventually. I won't give up on you. I know you are out there."

The single oil lamp Hornsby gave Madelaine spreads a warm yellow glow that gives the small room some light that does not seem to reach the corners. With no movement of the air in the small room, its flame does not flicker beneath the glass wind cover and so it barely moves in its dance of consuming oil soaking up the woven rag wick.

Madelaine is studying her small prison, the rough blanket wrapped tightly around her. Her shadow mimics her movements like a stunted ghost trying to keep hidden in the shadows, keeping her between it and the light it fears.

The walls look like they are made of one solid stone with no cracks where two stones would be mortared together, broken only by the door.

"That looks like stone, not concrete," she says miserably. "There is no way out. It's stone walls out there too, and I didn't see any windows. This must be a basement somewhere. Even if I yell, no one will ever hear me."

Giving up, she sits next to the lamp and stares at its motionless flame, the teardrop shape burning into her retinas.

Bored and miserable, Madelaine leans in and blows gently on the flame through the opening at the top of the glass cover. Not hard enough to put it out, just enough to make it gutter and dance, its light flickering and dancing merrily around her wretched prison. It makes her shadow twitch and dance on the wall too.

"I should save the fuel as long as I can. I don't know how long the lamp will last, or how long I will be trapped here alone. When my kidnapper will be back. If he will be back."

Madelaine blinks back tears, surprised she still has any left.

"There, I said it. Kidnapper. As unreal as it seems, that is what I have to admit this is. Hornsby is a kidnapper. That ugly old man kidnapped me and I don't know what he is going to do to me."

She turns the lamp's flame as low as she dares without it going out and sending her back into the darkness. At least it isn't complete blackness like before. She stares at the barely burning orange line of fire sprouting from the slit in the metal topping the lamp's base

"How long has it been since Hornsby left me here? It's been hours. How long have I been here before that? A day? Two? More?"

The hunger in her stomach is unsettling. Her mouth is parched and dry with thirst. Her lips feel dry and cracking.

She rubs them absently, imagining she feels the skin pealing like she sees in movies where people are dying of thirst.

"I'm going to die here all alone from thirst and hunger. I don't want to die here. If I had the choice, I'd rather kill myself. It's not that hard. I almost did it once already. Just swallow some pills and you go to sleep and you never wake up. Peaceful. Only I don't have any pills here."

Her thoughts are pulled to that memory. It was not peaceful. That is a lie. It was horrible. The strange feelings that came over her body were terrifying. The pills made her sick. It was the worst kind of sickness Madelaine ever felt in her life. Worse than the worst flu bug she ever had. It was a lot worse than she imagined dying would feel.

It hurt. First came the nausea washing through her, filling her stomach to bursting. Vomiting hot and hard, filling her whole body with a feeling she was sure was worse than death. Then came the real pain. The terrible cramps tearing through her stomach and making her curl up into a ball. They came and came, waves of them and then a stampede.

The violent vomiting seemed like it would not stop until it tore her stomach out through her throat. Her throat burned on fire with it by the time she lay there weakly wracked with gut wrenching dry heaves that would never end, sending pain slicing through her abdomen with every convulsing heave.

By the end she prayed for death to make it stop, even as she begged desperately for someone to find her and save her. She wanted to live. She wanted to die to make the pain and nausea and that horrible weak sick feeling stop, but she didn't want to die like that.

Her mind had filled with terror. The thought that would not let her go and still haunts her. What if how you died was how you had to stay forever in the life after? If there is an afterlife. What if she would be sentenced to eternity lying in a cold hot sweat on a chilled bathroom floor forever dry-heaving, wracked with agonizing cramps?

"This is my punishment," she thinks. "Right now, locked in this little room to die. This is what I get for putting my parents through that. And Zoe."

Madelaine wraps herself tighter in the wool blanket and curls up miserably on the floor. She forces her mind to go blank and think of nothing, staring mindlessly at the cool stone wall of her dimly lit prison. After a while her eyes lose focus and the wall becomes fuzzy.

"Hornsby, please come back," she sobs quietly. "Please don't leave me here. I don't want to die like this."

She closes her eyes and lays there for a long time.

Madelaine has no idea how long she lay there like that before she drifts off to sleep.

12   The Search for Madelaine Continues

A fresh wave of loss fills Caroline. She did not think it was possible for this overwhelming feeling of devastation to get worse. She was wrong.

Every update she gets fills her with new dread. Each time someone tells her they have not found Madelaine sends her spiraling deeper in despair. And now night is falling again.

"She can't stay out there another night," Caroline moans.

Clive feels her pain as an extension of his own. It makes his worse, feeling inadequate and helpless to do anything to ease her suffering.

His need to reach out for her, to touch her, to comfort her as he needs to be comforted himself, is a white hot knife in his heart. He hesitates and moves to put an arm around her.

Caroline angrily pulls away, turning away.

"No one is comforting Madelaine," she thinks miserably. "I don't deserve to be comforted when she is alone out there."

Clive feels her rejection as a rejection of him, her anger as being directed at him for failing her, for failing Madelaine.

He has the urge to walk out of the campsite, but pushes it away.

On the other side of the campsite where they are talking quietly, Zoe looks at Geoffrey.

"Do you really think Madelaine is still out there?" she asks quietly. "Do you think she's okay and we will find her?"

Geoffrey tries to hide his own doubts, giving her a small smile he does not feel.

"She's out there. Somewhere. Finding her? We just have to look in the right place. We just don't know where that is yet. If we can figure out where to look, where she would have gone, we will find her."

His look grows more serious. "I won't lie to you Zoe. Madelaine could be hurt. But, I believe we can find her and that she is still alive."

Zoe frowns, nodding. "We can't give up looking for her."

"We won't," Geoffrey says softly.

"The others want to rest," Clive says to Caroline. "We are all exhausted. I won't give up on Madelaine, Caroline. I just need a quick bite to eat and I'm going out searching again."

Her back to him, Caroline stiffens.

"You enjoy your bite to eat," she says coldly, her voice choking. "Madelaine doesn't have a bite to eat." She says the last words almost mockingly, regretting her harsh words as she is saying them.

Clive's head drops. He stares at the ground saying nothing. Turning, he walks out of the campsite and down the road, returning to his search for his daughter.

Zoe and Geoffrey watch their exchange, both feeling awkward. They watch him walk away with stunned shock.

"Mom, that was pretty mean," Zoe says. "How is Dad supposed to have the strength to hike all over the forest looking for Madelaine if you won't even let him eat?"

Caroline glances at her guiltily. She wants to call Clive back and apologize, but she is trapped in Zoe's accusing glare.

"I-I got to go," Geoffrey mutters, making a quick escape.

As soon as he is in the road he speeds up, returning to his bike and taking off on it at full speed. He wants to put as much space between him and the awkward moment as he can.

"I'll make you supper," Caroline says, turning away to hide the tears in her eyes.

Zoe angrily sits on a rock on the edge of the campsite, wanting as much distance between her and her mother as she can get without getting in trouble for leaving.

"I wish I could leave too," she thinks.

Zoe pulls the stone out of her pocket, looking at it. She rubs its smoothness with a finger, careful not to accidentally make any wishes she does not fully mean.

Gravel crunches under Clive's hiking boots, his walk angry and his face stiff with pain. The emptiness of his stomach is a distant echo to the devastated bareness in his heart.

"Caroline and Zoe hate me for not being able to find Madelaine. I can't blame them. I hate me."

It takes a long hike to get back to where they left off the search.

Alone, Clive looks up at the sky. It feels too vast, the world beneath it too large, the forest spreading out even larger. He feels too small.

With an unhappy sigh, he starts walking and calling Madelaine, his voice hoarse from calling the name over and over for hours.

"Madelaine! Madelaine!"

Ranger Davis Morgan and his team are riding their search grids in teams of two.

His mare plods along at a slow and steady pace, picking her way through large rocks and around trees, flicking biting flies off with her tail.

Owen rides next to him on a young dark gelding who keeps bobbing his head impatiently at the slow pace. He keeps a steady pressure on the reins to keep the animal in check.

Each man watches the ground on his side for any signs that could be human. They are on the return loop of their search, working their way back to the ranger station.

"How long are we going to give her before we decide she isn't going to be found?" Owen asks. "It's getting colder at night. Dressed in only a nightgown, this girl won't last more than a few nights out here."

"We are not giving up until we find her," Davis says, keeping his focus on the ground around him. "And don't start calling it a recovery. It's not a recovery until we find her. Until then it's a rescue."

Owen nods.

"What's the ETA on help? They should already be here. It's too much forest to search with only our small team."

"Tomorrow. I know, it's not ideal, but those forest fires over the next ridge are taking up a lot of resources. Numerous lives at stake versus one missing kid. They are putting the resources where the most lives will potentially be lost."

Owen shakes his head at the futility.

"Without a proper search group, she could be crossing from one search grid to another and we'd never catch her. We at least should have the tracking dogs in. The trail is so old now they may not pick it up from the campsite. If we knew which direction she went, we could focus there."

"The dogs were supposed to be sent right away. We'll be back at the station soon," Davis says. "I'll be on the phone again as soon as we are back to find out what's holding them up."

They reach a point where the path directly ahead becomes impassable.

"You take the left, I'll take the right," Davis says.

They continue riding, each alone on his own path now.

Half an hour in, Owen straightens in his saddle, peering ahead. He thought he saw movement through the trees.

Owen takes his bearings, realizing his location.

"It's quiet. Pretty close to town. The trees must be deadening any sounds from town."

He lets the horse speed up to bring him to it faster.

The movement in the trees resolves itself to be a figure wearing a long drab brown robe with a deep hood covering his face.

"He's weirdly dressed," Owen thinks, unsure at this point if it is a man or woman.

"Hello there," Owen calls out as he closes in.

The figure keeps going as if they did not hear him.

Owen urges the horse to keep moving, closing the distance.

"Hello." He rides up and ahead of the person, blocking their path and forcing them to stop.

The figure looks up at him, revealing glimpses of an age-gnarled face beneath the deep hood.

"Hello there," Owen says. "Out for a hike?"

The old man nods.

"Have you seen anyone else out here?"

The old man shakes his head.

"Are you mute or something?" Owen asks. "Can't talk?"

"Not well." The old man's voice is raspy and low, the words drawn out as if he has difficulty forming word sounds.

"I'm sure you heard about the girl missing in the forest." He pauses, waiting for a response, and continues when none comes. "Well, if you see a girl in the forest bring her to town and notify the police. We're looking for a girl about this high." He uses his flat hand to show Madelaine's height. "She won't be dressed for the weather. She is wearing only a night gown."

The old man nods and keeps walking, ignoring Owen.

"The guy must have had a stroke or something." Owen looks around.

"Maybe I shouldn't leave him out here." He considers the old man and shrugs. "He seems with it enough, just having trouble talking."

Owen clucks to the horse and urges him on; continuing the search for any signs Madelaine may have come this way.

Moving slowly down the other fork, Davis continually scans the ground and his mare plods along the path.

A white-winged butterfly with black veins and smudge of black at the tips of its front wings dances along on the air, flitting around the horse's head and before her eyes.

The mare bobs her head and shakes it, giving the insect a little snort. She makes as if to bite it without really trying.

Bouncing weightlessly in the air, the butterfly bobbles around Davis's head.

He makes a shoeing motion, looking at the distracting insect, and puts his focus back to searching for signs Madelaine may have come this way.

The horse plods on, passing by a girl-sized barefoot print going the other way. Davis misses it because of the distraction from the butterfly.

Caroline refuses to watch Clive go. She refuses to watch Geoffrey leave. She hates herself for the anger and resentment she feels for them both right now.

Letting the evening wear itself on, Caroline and Zoe are each lost in their own silent prison of misery.

Neither knows when darkness fell. It seems as if it has always been dark.

With a deep unhappy sigh, Caroline looks at Zoe.

"It's late. You should get to bed."

"Daddy isn't back." Zoe looks at her with empty exhausted eyes.

"You look past tired. I'll make sure you see him in the morning before he goes to look for Madelaine again."

With a disgruntled groan Zoe slouches to the tent.

"Take the light." Caroline motions towards a battery operated lantern.

Zoe takes it, clicking it on as she goes inside the tent. She zips the opening closed to shut out the night and her mother.

"When did that become a thing?" Caroline thinks with bland unhappiness. "It's like searching for Madelaine is our new normal. That can never be normal."

The shuffling in the tent stops. Zoe is finally still, the light still glowing inside.

Caroline sits there for a long time in silence, trying not to think about Madelaine or Clive. The night drags on, the clouds darkening the sky as they hide the moon and stars. Without the moon, Caroline cannot tell how far across the sky the moon has moved.

"Madelaine is alone out there and nobody can find her. Nobody, except maybe a dog who could follow her trail."

She looks at Mocha lying unhappily at the end of her leash, her watery eyes watching Caroline.

"A dog who wants nothing more than to find and be with her girl."

She swallows.

"I can't. Madelaine would never understand. But she can't even try, can she? She's alone out there cold and hungry. Alone through another night."

With a quick glance at the tent, Caroline goes and kneels next to Mocha. She looks for any signs of Clive at the campsite entrance and unties the rope from Mocha's collar.

"Go find her Mocha, find my Madelaine," she whispers. "Don't let her be alone."

Mocha doesn't believe it at first. She stares up at Caroline. She licks Caroline's hand to say, "Thank you."

Mocha trots to the entrance of the campsite, pauses, and stares back at Caroline. She has never felt and smelled such deep sadness from her before.

Their eyes meet for a moment and then the little dog turns and scampers off into the night.

Caroline stands there alone in the darkness looking very lost. She waves goodbye to the little dog.

Mocha stops in the road, searching for the aging scent trail, finds it, and turns and runs off into the woods, following the smell of the bad thing that took Madelaine in the night.

Clive doesn't know what time it is when he returns to the campsite. The sun will be rising in only a few hours.

The campsite is quiet and dark. Not even an insect makes a sound. In his exhausted state he can see nothing but the tent and bed.

He slips quietly into the tent, changing into his pajamas, and slides into their shared sleeping bag, careful not to touch or disturb Caroline.

Almost immediately he is snoring in troubled sleep.

13   Mocha's Search

Mocha races through the woods. She ducks under low branches and scrambles over fallen trees. The urgency to find Madelaine burns in her little heart.

She keeps following the smell of the bad thing that took Madelaine. Sometimes she loses the trail, but after running around in circles sniffing the ground for a while she manages to pick it up again.

A squirrel chatters angrily at Mocha when she startles it as she races by.

Branches from bushes catch in her hair, but Mocha ignores them, letting the momentum of her frantic race pull her free even though sometimes hair is pulled out in clumps and twigs are left tangled in her long hair.

Mocha dodges around a large tree and skids on the ground with her front legs straight and her back legs dropping so she is sitting on the ground as she tries to stop in her tracks.

She looks up, shivering, her eyes wide with fear.

Standing very huge above her, its sides heaving with heavy panting breaths and eyes also wide in panic is a deer.

Mocha has never seen a deer before. She is terrified.

She yelps and the deer bleats. Both scramble and bolt in opposite directions, running away from each other in startled fear.

Mocha's little heart feels like it is going to burst as she runs like she has never ran before. She runs blindly through the forest, urged on by the fear that thing is chasing her.

At last Mocha stops and falls down in a heap. She is exhausted and panting hard, trying to catch her breath, her tongue lolling out of her wide open mouth.

Mocha flops on her side, still gasping for air, laying there for a while panting in quick short breaths.

Her breathing finally slows after some time and Mocha gets up, looking around and sniffing at the ground and air.

She can't smell anything familiar except her own scent.

"Find Madelaine," Mocha thinks. "Find the bad thing."

The startled deer barges through the woods, nimbly dodging trees and bursting through bushes until she is tired and finally slows and stops running. She is a little out of breath, but not gasping like the little dog.

She stands still on her long elegant legs and turns her neck gracefully to look behind her, wondering what that little dog is doing all the way out here.

Stepping forward delicately, the doe goes on her way as if nothing happened.

Zoe is sleeping restlessly. She tosses and turns, moaning, harassed by bad dreams.

She dreams of an ugly old man, older than any man she has ever seen, with wrinkled cheeks and a wrinkled nose, swooping down from the sky. In her dream the old man snatches Madelaine away and carries her off into the sky with him while Madelaine struggles to break free. Madelaine cries for help but no one, not even Zoe, can hear her screams.

Zoe runs after them, but she cannot run fast enough. She reaches for the sky desperately, her heart pounding in her chest and her body feeling like it is floating in a sea of desperation, devastation, and loss, trying to grab her sister and pull her back. But Madelaine is already gone. The old man and Madelaine have vanished into the blackness of the night sky.

She screams for her sister, calling her name over and over, but no sound comes out.

Zoe wakes with a start, almost screaming. She covers her mouth to stop the scream. The dream feels so real that it takes her a few moments sitting there, heart pounding and terrified before she realizes it's only a dream.

"You're okay," she thinks, looking at her sleeping family for reassurance that it really was just a dream.

She looks around the tent. There is her mom and dad sleeping together in their two sleeping bags zipped together. Her dad's snores are quieter than usual tonight, his breath hissing in and out with deep exhaustion. His face is peaceful.

"How can he be so peaceful when Madelaine is lost? Nothing ever seems to bother him," Zoe thinks. "I wish it was that way for me too."

Her mom's forehead is wrinkled into an unhappy frown.

On the other side of Zoe is Madelaine's empty sleeping bag.

Zoe's eyes stop there, staring at the empty sleeping bag. Sadness washes over her and fills her up. "It wasn't all a dream. Madelaine really is missing, lost in the forest and alone."

"Madelaine is in trouble," Zoe whispers to the dark. "She needs help."

Zoe feels the conviction that Madelaine is in danger with such an overwhelming feeling of Madelaine's impending doom filling her up that she feels like it will burst out of her and fill the tent.

She stares at the tent zipper.

"Poor Mocha. They must have left her tied up all alone outside." She thinks about how unhappy the little dog must be. Her thoughts turn to the vast dark forest and how small and alone Madelaine must feel right now.

"Like me," she thinks. Being the youngest and smallest, Zoe always feels alone and small. The size of the forest is overwhelming. A shiver trembles down her back.

"I should stay where I am, safely tucked in my warm sleeping bag in the tent with Mom and Dad. But it isn't so safe here, is it? Madelaine was safely tucked in her sleeping too when she disappeared."

Zoe blinks in the darkness, thinking.

"Daddy and the searchers couldn't find Madelaine. She is gone. But how far did they go? The ranger said she wouldn't go far. Mom and Dad said she couldn't have gone far. But Madelaine would go as far as she thought she had to. She would not give up looking for Mocha. They are not looking far enough."

The vision of the old man in her dreams swims before her eyes.

"Did I see him for real? Did the old man take Madelaine or did she leave on her own? I woke up and she was gone, like she snuck out, but the dream feels so real."

She thinks about how heartbroken and afraid her mom is.

"If I can find Madelaine and bring her back-." She doesn't finish the thought in her head. She doesn't need to.

As quietly as she can, Zoe crawls out of her sleeping bag. She carefully picks up her jacket and shoes and crawls to the tent zipper.

She has a thought, puts her stuff down, and scurries back, reaching under her pillow for something. Zoe doesn't look at it. She finds it by feel and grips it in her palm. She returns to the zipper and picks up her jacket and shoes, reaching for the zipper head and pulling it up.

The zipper makes a small zipping noise as she opens it and Zoe winces at the sound. Crawling out, she slowly pulls the zipper back down. She puts her jacket on over her nightgown and puts her shoes on.

Zoe goes to the tree Mocha was tied to first.

"Mocha will find Madelaine. I know it. If I take Mocha, she will lead me to Madelaine."

She stops, staring in disbelief at the rope. One end is still tied to the tree, but the other end is lying loose on the ground.

"That wasn't a dream," she gasps softly.

Zoe was lying in her sleeping bag after her mother thought she was sleeping, peaking out the little hole at the bottom of the tent zipper where it was not quite zipped all the way down. She was in that sleepy moment of being neither quite asleep nor awake. She saw her mother let Mocha off the leash and watched as the little dog ran off. She convinced herself it didn't really happen.

"I can't believe Mom actually did that. Mocha is gone," she thinks. Hopelessness wells up in her and tears burn at her eyes.

"No, Mocha, where are you?" she whispers quietly. "How am I going to find Madelaine now?"

She steels herself, trying to feel determination that is not there. "I am not giving up. I have to find her."

"I'm coming Madelaine," Zoe whispers as she tiptoes to the edge of the campsite, grabbing one of the flashlights off the picnic table on the way.

Zoe looks back at the tent one last time.

"I will find Mocha and Mocha will find Madelaine," she says quietly. She turns on the flashlight and hurries off through the night. As soon as she is on the road, Zoe starts to run.

A sound breaks through into Madelaine's sleep. She blinks her eyes groggily, staring straight ahead in her dimly lit little prison. Her eyes are unfocused and not really looking at anything. She does not realize yet that it was a sound that woke her up.

She hears a muffled thud and her eyes come into focus, staring at the door. Madelaine catches her breath, holding it and trying to breathe silently through her nose. She listens.

Madelaine thinks she hears the soft shuffle of something being dragged or slid and then a dull thump.

"Is he back?"

Fear floods through her, but so does relief that she is not left here alone to die after all. The hollow pain of hunger rings in her stomach and she can't help licking at her dry lips, her parched mouth feeling like it had been dried out with cotton balls. Her thirst is painful, her need to drink urgent.

Madelaine gets up shakily, feeling too weak to pull herself to her feet, and goes to the door. She puts her ear to the door, listening.

She hears another dull thud.

Looking at the door with desperate hope, Madelaine bangs on it with her open palm.

"Hornsby! Hornsby, let me out! Please!" Her voice is cracked, raspy and weak, and dry. She fears it is not loud enough. It is as loud as she can yell.

It takes a painfully long moment before the lock disengages with a dull thud and the door is pulled open with a screech of its un-oiled hinges.

Madelaine blinks at Hornsby in the brighter light outside her tiny cell.

He looks at her for a moment, looks at the lantern and blanket in her cell, and turns and shuffles away.

She pauses before venturing out into the room beyond, looking around uncertainly. The moment she steps out she can smell his unpleasant sourness. It immediately unsettles her.

"Hornsby, you came back."

He grunts. "Hornsby is always here."

"I guess it would feel like you are always stuck here," Madelaine says. "So it must have felt good getting out."

She hopes to exploit his feelings, using them to get him to feel for her. If he sympathizes with her he might let her go.

"Hornsby does not go."

Madelaine looks at him with a confused look.

"You never left? But you said you had to go away and did not know when you would come back."

"Hornsby go."

"But- you just said that you did not go. Do you mean that you are going now?" Panic fills Madelaine. Her eyes are wide with it.

"I was left alone so long, and now he didn't even go yet," she thinks. "If he goes now, what if he doesn't feed me or give me any food and water?"

Her stomach rolls and growls hungrily. Its hollow emptiness feels like it is sucking her stomach into her spine.

Hornsby grunts and shakes his head. "Hornsby does not go."

"You are going, you are not going. Are you going to leave me here all alone locked up with no food and water to die? I'm dying in there already Hornsby!" It comes out shrill, more afraid than angry.

He shrugs. "Hornsby forgot." He shuffles nervously.

"Girl is hungry," Hornsby says, motioning to her. He motions to the little table again.

Madelaine looks and sees a very old looking silver plate and cup like before. It takes no coaxing this time to get her to sit down and eat and suck back the too little water. She is starving.

Mocha is huddled into herself, shivering and looking up at the looming trees crowding out the world around her. She is still feeling startled by her encounter with the deer and is distressed she cannot find any familiar scent other than her own.

The strange smells and sounds of the forest are frightening to the little dog.

She tucks her nose under her paws as if that might block out the smells. It doesn't work and it does nothing for the sounds. The wind in the trees makes the leaves rub together with a hissing that never stops. Strange birds call nonstop and there are a lot of sounds she cannot identify.

Mocha whimpers miserably.

Shivering harder, she gets anxiously to her feet. She tests the air, sniffing again for any smells she might have missed.

There are no familiar scents.

Then she remembers the bad thing and its trail leading to Madelaine.

With a new focus, Mocha's fears are pushed back just enough to let her turn her attention back to searching for Madelaine. She sniffs the ground and the air, circling around in widening circles, looking for the foul scent of the bad thing. She can't find it.

She starts shivering harder again. Mocha whimpers. She lets out a few barks and listens for any answer.

There is nothing but the continuous calls of the birds and hissing of the wind in the trees.

Mocha tries again, sniffing around on the ground, trotting back and forth in search of a scent trail. She focuses so hard on the scents that she forgets what she is sniffing for.

She finally hits on a familiar one.

"Me! That's me!"

With a nervous yip, still trembling, Mocha darts off through the trees, following the scent trail home.

"Home! Home! Home!"

Madelaine watches Hornsby while she eats.

He keeps shifting things around for no reason, looking busy. He never looks at her.

Her eyes go again to studying every inch of the room. There is only the one door that she can see, to the tiny dark room he keeps her locked in, and no windows hiding among the piles of clutter. She can't figure out how he comes and goes from the room.

She focuses her attention back on the old man.

"I'm a prisoner," Madelaine thinks. "I'm pretty sure Hornsby is the one who kidnapped me, even though it seems unlikely. He is so old and frail. I can't think how this stooped old man could steal a girl from a tent with her family right there and carry her who knows how far. But, if it wasn't him then who? He seems to be here all by himself, and has been for what must have been a very long time if he is forgetting how to talk."

She has trouble wrapping her head around that thought.

"No, who forgets how to talk? That's dumb. He must have something wrong with him; some kind of mental disability. He is a hoarder for sure. Look at all this junk. This place is a fire hazard."

One question haunts her. "Why did he kidnap me? What reason could this old man have to kidnap me and keep me prisoner?"

A gross feeling slithers through her. She heard partial stories, only hinting at bad things a man does to a girl he kidnaps. Her parents did not want her to know what those things were, protected her from knowing. The not knowing makes her imagination flounder at trying to think of what those things might be.

Madelaine has the unsettling feeling she knows what those things are, but her mind refuses to go there. She turns her mind away from it. She does not want to think those things.

A dark memory presses in on the edges of her mind, another time she was trapped, and Madelaine suddenly feels the room spin and swoop. Nausea washes through her and she breaks out in an icy sweat.

She pushes it away, closing her mind to it and refusing to let it in. She continues her thoughts, pretending the dark memory does not exist.

"He looks too old to do anything," Madelaine thinks, "so whatever his reason for taking me, it can't be those gross things. I have to find out. If I can find out why he kidnapped me, maybe I can figure out how to escape, or talk him into letting me go.

If I can get him talking, get him to see me as a person with feelings, maybe he will let me go and not do anything to hurt me." That weak hope gives her the small piece of bravery she needs.

Madelaine struggles to muster up her courage to speak.

"Will you let me go?" she asks hopefully. Her voice sounds small to her.

"Can not," Hornsby says in his slow struggling speech.

"Why not?" Madelaine asks with a sinking feeling. She wants so badly for him to say yes, to tell her he will take her back to her parents.

"Why can't you?" Madelaine's voice is choked. She is close to crying again. "I won't tell anyone it was you. I-I'll say I got lost in the forest. I promise, I won't tell. Please, I just want to go home."

"Can not," Hornsby says. He shuffles out of the room through a door Madelaine had not seen before he went through it. The room is that cluttered.

"Is there any other doors hidden in the clutter of this room?" Madelaine wonders.

"Please let me go," Madelaine calls after Hornsby. She gets up to follow him out of the room and hesitates.

"It feels unreal," she thinks. "Being kidnapped, locked in a small dark room, abandoned-."

She stops after a few steps, stunned, realizing.

"And now this sudden freedom. He isn't locking me right back up," her mind swoons with the thought and another rush of hope.

She hears Hornsby shuffling beyond the door. Madelaine moves again to follow him uncertainly. She has a bad feeling about this now, looking around the gloomy space.

"You have no reason to keep me here," she says after him. "I'm just a girl."

Madelaine feels a rush of anger and defiance.

"I'm going to escape, you know," she says a little louder.

"Maybe that wasn't a good thing to say," she thinks, instantly sorry.

"No escape," he rasps back to her. "No way out. Nothing out side. Only trees. Trees. More trees."

"If there is a way in, there has to be a way out," Madelaine mutters to herself, approaching the door he went through.

She hesitates, filled with a sudden rush of fear of what might be waiting on the other side.

"Not for girl," Hornsby rasps back to her. "Girl does not know way in."

He looms before her, startling her and blocking the doorway.

She blinks at him, wondering how he could have heard her.

He points one craggy finger at her. Past her.

A cold sinking fills Madelaine's stomach. She doesn't have to turn and look to know. He is pointing at her dark pit of despair; the tiny room she has been kept locked in the dark in for so many hours.

"How many days has it been?" The thought is small. Weak. Like she feels right now.

"Back," Hornsby croaks at her. "Girl go back."

"No Hornsby, please." Madelaine tries to look convincing. She doesn't feel convincing. She only feels wretched.

"I'll be good. Please don't put me back in there." Her voice cracks and weakens into helpless whimpering by the end.

"Girl back. Now."

Madelaine steps towards him, hands out pleadingly. The idea of actually touching him sends revulsion oozing through her, but she feels the urge to fight back.

Hornsby steps closer, sending a surge of fear through her. Madelaine falters.

"Go in room," he rasps.

She can't tell if he sounds angry with his guttural hoarse voice.

"I-I'm not going back in there." Madelaine tries to sound strong and defiant, and fails.

Hornsby closes the space between them with surprising speed. She never imagined this shuffling stooped old man capable of moving half that fast. He is on her, grabbing her by the arms and propelling her backwards. The grip of his withered bony hands is painful and his force pushing her backwards unstoppable.

Madelaine tries to push back and instead loses balance with the backwards momentum.

"How is he so strong?" her mind reels. She is unable to utter anything more than a shocked squeak.

It is over so fast she barely blinked. Hornsby's grip on her the only thing keeping her on her feet; he shoves her back into her little prison and closes the door, its hinges squealing rudely.

Madelaine staggers, almost falling, when he releases her. She barely manages to recover, clumsily leaping at the door as the gap of light narrows.

She throws herself against the door as the lock clangs into place, pounding uselessly on it with her fists.

"Hornsby! Please! Don't leave me in here!"

Madelaine throws herself against the door over and over in a frenzy, clawing at it, pounding, throwing the weight of her body against it. The noise reverberates in her tiny prison, amplified by the small space.

She keeps at it, screaming and sobbing, over and over, "Hornsby! Don't leave me in here! Please!"

Finally, Madelaine sinks to the floor in a wretched puddle of misery, moaning and sobbing in desperation-weakened mewling sounds.

"Hornsby. Please. Don't leave me."

She softly sobs the words over and over until she is too exhausted to repeat them anymore.

14   Determined Zoe

Keeping the flashlight aimed on the ground ahead of her, Zoe keeps going, following the road taking her further away from the campsite and determined to not let her fear of the dark stop her.

Every now and then she whispers as loud as she dares, calling Mocha.

She comes across it by accident, a footprint in the soft mud on the edge of the road.

Zoe stops and kneels down, shining the light on it. It looks like a dog print and it's the right size.

"That has to be Mocha."

She studies the ground carefully, looking for more. When she doesn't find any, she goes back, searching until she finds the print again.

Zoe studies the print, then turns and looks up the road.

"I think she's going that way."

Zoe moves slowly, swinging the light left and right on the road directly in front of her, searching for any more signs as she goes.

She comes to a narrow hiking trail branching off from the road and pauses at the entrance.

"Should I try it?" She looks up at the branches looming above and down at the spooky darkness of the trail. She can't see very far down the path before it vanishes in the darkness.

"I will go just a little way. If there is no sign of Mocha, then I go back to the road."

Zoe hesitantly moves ahead up the narrow trail, trying to focus on looking for dog prints, but getting distracted by her nerves and the need to look and see what else is out there waiting for her in the dark.

"There's nothing here. No signs of Mocha. I'm going back to the road."

When Zoe is turning around, she spots a dog print in the light from her flashlight. She stops, kneeling to study it closer.

"It has to be Mocha. She did go this way. I wish I was wrong so I can go back to the road instead of deeper down this trail, but I'm sure she went this way."

Zoe looks down the trail. It is narrow and dark. She looks back to the less dark and wider road longingly.

"I can't take the chance. I have to follow them."

Steeling herself, she takes a deep breath to build her courage and continues on down the trail, feeling the darkness pressing against her like it would suffocate her. Her muscles are tense and her stomach tight with her fear of the dark. She feels like she is being pulled along by a tight string that goes right through her, like she can feel the vibrations of every step on that string going through her gut.

Both the trail and the night seem endless.

After walking for what feels like forever she comes to a fork in the trail and stops, staring up the two paths leading in different directions.

"Left right left right, which one?"

Zoe searches for any signs and finds nothing. Not a dog print, tuft of hair, or anything.

Tears fill her eyes. She feels alone, afraid, and helpless.

Zoe puts her hand in her pocket and feels the smooth stone there. It is what she slipped from beneath her pillow when she left the tent. She rubs it between her fingers, taking comfort from its smoothness, and closes her eyes tight.

She tries to see the twin trails in her mind, tries to picture Madelaine and Mocha, which way they went.

"Please let me find Madelaine. Please let me pick the right path. I wish Mocha and I both find Madelaine." Zoe wishes it as hard as she can.

"It's stupid," she thinks. "It's just a dumb stone." Pushing the thought away, Zoe concentrates on willing what she needs to happen.

With her eyes closed tight, Zoe steps forward slowly, one foot after another, choosing blindly which fork to take.

Zoe keeps going, squeezing her eyes closed tighter when she has the urge to look, and hopes she doesn't walk into a tree. Right now she doesn't want to know which path she is on. She feels like somehow knowing will jinx it.

She keeps walking blindly, clutching her flashlight in one hand and holding it out ahead of her, feeling for anything she is about to walk into. She keeps her other hand in her pocket, rubbing the smooth stone with her thumb and taking comfort from the smoothness and warmth of it.

"Please let me find Madelaine. Please let me pick the right path. I wish Mocha and I both find Madelaine. Please let me find Madelaine. Please let me pick the right path. I wish Mocha and I both find Madelaine." Zoe repeats the words over and over under her breath like a mantra.

Time seems to have stopped as she puts each careful step before the last.

Finally, unable to stand it anymore, she stops and opens her eyes.

The bushes have thinned out and the branches of the trees above grow together, creating a canopy that blocks out much of the light when the sun is shining.

Zoe turns in a circle, looking around her, shining the flashlight into the darkness.

She is no longer on any kind of path at all. She can't find where the path was. Zoe is lost in the forest.

"Where am I?"

Suddenly, she feels very tired, the nervous energy that kept her going leaving her. Zoe looks around, wishing she has a safe place to sit down and rest.

"I'm so tired; I don't think I can take another step. But I have to keep going."

She pushes herself on, making herself run now that there are no thick bushes to slow her down and she can see further with her flashlight. She bobs along, her gait lopsided from the exhaustion and her arms flailing in a way she would never let them any other time.

Zoe runs until she cannot run anymore and staggers to a stop, panting hard.

"I have to rest." The words come out staggered between gasps for air.

She looks for the best place and settles on the base of two trees growing close together.

"If any hungry animal comes looking for me, hopefully it will come from the right direction and the trees will hide me."

She sits down, leaning against the trees staring fearfully at the darkness surrounding her with only her flashlight to hold it back. Her eyelids grow heavy and in time the world goes black.

15   Madelaine Learns Her Fate

Madelaine is huddled on the floor against the door of her dark little prison, seemingly oblivious to being cold; her rough blanket abandoned within arm's reach. The lantern flame struggles to put out the barest light. Its wick, having soaked up the last of the oil, is dying.

She blinks slowly in the deepening darkness but is otherwise completely still.

The sudden clang of the lock echoing in the small room startles her and she awkwardly skitters away across the floor, looking more like a frightened animal than a girl. She stops only when she hits the far wall, pasting herself against it.

Trembling, she stares at the door, her eyes large in her dirty face framed by tangled greasy hair.

The door opening is louder after the hours of absolute silence, rudely loud, making her cringe.

A vertical bar of light is born and grows with the widening gap of the opening door. The light splashing on the floor spreads across to the far wall, widening with the door until it finally touches her.

The light, and being seen, makes Madelaine cringe again. She trembles harder, wanting to scurry away back to the darkness like an insect. Unlike a tiny insect, she cannot squirm into the tiniest hole. There is nowhere to go.

When the door is open all the way Madelaine is cut in half by the light. She blinks, torn by the need to scream and jump up and run, and the desire only to be gone, invisible.

"If I don't move, he won't see me and he'll go away," she thinks irrationally.

He steps into the doorway, blocking out much of the light and putting Madelaine almost entirely back in shadow.

"Little Kitten. Come."

Hornsby steps back and turns, shuffling away from the door. He is wearing the same worn floor-length cloak he always wears, the deep hood pulled up and hiding his face.

Madelaine stares up at him.

He motions to her, a "come here" motion.

"Come, Little Kitten."

He moves further from the door and vanishes from sight.

Madelaine blinks at the light of the doorway and the room beyond, her breath coming in shallow frightened pants.

When nothing happens beyond the door, she finally moves hesitantly. First an arm then leaning forward. She shifts a foot, and finally crablike shifts to squat on her hands and feet, keeping her eyes glued on the open door.

Still nothing happens in the room beyond.

Rising slowly on unsteady legs, Madelaine cautiously approaches the door. She stops in the doorway, looking out. Even though she expected it, she is startled when she sees the robed figure standing across the room.

"Come." He motions her to follow and walks out the door.

Madelaine swallows, feeling no courage whatsoever and almost stumbles when she steps forward. She only realizes now that she doesn't feel her legs and feet, but only the slow numb tingling of circulation returning after endless hours of lying huddled motionlessly on the floor.

Madelaine steps through the doorway of the small cluttered room into another room. This room is larger, just as dark and gloomy, and as cluttered; an extension of the room with the prison closet.

She has an image of herself trapped inside the layers of a nesting doll in the form of endlessly cluttered rooms. Each wooden painted doll encasing a smaller almost identical doll until at the very center is her, Madelaine, trapped and squished unmovable inside the blackness of the smallest doll, unable to breathe.

Following him through another doorway, she stops the moment she steps through into what lays beyond. She stares in awe at what she sees.

It is dark and gloomy with only widely spaced lighted torches on walls creating little spots of orange light between the deep shadows all around. Dust coats every surface and groove she can see.

Madelaine walks in a circle, staring up at the high ceiling and wondering at the grand wide hallway. The ceiling and walls look like they are carved from one huge stone like the other room, only on a scale that dwarfs her with its tall elegance.

Madelaine swallows. She wants to pinch herself hard to see if she is dreaming.

"Impossible," she gasps in disbelief. "It's like some kind of forgotten castle. This must be some kind of tourist attraction. But, it looks abandoned. Is it closed? It must be. How long?"

The hallway seems to go on forever, lit by torches burning in holders on the walls. The torches are like softly glowing beacons of light, fading to dusky shadows as the light reaches towards the next torch. The stone itself is nearly white, smooth, and lacking in the usual veins of other colors of minerals one would expect of a stone of significant size. Closer inspection would reveal the grains that make up the stone, almost able to glint softy with the reflection of light, except that the stone seems to almost absorb the light, rather than reflect it.

"Is there no electricity?" Madelaine wonders at the torches along the walls, seeing no signs of electric lights anywhere.

Great arches loom tall and wide at evenly spaced intervals down the hallway, adding both support and elegance to the large hallway. More arches on each side are spaced along the walls, some with tall statues of people in long flowing robes and strange creatures, and others opening to other hallways or holding closed doors made of heavy looking wood.

Paintings from a long ago era hang on the walls in places, their heavy frames ornately carved works of art in themselves. The subjects of the paintings vary, people on horses in the woods, people with golden cups and plates of food at a table, scenes of battle, and strange looming formal portraits of very serious looking people alone. Like the statues, some are strange looking creatures.

Like the small rooms they came from, there is not a single window.

"Come," Hornsby rasps at her, motioning with one withered hand.

Madelaine turns her attention back to the old man and starts walking towards him as he starts down the wide hallway. She jogs to catch up and walk beside him.

"What is this place?" Madelaine gasps. Her awe of how big and beautiful this place is despite the deep shadows, darkness, and dust of the ages has pushed her fear aside for the moment, but not all the way. Fear of what she doesn't know, of being kidnapped and not knowing why, still presses urgently at the back of her mind.

"Castle Blachedone," Hornsby says.

"It's a castle? I never heard of it. I didn't think there were castles here. Is this some kind of tourist attraction?" Madelaine asks, unable to stop gaping at everything around her.

"No," Hornsby says.

"Does anyone ever come here?"

"No."

"Ugh, can't he answer in more than one word?" Madelaine thinks, getting frustrated with his one word answers that give her no information.

She decides to try a different tact.

"Where do you live Hornsby?"

"Here."

Madelaine considers this.

"You live here? In this place?"

"Yes."

"So, you are like a caretaker or something? You live here and look after this place?"

It gives her a small hope. Whoever owns or runs this place must come around sooner or later.

"Some thing."

Madelaine wrinkles her brow in frustration.

"You live here and are the caretaker? Or is it something else? Is it a museum? A tourist attraction? A mansion?"

Hornsby only nods.

Madelaine feels like screaming.

"Who else lives here?" Madelaine asks. She tries to not let her frustration show.

"Only Hornsby."

Hornsby stops and turns to her. He looks like he is annoyed by all her questions. It sends a small shiver of fear down her back.

"No more. Girl asks too much."

He waves at her, a stop motion.

"Girl stop. Stay here. Wait. Hornsby will come."

He turns and starts walking in another direction.

Madelaine moves to follow and he stops again.

"No. Girl stays here." His voice is more gruff, annoyed.

Madelaine swallows and watches him turn and go.

"He calls me Little Kitten and is nicer then he calls me girl and is grumpy. He has two moods and it feels like I'll never know which Hornsby I'll get."

She looks around her, studying her surroundings.

"I can go. I can run. If I go the other way, he would never be able to catch up to me. I can find a way out."

"Come," Hornsby says from behind her.

Madelaine turns, startled, staring at him.

Hornsby walks on at that same slow steady pace, down the hall in the direction they were going before.

"Where did you come from?" she asks.

"He went that way," she thinks. "This place is a maze of hallways and doors. He circled to come up on me from behind. And why does he talk about himself in the third person?"

Hornsby waves her to follow.

Feeling a little hollow and off, Madelaine follows.

She watches him to see if he is still angry. He seems fine now.

Madelaine picks up the conversation where they left off. She is uneasy now; worried her questions will anger him again.

"I have to find out everything I can so I can try to escape," she thinks.

"Hornsby," she says, "this place must be huge. It can't be just for one old man. Someone must have lived here before, kings and queens maybe."

"Ones before," Hornsby nods.

"Yes, who lived here before?" Madelaine crinkles her nose at him, thinking it an odd choice of words. "Do you mean people who lived here before you?"

Hornsby nods. "Ones before." He thinks and seems to struggle with how to put the words together before he repeats, speaking even more slowly. "The ones what-," he pauses, shaking his head slowly at his error, "who-."

He looks at Madelaine for help. "That?"

Madelaine stops herself from laughing. "Who or that, whatever." She shrugs.

"What ever?" Hornsby looks at her confused.

This time Madelaine can't stifle the smile, although she manages to keep her laugh at bay. "It probably would not be smart to insult my kidnapper," she thinks.

The thought pushes away the moment of light-hearted humor, bringing back the dark cloud of her reality. The smile drops from her eyes and mouth and she shrugs again.

"I meant that both would work; who or that." Her voice is now dull with unhappiness.

Hornsby nods understanding. He tries again.

"The ones," he glances at her for approval and gets none, "who- come before."

"Where are they now?" Madelaine asks flatly.

"They go. Gone." He waves his hand in an upswing. "Pssshhht."

"Okay, so they were here and are gone." Madelaine can't help it. Curiosity is filling her up again. "Who were they?"

Hornsby thinks harder about these words. His forehead wrinkles with the effort.

"Old ones. You would-," he thinks again, "call them-."

Madelaine is feeling impatient now with the slow progress of words coming from him. She is opening her mouth to complain when he finishes.

"V-v- vam- vamp pyres." Hornsby looks a little uncertain.

Madelaine stops in her tracks, staring at him. She can't believe what she heard.

"He must be joking," she thinks, but a cold chill washes down her spine and makes her feel dizzy.

"Vampires?" she asks doubtfully, walking forward again. "I don't believe it." She catches up to the old man.

"You are playing me," she says angrily. "This is a joke and it's not funny. I don't feel like joking. You are keeping me here against my will and I just want to go home."

Hornsby shakes his head. "True."

"Does that mean you are a vampire too? Show me your fangs then," Madelaine demands, looking up at him.

Hornsby shakes his head, smiling as if she said something funny.

This makes Madelaine angrier. She stops, standing firm, hands on hips, and glares at the old man.

"I'm serious," she says angrily. "You are playing tricks on me. You kidnap me and lock me in a dark room, you almost kill me giving me no food or water, and then you tell me we are in some place where vampires live. Vampires are not real!"

"Real, Little Kitten," Hornsby says. "Live here once. Only Hornsby now."

"If they're real then show me your teeth," Madelaine demands.

The old man grins at her, spreading his lips with his fingers to show off his teeth.

Madelaine examines them.

They are old looking and crooked, yellow with age and ugly. But he does not have fangs.

"You don't have fangs," Madelaine says with a pout. She sounds disappointed.

Hornsby chuckles, his shoulders shaking with it.

"Vamp pyres real, Little Kitten. One I am not," he says.

"Well then what are you?" Madelaine asks.

"Their keeper," Hornsby says, "like bees. Buzzzzz buzzzz.

Madelaine wrinkles her forehead at him in annoyance.

"You mean their caretaker, as in someone who looks after them; cleans up after them."

Hornsby nods, pointing at her. "Care taker. Clean. Look after Castle Blachedone."

"Who's caretaker?" Madelaine asks, "The vampires?"

Hornsby nods.

Madelaine gives him an odd look, taking in his very old appearance. She is skeptical anything he says can be true.

"Vampires," she thinks, "as if."

"How old are you?" she asks.

"Old," Hornsby says, "older than hills," he motions, "older than trees."

"Humph." Madelaine grunts. He obviously is toying with her and she doesn't like it.

"I'm older than some trees," she huffs at him.

"Not these trees," Hornsby says. "Big. Wide and tall as sky. Wood of Blood. You call them," he pauses again, searching his mind for the name, "The Red Woods."

"Wood of Blood?" Madelaine asks, frowning at him. "The Red Woods? That doesn't make sense. Do you mean redwoods? Daddy said redwood trees can be hundreds of years old. Nobody is that old."

Hornsby nods, pointing to himself and motioning as if to another, or to the forest surrounding Blachedone.

"Hornsby planted," Hornsby says with a wink, "Hornsby plants and Hornsby plants. Bit of devil in them."

"Why do you call them such an odd name, Wood of Blood?" Madelaine asks. "And how could you have planted them when they are so old and so big?"

She does not like the way this conversation is going.

"Either he is completely mad in the head, or he is delusional," she thinks. "No, he is definitely playing me." She reconsiders with a frown. "Or he is crazy as a delusional bat crazy?"

"Soak seed in little vamp pyre blood and wine," Hornsby makes the motions with his hands, then counts off his fingers. "One two three," he gives up with a shrug. "Many. Many moon cycles. Plant in light of full moon in-."

He looks at her.

"How do you say? Un hollow ground?" He nods. "Make them grow big and live long. Yes, Little Kitten, Hornsby plant Wood of Blood, your Red Wood. Lot. Lot of trees. Lot of planting."

Madelaine looks at him in disbelief.

"So, you are telling me that you planted the whole redwood forest."

He nods, thumping his aged chest. "Hornsby plant the Red Wood. All the Red Wood. Hornsby and Hornsby and-." He stops and starts counting on his fingers, gives up, and shrugs.

"You planted this whole forest by yourself?"

"More Hornsby once." He struggles with this next bit, mouthing each word slowly and carefully, "Keepers of Those Who Sleep."

"You are telling me there were more like you? And you all lived here together?"

Hornsby grunts agreement.

Madelaine pauses. "You called them the ones who come before. Now you say they are the ones who sleep."

"Yes," Hornsby grunts.

"And you all planted the redwood trees?"

Hornsby nods. "Planted. Planted whole forest. Hide Castle Blachedone."

"This place is hidden by the trees?" Madelaine's heart sinks.

He nods.

"Wait, you are telling me that you are hundreds of years old?"

He nods again. "Old. Many-," he struggles for the right word, "cycles. No."

"Do you mean years?"

He shakes his head, pointing up with his thumb. "Bigger."

"Decades?"

He shakes his head again, once again pointing up with his thumb to indicate something higher.

Madelaine blinks at him. "Centuries?"

He points at her, nodding. "Cent yure ees."

"This guy is wacked out nuts," Madelaine thinks.

"You are lying. How can you be so old? It isn't possible." She is finding his story very hard to believe and is certain he is just fooling around. But it is very strange to wake up and find yourself a prisoner in a giant stone palace after going to sleep in a tent in a campground in the forest with your parents.

"They give Hornsby blood of," he pauses to remember her name for them, "vamp pyre. Not enough to turn. Only enough Hornsby never die."

Madelaine tries to digest this last madness. "Does he really believe he will never die?" she thinks. "This is getting weirder and weirder. No. He can't believe that. It's just some stupid game he's playing."

"Why would you want to hide this place? Who are you hiding it from?" Madelaine asks.

"Enemies," Hornsby says.

Madelaine looks at him skeptically.

"I wouldn't want to live in hiding," Madelaine says, imagining what it might be like to skulk around, always afraid of being found.

Hornsby nods to himself as if somehow hearing her thoughts.

Hornsby starts moving on again; shuffling down the hall in what might have been a run for him.

"Enough talk," he rasps. "Too much talk. Tired."

He waves her on to follow. "Come Little Kitten."

Madelaine watches him go uncertainly and then moves to catch up. She has no trouble keeping up with him at a brisk walk.

"Why am I here? Why did you kidnap me?"

"Little Kitten will be vamp ire."

Madelaine stumbles, blinking. She suddenly feels numb. The world just got less real.

"He's crazy. He is bloody crazy," she thinks.

She swallows, staring after Hornsby shuffling down the hallway. A chill slithers through her. Her body suddenly feels too weak to keep her standing and hot tears fill her eyes.

"He's going to kill me."

16   The Way to Madelaine

A scream pierces the quiet morning of the campground, echoing off the sky and the trees and carrying far across the forest.

"ZOE!" Caroline screams. "ZOE, SHE'S GONE! ZOEEEEE!!!!!"

Clive sits up in a shot, looking around fearfully and still half asleep.

"What? What?" he gasps. "What's going on?"

"Zoe is gone," Caroline wails. "My baby, she's gone!"

Clive scrambles out of the sleeping bag and rushes out of the tent so fast that it looks like he is falling out of it.

"Where's Zoe," he asks numbly, looking around. "Where's the dog?"

His mind works in what feels like a staggering slow confusion. "Could Zoe have taken Mocha for a walk?" he thinks. "Not likely, unless she took the dog to go looking for her sister." Suddenly he feels years older than he had a moment before.

Other campers come running to see what is wrong.

Caroline is standing in the middle of the campsite looking around in shock, trembling and pale. All she can say is, "She's gone," while staring at them imploringly.

"Zoe, our other daughter, is gone," Clive says urgently.

The growing crowd murmurs and gasps with the shock of learning that another child has gone missing.

Parents pull their kids closer, holding them tight in case they might vanish too.

"Someone is stealing children," a woman wails.

That is the closest anyone would come to the truth.

Some in the crowd grumble and turn on her, complaining about the ridiculousness of her suggestion or pointing out the unlikelihood.

A few give her warning looks, trying to shush her and casting anxious looks at Caroline and Clive. The last thing anyone wants to do is give them reason to fear all hope of finding their daughters alive and well is lost.

"She must have gone looking for her sister," Clive says with a frown, hoping the woman keeps quiet.

Ranger Davis Morgan is driving around with his windows down scouting out the campground.

"I don't want to bother the family too early if they are still sleeping," he thinks. "They will need all the sleep they can get. If we don't find their daughter, they likely won't sleep much for a very long time."

A scream piercing the morning interrupts his thoughts.

Davis hits the brake, bringing the truck to a stop. At the same moment his head snaps around, looking for the source instinctively.

He studies the surrounding trees, looking ahead and behind him in the road, listening. He hears a woman's voice shrieking something, but can't make out the panicked words.

"The Winslows. It has to be."

A sickening sinking feeling slithers down to the pit of his stomach and he blanches. He has heard that same soul-shattering tortured scream before; on more than one occasion. It is the scream of a mother who has found her child drowned in the lake. As she witnesses a mountain lion snatch her child from the hiking trail right in front of her. The mother's gut-wrenching reaction to knowing her baby has been forever ripped from her arms and her heart.

It is the scream of un-repairable loss and devastation.

His hand shaking as it reaches for the gear shift, he puts the truck into reverse, spinning the wheel into a hard turn as he backs up, and turns around in a four-point turn in the narrow road. Driving too fast, he hurries to the campsite.

Davis pulls up to the Winslow's site in his truck and jumps out. He pushes his way through the growing crowd into the campsite.

"What happened?" he asks, looking around at all the people. He looks through the crowd for Clive and Caroline.

"Another child has been stolen," the woman who believes they are being stolen wails. Two women try to comfort and quiet her, glancing at Caroline and hoping she didn't notice the implications of what the woman said.

"Another child got lost," a man says.

"The little dog too," the man who twice caught Mocha adds.

Davis groans, trying to keep his response casual and unresponsive to the gravity of the news.

"Has anyone checked the bathroom or the park yet?"

Clive shakes his head guiltily. "We found the dog. The dog is gone too."

Davis nods at this.

"Check the bathrooms and the park. Maybe she took the dog with her. The girl is probably scared after her sister got lost."

"I just came from there," a woman says. "There was no one there. No kids or dogs."

Davis looks directly at Clive. This is addressed to him. "Someone who knows her, go check the bathrooms, all the outhouses, the playground, and anyplace you think she could have gone."

On the edge of the crowd, Geoffrey stands, unnoticed. He feels chilled by more than the cool morning air.

"I have a bad feeling Zoe went looking for her sister herself," he thinks. "Madelaine would not want Zoe putting herself at risk looking for her. She would be even more upset if she knew her dog was found safe and taken out to get lost again."

Davis scans the crowd, taking stock of what he has to work with. His eyes stop briefly on Geoffrey and Geoffrey meets his look. His eyes move on, continuing his assessment of the group.

Davis turns to the group now.

"If she isn't there, the little girl may have taken the dog to find her sister. If anyone has seen a girl and a dog, we need to know."

He turns back to Caroline and Clive again, looking to them for confirmation.

Caroline steps forward, her eyes and nose red from crying, and shakes her head no. Her expression is of abject misery and guilt.

"No," she chokes out. "I let the dog go last night. Zoe was sleeping in the tent. I thought maybe Mocha could find Madelaine and bring her back, or at least keep her company out there in the forest."

She sobs, covering her face with her hands.

Clive gives her a stunned look.

"Zoe must have gone looking for the dog," Clive says. He can't completely hide the accusation of his words.

They are a knife to Caroline's heart. It is her fault Zoe is missing.

"He blames me," she thinks miserably, feeling betrayed. "He's right. It's my fault. She probably went looking to Mocha."

Caroline has never regretted anything in her life like she now regrets setting Mocha loose.

Everyone starts talking at once.

Ranger Davis tries to quiet them so he can talk, but they won't hear. At last he blows a loud blast on his whistle.

The whistle's piercing shriek shocks everyone into silence. They all turn to stare at him, wide eyed with the stunned alarm of adults frightened for the safety of two children lost alone in the big forest.

"Ok, now this is what we will do . . ." Davis starts organizing a massive search for the missing children and dog.

After he finishes giving the group their instructions, he waits for most of them to disperse in search of the missing girls.

Geoffrey comes forward to stand before him.

"It doesn't look good, does it?"

Davis sighs. "It could be worse. It didn't get that cold. We still have time to find them before the nights get really cold."

He turns to Caroline and Clive.

"Have you noticed anything missing? Do you think either of the girls took anything extra with them? Jackets, blankets, food, water?"

Clive shakes his head. "Even Madelaine's shoes and jacket are here. Wherever she went, she went barefoot and dressed in only a nightgown."

Geoffrey looks stricken. "Nobody goes wandering the forest barefoot," he thinks, "especially someone not used to being out here."

"Zoe's shoes and jacket are gone," Caroline adds.

The others look at her. You don't take your jacket and shoes if you aren't planning to leave.

Davis's frown deepens. He has to force himself to keep a bland expression. Suddenly the story that Madelaine wandered off to find her lost dog does not feel right.

"I should have asked this yesterday," he thinks. He regrets the lapse. This changes everything.

"It's possible, I suppose, that Madelaine crawled out of the tent when she heard a noise and thought it was the dog," he says. "She could have seen something. Maybe even the dog. And tried to catch it and didn't think to grab shoes."

"Being barefoot could mean she's laid up somewhere with a foot injury and unable to make it back on her own," he thinks. "But if Zoe took her jacket and shoes, that tells us it was planned. She knew she would need them."

He turns to Geoffrey. "Get on your bike and cover as much ground as you can. Check everywhere a kid her age might have gone; any trails you think she or the dog might have taken."

Geoffrey nods and leaves.

Davis turns to Caroline and Clive.

"That boy knows this campground almost better than I do. We won't give up searching for your daughters."

Caroline watches Geoffrey go.

"That boy is always there," she thinks. "He was with both Madelaine and Zoe before they disappeared, and hanging around after."

The heat of shame flushes her cheeks, but she can't push away the nagging doubt and suspicion.

Zoe wakes up slowly, looking around. She is cold and shivering. At first she doesn't know where she is. The sun is coming up with the pale light of early morning beginning to chase away the darkness. A weak beam of light is splashed across the ground.

Her flashlight.

She picks it up and swings the light around, revealing the woods around her. The light is dim, the batteries weak from being left on all night.

She frowns down at it and turns it off.

"I have to save it now for when I really need it."

Really looking around now, her heart sinks in her chest and her stomach feels sick.

"I'm lost." Her voice comes out smaller than she remembers hearing it sound in a long time. Like a little kid.

Zoe doesn't know what else to do, so she calls out.

"Madelaine! Mocha!"

She listens and hears nothing. The forest is eerily quiet. Even the wind is not hissing in the leaves.

Her heart is beating faster now. She feels panicked.

Zoe starts walking and then running; calling Madelaine and Mocha over and over. Her heart feels like it is going to burst with fear and sadness. Tears burn at her eyes.

"It's my fault Madelaine and Mocha are both missing. It's my fault I'm lost alone in the forest now too. What if I never find them? What if I never find my way back? What if nobody ever finds any of us?"

She runs faster, pushed by fear, running blindly and calling, screaming for Madelaine and Mocha again and again until her throat hurts and her voice is hoarse.

Zoe has no idea how long she has been running through the woods, calling Mocha and Madelaine.

She does not hear a sound of warning.

Suddenly she is grabbed from behind and yanked off the ground. She feels herself swinging up through the air and it is dizzying. Her captor came silently from behind, scooping her up and walking on without slowing down.

Zoe shrieks with fear, her scream piercing and loud echoing off the sky.

Like her dream. Only, in her dream the faceless captor flew up into the sky with her. Except it was Madelaine he flew away with. It was Madelaine who was taken, but for those terrifying moments Zoe experienced it as though it was her. Then she was on the ground watching helplessly as they vanished into the sky.

The thought that it could be just a bad dream comes and quickly goes. It doesn't feel like a dream. And when she is dreaming Zoe always knows it's a dream. At least, in the ones she remembers.

She has no idea what has her at first, if it is animal or human. She realizes it has to be a human from the shape and the feeling of being in someone's arms like when her dad used to carry her when she was smaller.

Zoe twists and fights, struggling and kicking.

She screams again, a blood curdling shriek of fear and anger. She tries to bite the man carrying her, and she knows now that it is a man. She knows it has to be a man because he seems so strong. She cannot see what he looks like because he is wearing a deep hood that hides his face. His cloak and hood are old and worn, looking like they belong in a fairy tale story not something anyone would actually wear. She wonders how he can see where he is going.

"Why doesn't he say something?" Zoe thinks in a panic, "This doesn't feel right." She senses she is in very serious danger.

Zoe keeps fighting and kicking, screaming and trying to hit him, but he keeps going as if she is a lifeless doll in his arms.

"Let me go!" Zoe demands, her futile struggles exhausting her. She knows in her heart this is not a rescuer searching for her or her sister in the forest. This man has another purpose and it is not good.

The man ignores her and walks on and on and on through the forest as the sun rises and the morning grows brighter.

"How is he still going?" Her mind reels with the impossibility. "How is he not tired?"

Zoe goes still, quiet now and listening.

She thought she heard a noise. It is a far away sound, echoing off the sky and distant mountains.

"Was that a scream?" Zoe wonders.

Suddenly she feels very bad. She is alone and afraid.

"I am being kidnapped by some strange man who doesn't talk," she thinks. "Could he have taken Madelaine too?"

"Mommy," Zoe whispers. She is pretty sure that was her mother's scream.

The scream sounded so scared and desperate. Zoe feels guilty knowing her mother is scared because of her, because she is missing too now.

"Sorry Mommy," Zoe whispers sadly.

The man carries her on.

Mocha lifts her head to listen. Something woke her up.

She hears it echoing from far away.

A scream. The mother.

Her tail wags and thuds on the ground, then stops. Mocha's ears droop.

It is a sound of pain and fear.

Mocha thinks about what might make the mother scream like that. She smelled bears and bad dogs, the ones with the wild danger smell, coyotes. That might make the mother scared.

The scream sounded lost. Lost and afraid, and in pain; not just scared.

Mocha starts panting short quick anxious breaths in worry. She jumps to her feet and looks around. She is still lost.

Mocha sniffs hard at the air and the ground, running in circles. She catches her own scent and begins to follow it back.

"Home, home, home," she thinks as she goes.

Mocha runs as fast as she can. Sometimes she forgets and has to stop and double back to find her trail again, following her own smell.

Mocha runs on through the woods, panting with the effort.

Suddenly, she stops and listens. She sniffs the air.

Mocha heard something familiar.

And there, right there. She sniffs again. Yes, right there is a familiar scent. It is very faint, barely there at all. But she knows it is there without a doubt. The bad thing.

Mocha yips with joy, suddenly remembering her mission.

Madelaine. She barks. Sniffing the ground to get a direction, Mocha takes off running through the forest.

The familiar thing she heard is completely forgotten.

Hornsby turns ahead of Madelaine and vanishes through a doorway.

She almost misses seeing him go in her shocked staring at the grand hallway as she follows his slow shuffling walk.

Madelaine stops in the doorway and looks around the room. It is just as dimly lit and more filled with dusty old books and bookcases than the other one was, but the room is a little larger.

It takes her a moment to spot Hornsby standing against a wall in the dim room.

Hornsby motions towards another doorway on the other side of the room. The brighter light coming through the doorway gives her little relief from the dread. It is still a big unknown.

Madelaine looks at the open doorway and then at Hornsby uncertainly.

"I don't like this," she thinks. "What or who is in the other room?"

She looks back to Hornsby and he motions towards the doorway again, nodding as if to say it is okay.

Steeling herself, Madelaine walks stiffly across the darker room towards the brighter rectangle doorway. She walks through the doorway and into another room.

The room is an explosion of brilliant light in comparison to the gloominess of the other room. The light comes from a row of tall rectangles in the far wall, filling the room with blinding light after the virtual darkness of the rest of the castle she has seen. Her eyes burn from the sudden light.

Madelaine blinks numbly, trying to take it in and make sense of it. The room is so bright with sunlight after hours of darkness that she thinks at first it will blind her. The details come into focus as her eyes adjust.

She looks around and sees no one in the room. She stares at the windows. Madelaine forgets herself.

"Windows! Big wonderful tall windows!"

A draught of fresh air caresses her face. It feels deliciously fresh and crisp. It takes a moment before she realizes these windows have no glass.

"No glass! I've never seen a window without glass before, except once when we passed an old abandoned farm house. Oh, and when we visited that old ruined fort, what was left of it."

She rushes forward in her excitement, forgetting for a moment that she is a prisoner, kidnapped and being held against her will.

"That old farm house leaned to one side, the door was gone, and half the roof had fallen in. The windows were all smashed out. But this place is like a castle."

It all comes crashing back on her just as suddenly. Madelaine stops halfway across the room, feeling her world yanked out from under her once again. She blinks back the tears.

"Come on Madelaine, be brave," she thinks. "Don't show how hurt and scared you feel."

The return of the reality of her captivity after the false surge of hope and very brief feeling of freedom and joy feels like the ultimate betrayal.

Trying to keep her expression from showing how wretched she feels, Madelaine turns and studies the room.

She looks at the windows again, blinking in confusion. She can't help but think of Hornsby's crazy story. It feels unreal. She turns to him.

"But-but," she stammers. "Vampires. The sun."

"This proves it is not real," she thinks smugly.

Hornsby chuckles, shaking his head.

"Human child needs light to grow," Hornsby rasps. "Those who come before," he shakes his head again, "do not." Madelaine automatically bristles at this. She does not think of herself as a child.

"Child sounds so, immature, so young, so- childish," she thinks. Madelaine wants to tell him this, but stops herself. "Don't, Madelaine. He is crazy and maybe dangerous. He kidnapped you. Don't forget that. Who knows what he might have done to your family when he did."

The thought brings pain, guilt, and a wave of mind-numbing loss. It is the first time she let herself think about that possibility, that he may have hurt or even killed her family.

"What if he hurt them?" she thinks. "Are they still alive? Do I still have a family?"

Madelaine feels weak. She feels her body slipping to the floor and it takes every ounce of willpower she has to keep standing.

She looks at Hornsby again. He is still in the darkness of the other room, on the edge of the shadows where the light goes through the open doorway.

Forcing the horrible thoughts from her mind, she tries to boost her courage.

"Be brave Madelaine," she thinks. "You still don't know what this is. He let me out of that room and is showing me the castle. I've got to keep my eyes open for a possible escape."

The thrill of the sunlight and open windows starts to draw Madelaine out of her funk a little bit again. She can't help it.

She looks around the room again. The light feels so wonderful after the dark little room and dim torches lighting the halls.

The sunlight has that soft glow that it has in the early morning as the sun rises. It is also the first time she has had any idea whether it is day or night.

"How long have I been trapped here?" she wonders. "How many days?"

Time has moved with the endless slowness of days without light and dark or a clock to show the passing of the hours.

She goes to the window, looking out at the forest spreading out before her. Below is a sea of trees as far as she can see. Above is empty sky, pale blue with the last color of dawn washing away and a few light clouds hanging high in the sky above.

She turns from the window to look at Hornsby.

Hornsby is still hovering on the other side of the doorway between the two rooms, hiding in the shadows.

Madelaine thinks it odd. Then it dawns on her.

"Hornsby," Madelaine asks, "don't you like the light?"

Hornsby shakes his head. "Burns," he rasps, "hurts."

"He's afraid of the light?" Madelaine thinks. "Maybe I can use that." Her thought is unfinished, interrupted.

Madelaine hears a distant echo. She turns to the window where the sound came from, echoing off the sky and distant mountains.

The sound sends a chill down her spine.

"What was that?" she asks, turning to look at Hornsby questioningly.

Hornsby looks at the floor guiltily.

"Little Kitten's mother," he says sadly.

"My mother?" Madelaine is alarmed. She listens hard and hears it again and then once more for the last time.

"Is that my mother? Why is she screaming?" She turns to him, her eyes wide with worry, feeling panic.

"Little Sister," Hornsby says. "She ran away to find Little Kitten."

Madelaine gasps.

Hornsby nods sadly.

"Zoe, no," she breathes. "She'll be lost in the forest."

Hornsby shakes his head.

"Little Kitten not worry," Hornsby says, "Hornsby will look after."

"Why? Why would you do that?" She looks at him, pleading. "I mean, you kidnapped me. Now you are kidnapping my sister too?"

"Hornsby does not take Little Sister," Hornsby shakes his head. "Little Sister is lost. Hornsby will help."

"Why? Why do you even care if she is lost?" She is burning inside with the need to understand.

Hornsby stands on the other side of the doorway, still in the shadows of the darker room.

"Hornsby wants Little Kitten to be happy. Little Kitten is not happy if Little Sister is hurt. Hornsby will find Little Sister. Make Little Sister safe."

Madelaine's eyes water with tears. They fill her up to the point she feels like they will burst out of her chest. She feels so desperately alone, but she wants more than anything right now for Zoe to be home safe with their parents. Her mother's scream echoing in the distance with such loss and sadness feels like a knife cut her through the heart.

A thought strikes her and she utters it out loud before she realizes it.

"If I can hear her scream, she would be able to hear me."

"No," Hornsby says.

Madelaine flushes and turns to look at him, scared of what his reaction to her betraying thought might be.

Hornsby points to the windows.

"Echo is tricky. Sound comes here. Okay."

He motions a swooping gesture towards them.

"Mountain makes sound echo away. Nothing there. Only trees. More trees."

His motion is swooping away in the opposite direction.

Madelaine's lower lip trembles. Her eyes burn hot with tears. If this is true, she can scream as much as she wants out that window and no one will ever hear her.

"Little Kitten read now," Hornsby says. "Not worry."

He steps away from the doorframe, retreating into the darker room they entered first from the hall.

Madelaine turns and looks at him through the open doorway.

He points one long withered finger at one of the book cases.

"Stay here." He turns and leaves.

Madelaine stares after him for a long moment after he'd gone from sight. She considers sneaking out, but fear holds her back.

With nothing else to do, she turns her attention on the book cases, walking along them and running a finger along the spines as she looks at them. She stops and considers a stack of dusty books on a small table in a corner.

Madelaine wipes a swath of the dust off the cover. It is so old that she cannot read the title on the cover.

Taking the book and sitting in a chair at the table in the middle of the room, she opens the book and turns the first few pages. The pages seem thicker than normal paper, tainted yellow-brown with age, stiff and almost brittle.

She leans forward, sniffing it. Somehow picking it up feels wrong, like she might risk damaging something very old and rare. It even smells very old.

Madelaine carefully flips through the pages of front matter.

Not knowing what else to do, she begins to read. It feels very strange to her; to be here held captive and sitting calmly reading a book with an open door only feet away. The book itself is strange too.

"It's like reading an old fairytale storybook that must have been written hundreds of years ago."

She looks closer at the pages. "This isn't even printed. These pictures and words are painted right on the pages."

Watching out of sight, Hornsby quietly moves back from the doorway, vanishing down the hallway.

Ranger Davis Morgan and his crew are readying the horses at the stables to mount up for another day of searching the forest. Only this time they have two missing girls to find.

He pulls at the strap angrily, tightening the saddle. The horse puffs out her stomach and stomps a hoof to let him know she is not happy. She is already agitated, sensing his mood.

Davis is angry at the stupidity of people who let their kids go wandering off into the forest to get lost. Angrier that they did it not once, but twice, letting a second kid get lost. The forest is no place for kids.

"It was bad enough they let the dog take off the first time," he mutters angrily, pulling on the strap again. "There are always dogs lost to the forest every year. They don't survive long. Then they let first one then the other kid wander off and get lost."

The rangers don't look for the dogs. He will not put his people in danger for a dog. It pains him. It is completely unnecessary and avoidable. But when a child is lost and not found, that leaves a special kind of hurt on the soul.

The horse stomps again to show her displeasure.

"Sorry about that, girl," Davis apologizes, patting the horse on her shoulder and loosening the strap to be more comfortable. It needs to be tight enough the saddle won't shift, but not so tight it leaves the animal sore.

With the saddle cinched, he checks and flattens the blanket, making sure it is not bunched anywhere to rub her raw and moves to her head.

Taking the bridle off the fence where it was hanging, he reaches to slip it over her head.

She turns her head away from him, ignoring him.

"Don't be like that, I said I'm sorry."

She continues to ignore him, head turned away.

He reaches out, gently taking her nose and turning her head to him. She quietly lets him until he reaches again with the bridle.

She turns her head away again.

"So, it's going to be like that is it?" He gently pulls her head back, holding it in place with one hand this time while he brings the bridle closer to pull it up over her nose.

She pulls her head up sharply with a snort, bobbing it in her way of saying, "No".

Davis sighs. "I need you on this one. We have two lost kids in the forest. One already spent a few nights out there. It's not looking good for her, girl."

As if understanding, the mare brings her head down and stands still, allowing him to finally bridle her. She opens her mouth to take the bit in her teeth, bobbing her head and mouthing it in her dislike of it.

"I know you don't like the bit. I don't blame you."

He moves on to filling the saddle bags with supplies and carefully placing a rifle in the rifle holder.

Davis takes the reins and leads her to the others to see if they are ready to go. This is his crew, the park rangers who work under him, three men and a woman. Not enough to search this forest for a missing child, but good at what they do.

Two are already mounted and ready to go and the others are finishing packing their gear including rescue gear.

"All ready?"

"Ready," they nod.

"You each have your area to search. Radio if you see anything at all. The dog is out there somewhere too. She might be our best chance at finding these kids. Pay attention. If you hear any barking, radio it in."

The rest mount up and they head out, riding together for the forest to search for Madelaine and Zoe. They split off to go their separate ways to search their designated areas as they enter the forest.

Geoffrey is riding his mountain bike hard through the campground trails. His breathing is rough and ragged from exertion. The bike is sturdy enough to handle the abuse. Wheels spinning and legs pumping, he presses on uphill along the trail.

He knows what is coming. Geoffrey is familiar with all these trails. He grips the handlebars tighter and eyes the path ahead. It appears to be a dead end, ending at the wall of trees ahead.

"Come on, you've got this," he mutters through ragged gasps, his eyes burning with determination. He grits his teeth harder in a grimace of effort.

The dead end ahead comes at him swiftly as he speeds up the trail. Instead of ending, the path takes a hard bank turn to the left. Taking the corner without slowing, he leans left, putting one foot down and ready to hit the ground if he wipes out. The tires skid on the dirt path with the dull grinding of rubber on dirt. He feels the traction go, the tires sliding, and tries to counter it.

He lets out a low animal growl, a mixture of dread and thrill, as he struggles to keep control of the bike.

Geoffrey manages to barely avoid a total wipe-out on the bike, the bike wobbling and tires not quite getting traction again. He grips the handle bars harder, bearing down on the pedals and pushing the bike's limits. He has no time to lose. He has to be in complete control. A tight knot of anxiety clutches his stomach.

Putting his head down, he puts everything he has into pedaling harder. A small thrill of hope pushes up through the knot of anxiety as he feels the tires grasp at the traction. The bike surges with a small burst of speed, the tires still spinning faster than the bike is moving, kicking out dirt behind it.

The ground slopes down and Geoffrey bears down harder. He tries to pedal faster, his knuckles white on the handlebars. The slope grows steeper and he is no longer controlling the bike.

All he can do now is steer and hold on.

He flies down the path, his momentum and the down slope adding speed to the bike.

With a sickening lifting feeling in his gut, the bike hits a small rise in the ground and they are airborne. The bike flies over the open expanse where the ground falls away sharply below. He looks at the path continuing a few feet below on the other side of the deep cut-out and closes his eyes. Geoffrey can't help the howl that tears loose from his throat, expressing his fear and the incredible thrill rush that makes his whole body feel like it is vibrating.

For a long moment Geoffrey feels weightless, clinging to the handlebars. The bike beneath him soon begins to fall away. He does his best using his grip on the handlebars to keep the seat from falling too far beneath him. He lets his legs spread just enough. Keeping the front wheel up, he has to catch the pedals on the way down before he hits the ground below.

The bike starts swinging away beneath him, swinging too far to the right. He is in danger of not landing right and being seriously hurt. If he gets injured out here, it could take a while for anyone to find him. He knows. It happened before and he was stuck laying in a gully for hours with a broken arm, leg, and collarbone.

"Come on," he urges under his breath, opening his eyes.

Geoffrey manages to straighten the bike a fraction of a second before it is too late. The ground below is rushing up at him with incredible speed.

Bringing his feet in, he fumbles for the pedals, still gripping the handlebars tightly. Steeling himself for the impact, he tries to keep his legs stiff but loose enough to bend with it.

Just as Geoffrey feels the tease of the pedals beneath his feet, he feels the sudden impact of the back tire hitting the ground hard. The pedals slam against his feet, he bends his knees a little to take away some of the shock, and the front wheel hits the ground, sliding and almost sending the bike skidding out of control sideways. The force pushes some of the wind out of him.

Geoffrey lets the momentum take him, not pedaling, allowing the bike tires to spin at their own pace. He works only to keep the bike upright, to keep from sliding and skidding out of control.

Finally, the bike stops fighting him for control and he can steer, just in time to avoid slamming full force into a large tree.

Slowing the bike, Geoffrey finally skids to a stop and looks back. It is too far of a drop to jump without risking breaking anything, but with the momentum of the bike he made it alive and uninjured.

His heart is pounding in his chest and his breath is coming in ragged gasps. The rush of adrenaline surging through him from the fear and daring of the dangerous jump is dizzying. He feels jarred, a dull ache in his bones mimicking the stronger ache in his muscles.

Geoffrey stares up at the path he left, feeling weak with the draining adrenaline. He has to focus to keep his knees from buckling under him.

Reaching to wipe the sweat from his forehead, Geoffrey pauses to stare at his trembling hand.

"I made it. It was stupid, but it's the fastest way to get down here. Nobody would have searched these trails. None of these weekend campers know these trails exist."

Still breathing heavy and feeling shaky from the risky move, Geoffrey opts to walk his bike for a while. He starts off down the path.

He looks up at the sky, judging the light, and glances at his watch.

"I've still got a few hours to search for the girls."

17 Discoveries

Davis has been riding for some hours, his horse picking her way through the trees at a slow plodding pace while he studies the ground for any sign either of the missing girls have been there. His two-way radio crackles to life. He can barely make out who the garbled static-filled voice belongs to. The same words are repeated three times, the words garbled each time but understandable.

"I found something."

Davis presses the button, speaking into the radio.

"Davis here. Where are you? Over."

The person on the radio gives map coordinates, repeating them three times followed by the call sign "over" to indicate they are done talking. They all know the power of repetition. Their radio signals only work within a certain distance and they are pushing it spreading out their search with the rough terrain interfering with the signal.

"Got it. On my way. Over."

He pulls out his map, studies it, gets his bearing on where the coordinates are, and tucks it away. He urges his horse into a jog, then a trot, and finally pushes her up to a gallop, dodging trees racing through the forest. He slows when the terrain requires it, speeding up again when he can.

The horse is lathered with sweaty foam and breathing hard by the time he arrives at the coordinates, her sides heaving.

It takes a moment to find him in the trees. One of the men on his team is standing there studying the ground. His horse is patiently eating leaves a short distance away.

"What did you find?" Davis asks as he gets off his horse.

Jacob points to the ground.

"Footprints. One of the missing girls was here."

Davis comes closer, studying the ground. The prints are of smallish shoes the size you might expect a pre-teen girl's to be.

"She slept here," Jacob says, walking away and directing him to the base of two trees growing together.

"Smart girl," Davis says. "It wouldn't protect her from any predators, but at least she has the sense to try to find shelter."

He stares off into the forest as if she might appear at any moment in the trees.

He sighs heavily. "At least we have a starting point to search for one of them."

"Which one do you think it is?" Jacob asks.

"These are shoe prints. Definitely the younger girl. The other one is barefoot."

"That should make us feel better. We could be close to finding the younger one."

"Does it make you feel any better?" Davis asks.

"I won't feel better until we find them both," Jacob says with a sad shake of his head. "Are we going to pull the others in? Redirect their search to this area?"

"No." Davis pulls out his map, studying it again. "The other girl has been missing for a full day and night longer. She could have gone much farther in that time, even barefoot. We will keep ourselves spread out. We have a lot of ground to cover. Let's follow this trail and see where it leads."

They both lead their horses, studying the ground as they go, following the marks Zoe's shoes left behind.

They continue on for some distance and then stop, staring at the ground.

Jacob looks around and then up at the trees above. He turns to Davis. "The trail, it just stops." He searches the ground for the trail again.

Davis stares at the ground, a chill pricking his spine.

"It's like something scooped her up and she's gone," he says.

"Something that doesn't leave a trail?" Jacob asks in disbelief.

They turn and look at each other, their eyes hollow with shock and disbelief.

"It's impossible. There has to be a trail," Jacob says.

Davis stares off through the trees, his eyes narrowing.

Madelaine feels like she has struggled for hours to concentrate on reading. It's no use. Sitting here alone, all she can think about is home.

The absolute silence is unnerving. Like in the small dark room Hornsby kept her in. She has never experienced such silence. Even when the house is quiet there is the almost inaudible sound of all the things in the house powered by electricity. It is the sort of absolute silence you get only when the power is out, but then the dog barks to complain about the strange silence.

It makes Madelaine afraid to even breathe. As if somehow even that small noise is an unwanted invasion on the expected total silence of this place.

"It feels like a tomb," she whispers. "Like some cold dead ancient tomb."

Homesickness washes over Madeleine with a deep sadness and loneliness that adds to the constant fear hanging over her.

"I want to go home."

The thought of trying to escape makes the fear knot in her stomach tighten.

She looks at the empty doorway.

"Outside that doorway is the other room and after that is who knows how many hallways and rooms. Somewhere after that is freedom and my family in the campground."

She looks down miserably.

"If they are still alive. Hornsby could have murdered them all in their sleep to kidnap me."

Madelaine looks at the open window again.

"He is a kidnapper and crazy. He could have lied about that being my mom we heard."

She looks at the doorway again. She is too afraid to go off wandering to search for the way out but that doesn't stop her from thinking about doing it.

"What would Hornsby do if he caught me wandering around? What if he locks me back in that tiny room with no light?"

She shivers at the thought.

Madelaine tries to force herself to focus on the book again. Her attention keeps being pulled away, listening for Hornsby or anything else living in this empty place. She is so tense with the stress that she feels like she will snap like an old crunchy elastic band that has been stretched until it breaks.

Madelaine looks down at the ancient book again, trying to force her eyes to focus on the text.

She has reread the same half sentence more times than she can count. She squints her eyes at the words on the page and wrinkles her nose at them.

"Come on, at least it's something to do. Just read."

She focuses hard on the page, reading those wretched words again, and finally gets to the end of that sentence and into the next. Madelaine pushes down the urge to throw the book across the room. She reads on, sentence after sentence.

And unbeknownst to the Maurader, the fae maiden had hidden herself away deep within the roots of that ancient tree.

She watched the wretched creature as he mucked about searching for her.

His search grew frantic as the light waned. He could not return without the fae maiden prisoner.

"Maiden!" He called. "Maiden! Come now. You must know you cannot get away. There is no place to run."

His search brought him to that tree. He stopped and stared at it as if he might see through the leaves and branches, through the wood of its stout trunk and down to the bramble of twisted roots, some roots stretched deep beneath the earth to where the underground springs lay in secret, and some pushed up as though the wooden beast would step from the ground and walk.

"Walk. Walk now and take me far from here," the fae maiden whispered to the twisted roots hiding her.

The ancient tree only sat as silent and stoic as ever. It deigned not to answer her plea. The fate of those like her were beneath the grandfather tree's notice.

The Maurader searched too close to where she hid.

> *Fear sent its icy chill through her and she must swallow it to not cry out.*
>
> *With the smallest whimper, the maiden pressed herself back against the roots. She felt behind her for any space to fit so that she might move deeper within the roots.*
>
> *Under her questing fingers one root moved and then another.*
>
> *In her shock she turned to look and there she found an opening.*
>
> *The fae maiden in her fear did not know to be afraid of such things.*
>
> *Without consideration of the consequences, she squeezed down the hole to find what she shall find.*
>
> *She moved down, climbing down through the tangled roots, the Maurader calling above.*
>
> *"Fae maiden! My fae maiden! Please come back to me."*
>
> *The desperation in his voice did not warm the icy fear in hers.*

Against her will, Madelaine finds herself drawn into the story she is reading despite wishing only to throw the book away and run for her life.

She sniffles at the book. "At least they are consistent in spelling marauder wrong," she jokes sarcastically. Madelaine returns to reading the story.

> *As the fae maiden descended further, the climb grew more difficult, her world darker, and the Maurader's calls more distant.*
>
> *"How much deeper must I go?"*
>
> *She looked up to the faint light above, such as it was. It was her only known escape from the depths beneath the tree.*
>
> *Below was darkly unknown territory.*

"The old stories tell of frightening things which dwell beneath the earth. I hope I do not come across any."

She continued her downward climb, struggling through the spindly tangles of roots. The fat roots grew thinner as she went; their nature all that gave them the strength to hold her weight.

The fae maiden heard the strangest sound. She stopped climbing down to listen. She held her breath and tried to breathe softly through her nose. Her ragged breath pushed through, rough and too loud. Her heart pounded fearfully.

"What makes that sound?"

It was a dull thocking, as of a woodpecker who had a wooden dowel for a beak. Rhythmic. Thock thock thock. Thock thock thock.

It sent a chill through her. An instinctive fear.

A rough slithering came from her left.

She turned and stared through the dark, but saw no movement.

A sound interrupts Madelaine's reading. She looks up.

"What was that?"

Her chest is tight with sudden fear, feeling the fae maiden's fear as her own with the interruption by the strange noise. She imagines it is the dull thocking noise or the rough slithering.

She looks around for Hornsby, afraid to get up from her chair and approach the darker room he would have entered from the hall. He is nowhere to be seen, but he could be out of sight.

"No, I would have heard him. He shuffles his feet and that's not what I heard."

Madelaine listens again, her heart pounding in her chest. "Come on sound, I need to hear it again," she thinks.

A distant noise barely reaches her ears.

"Could it be? Impossible."

She listens again, leaning forward in her intensity. There it is again.

"It is!" Her heart beats faster and her breath comes faster, excited. She hears the familiar high bark of her little dog again.

"I'm sure of it!"

"Mocha! Mocha!" she cries, jumping up from her chair and rushing across the room to the open doorway between the rooms, looking around excitedly and half expecting to see the little dog appear before her in the old library room.

Madelaine runs into the other room and stops, looking around expectantly. She runs to the doorway opening onto the great hallway and looks up and down the hall, quickly becoming unsure.

"I was so sure I heard Mocha's bark. It sounded far way but much closer that Mom's cries, like she is someplace in the castle."

Madelaine's shoulders sag with the crushing pain of disappointment filling her.

"It's too good to be true. I'm wrong. It's just wishful thinking and my imagination. Of course Mocha isn't here. How could she have got here?" The thought sits hollow and empty inside her stomach.

Mocha whimpers and cries out in a sharp bark, digging frantically at the ground.

She digs through the mud to find her paws blocked by hard rock. Her paws scrabble at it uselessly. She can't dig through that.

The little dog presses her nose against the stone and puffs and snorts through her nose unhappily at it.

She can still smell it, the smell that is distinctly Madelaine, and the putrid ancient grave stink of the bad thing. The smell is coming from somewhere nearby.

Mocha looks around, sniffing the air. She takes a few steps, following the scent, and a few more steps.

There, very close, Mocha sees the darkness of a hole. She pounces on it, pressing her face to it, pushing her nose as deep as she can and snuffling loudly, smelling dirt and smoke and the other smells that increase her feeling of urgency; Madelaine and the bad thing.

Mocha barks a few times, then attacks the hole. She digs at it, her paws working frantically and whimpering eagerly. She sends dirt flying behind her as she makes the opening bigger.

When it is big enough she squeezes and squirms her way inside. Mocha scrabbles against the narrow hole, digging urgently and kicking more dirt behind her, widening it as she burrows deeper.

She barks again.

Mocha's urgency pushes her to move faster than she can dig, wriggling and digging, the hole closing around her until she is stuck.

"Yiyiyiii," she cries; the sound high and drawn out.

Madelaine's head snaps up and she looks around at the muffled sound of a high keening crying, her eyes large.

"It sounds like something is crying. Like whatever is making that sound is hurt."

She listens, focusing on the sound.

"Mocha?"

A surge of panic fills her with the certainty that despite the impossibility of it, the sound is Mocha.

Madelaine starts moving down the hallway in what she thinks is the direction the sound is coming from. She moves hesitantly at first, afraid of being caught out of the room Hornsby left her in. As she puts distance between her and the room a sense of doomed inevitability fueled recklessness takes hold and she starts walking faster. The growing volume of the cries as she goes spurs her to speed up more.

And then they suddenly stop.

She stops, staring wide eyed and listening. Madelaine is holding her breath, fearful even the faint noise of her own breathing will make her miss a crucial sound.

"It's gone," she thinks. "Was it even there? Did I imagine it? There's no way Mocha could be here. Whatever it was, if I even heard it, it's probably dead now."

The thought of Mocha paralyzes her with sorrow and loss. She tries to push it away.

"It's not Mocha. It can't be."

But that foreboding recklessness moves her forward to investigate.

Expecting to find nothing, Madelaine starts walking again.

"I should go back before he finds me gone. This is ridiculous. There won't be anything."

She reaches another hall branching off this one and pauses, looking up both halls.

"Which way do I go?"

Shrugging uncertainly, she starts walking up the new hall. The ceiling is not quite as high as the other and it's not as wide. The torches lighting the way are further apart and the shadowy areas between them wider.

"How does he keep this whole place lit?"

The hole is tight and very hard to move in, but the little dog doesn't give up. Mocha stops crying and wriggles and squirms and scratches herself forward one tiny inch at a time.

There is light ahead. She snuffles at the air coming from it, sucking in the smells.

That pushes Mocha to try harder, digging and inching her way frantically.

She reaches the end of the narrow tunnel and it opens to nothing. Air. Spacious dimly lit air.

Mocha hesitates at the drop below. It is a long way to fall for a little dog.

She pushes and pulls, wriggling herself forward out of the tunnel.

The little dog twists in the air as she falls, like a cat trying to land on its feet. She lands hard on the stone floor below with the dull sound of her body hitting stone and a strangled sound that is quickly cut off from the breath being knocked out of her.

Mocha lays there motionless except her labored panting and wheezing. It is too hard to breath.

When she is able to wheeze a little air in and out she struggles to her feet. Mocha shakes her whole body as if to shake off the shock and pain of the hard landing.

She stands there, sniffing the air, and lets out a small whuff. The bark sounds off because she is still struggling to catch her breath.

Mocha listens and smells the air again then lets out another strained bark. Her head pops up and she listens. Her ears perk up.

She hears a quiet sound echoing to her from somewhere down the wide hallways.

Mocha rushes forward, her feet not getting a grip at first and scrabbling on the stone floor. Her feet find their grip and she darts away. She follows the dying echo of Madelaine's voice as it echoes off the stone walls.

Madelaine stares in disbelief when she sees the little chocolate brown and white cocker spaniel bounding towards her. She shrieks with delight.

"Mocha! Mocha!" Madelaine cries happily. "I can't believe it. Mocha is actually here! She found me!"

Mocha nearly skids into her trying to stop on the stone floor, looking up at her, her tail wagging so hard that her whole bum wags with it.

Madelaine grabs the little dog, scooping her up and holding her so tight Mocha squirms uncomfortably.

"Mocha, oh Mocha," Madelaine sobs into the dog's dirty fur. "That awful old man, Hornsby, he kidnapped me and brought me here. Hornsby talks like he thinks vampires are real. I'm not sure, but I think he really does believe it. He's crazy and said he's going to make me a vampire. I think he's going to kill me Mocha."

She buries her face in Mocha's fur.

"I know it all sounds too stupid and unreal. This whole thing is stupid and unreal. It's just a crazy story Hornsby told me. He is totally delusional and that's what he thinks he is going to do. He says that's why he kidnapped me."

She sobs harder into the little dog's fur.

"Oh Mocha, I don't even know what this place is or where it is. I think it's somewhere in the forest. He talked about the redwood trees hiding it. It has to be not that far from the campground because he's going to go looking for Zoe, and you found me, and, and-."

Madelaine trembles and almost falls to the floor as her knees suddenly become very weak. The shock of everything that happened has finally caught up to her.

She sinks to the floor, still hugging Mocha tight.

"Mocha," she gasps into the dog's fur, "we have to escape!"

She sobs harder again, her shoulders shaking with her sobs.

"All that crazy stuff about vampires and planting the forest, he's crazy! They aren't even real. But this place-."

She trails off, not knowing what to say.

The thought hits her.

An earthy stench of forgotten decay seeps into Mocha's nose. She stiffens, but Madelaine does not notice. The oily smell of something that should have been dead a very long time ago fills the air, distant and approaching, but only Mocha can smell it with her keen sense of smell.

"Mocha, if you found a way in, then there has to be a way out!" Madelaine sobs.

Hornsby comes up behind her.

Madelaine is still oblivious.

Hornsby looks down at Madelaine and the dog. He does not seem surprised to see Mocha.

18   Everyone is Lost

The light is fading from the world. Geoffrey looks up at the darkening sky with a frown.

"It's going to be dark soon. I have to stop searching and try again in the morning."

He looks around him grimly.

"Madelaine, where are you? You are out there somewhere. I know you are. How far could you have gone? I searched every trail without going deeper into the forest, even the ones you probably couldn't have gotten to or would not have taken because they are too hard."

He starts riding again, the wheels of his bike spinning fast, bouncing over the rough terrain; heading home for the night.

Geoffrey is riding without thought about where he is going. His thoughts instead are on running routes through his mind. He is planning out his search for tomorrow. Ranger Davis Morgan told him to never search blindly. Always have a plan. Always have a search pattern mapped out. Otherwise you waste a lot of time searching areas you already searched or risk leaving holes in your search that could make you miss finding the target. That's how people don't get found. That and because they don't stay where they are, making finding them all but impossible as they move deeper into the forest or into areas that have already been searched.

He looks up to get his bearings and realizes he is riding through the campground instead of towards home. He is riding towards Madelaine's family's campsite.

He groans.

"I don't want to see them. I don't want to face her parents. What do I say? Why did I come this way?"

Geoffrey knows deep down that he needs someone to feel what he feels. He needs someone who feels the same loss and desperation he does.

"Why do I care so much about some girl I just met and don't really know?" he groans as he continues riding towards the campsite.

He arrives at the campsite and stops his bike a few sites before it. He stands there in the growing dark, one foot on the ground to steady himself and one on the pedal, looking at Madelaine's campsite up the road ahead.

"No one understands," he mutters, feeling the pain flow through him with a fresh surge. The pain he felt like a large knife slicing through him when he learned the girl he met the day before had vanished during the night and is lost in the forest.

"They don't think I should feel anything. They tell me I don't know Madelaine because we only just met. But, I know her. I don't know what it is about her, but I feel like I've known her forever. There is something about her. It's stupid, I know, but I feel, I don't know, some sort of connection to her. And now Zoe is missing too; lost out there somewhere alone."

Geoffrey pushes down the feelings of pain and loss, blinking back the burning in his eyes, and swallows. Steeling himself to be strong and stay calm, he rides on to the campsite.

He stops outside the entrance to the site, looking in uncertainly.

There is a small fire burning in the fire pit, not putting out very much light and just as little warmth. The sound of the meagre fire crackles too loudly in the still darkness.

It seems fitting somehow, seeing Madelaine's parents sitting there across from each other around the small fire, the darkness pressing in as if to swallow them up like the forest swallowed up Madelaine, Mocha, and Zoe.

The chill filling the scene feels more like the cold of misery and loss than the night air in the darkness; the fire unable to push back that chilly darkness because they are all so small and helpless against the forest.

Caroline notices him first, hiding quietly in the dark at the edge of their site. Caroline, who so clearly did not approve of Madelaine talking to him and who was so cold towards him, making him feel awkward and uncomfortable.

Geoffrey stands there still, silently, feeling awkward and unsure of his welcome. He is afraid to enter the campsite and face them. He is sure he can feel dislike and distrust oozing out of the campsite.

"Their mom hates me," he thinks. "They both probably blame me."

Caroline nods acknowledgement of his presence. She stares at the shape in the darkness, knowing who it is and unsure how to respond.

"This is the boy we let our daughter go off alone with," she thinks, "after what happened." She pushes down the rest of the thought. That is a dark place that she cannot visit right now. Not when their world is already so dark and empty with both their girls missing in the forest.

"And then I let him go off with Zoe and now she's gone too," she thinks miserably.

She can't help the flare of white hot blame she feels towards the boy. The doubts. The nagging questions. What if he did have something to do with their disappearances?

Caroline chokes back a sob, trying to be quiet and calm.

Clive continues staring down at the fire as if it is the only thing that exists in the world, oblivious to the silent standoff between the woman and boy.

"Go away," Caroline thinks, staring at the shape whose features and expression she cannot make out in the dark. "Just go away."

She sighs.

"Hello Geoffrey," she says quietly. Her voice seeming to carry louder than it should on the quiet night air.

Clive looks up, startled, and looks around until he spots the boy in the darkness at the edge of the campsite. He relaxes, waving him over.

"Geoffrey, have a seat." His voice is heavy with the fear and loss weighing him down.

Geoffrey stands his bike on its stand and comes into the campsite, feeling awkward as he sits in one of the empty camping chairs. He looks at Caroline and Clive. Their eyes and faces hold a depth of loss and pain he never thought possible.

He swallows, his eyes shifting away uncomfortably, and forcing himself to look at them again.

"We'll find them," Geoffrey says, his voice rough with uncertainty and the heaviness of the moment.

"Thank you," Caroline says, her own voice rough with the tears she has run out of and the overwhelming loss and sorrow filling her.

"Is that what you are doing out so late?" Clive asks. "Were you out looking for them?"

Geoffrey nods. "I had to stop. It's too dark."

Clive nods his appreciation for the help. "Thank you."

"I have to get home." Geoffrey gets up awkwardly, still feeling the tension of the strained moment. He hurries to his bike, gets on, and rides off into the darkness.

After a moment of silence to give him time to get out of earshot, Caroline speaks quietly.

"Do you think he had anything to do with it?"

Clive looks at her in surprise.

"You mean with Madelaine's and Zoe's disappearances?"

"Yes."

"Are you really going to go there?" Clive's voice has a hard edge of anger to it. "Are you really doing this? No, I don't think he had anything to do with it. Jesus, Caroline, you really are an untrusting hateful person, aren't you?"

The words are barely out of his mouth and Clive already regrets the hurtful remark.

Caroline's expression is pained, cut to the heart by Clive's harsh comment.

She looks down at her lap, not wanting to look at him anymore. Her bottom lip quivers and a cold chill fills her with the crack that just split in their relationship.

"I mean, you don't really think Geoffrey kidnapped either of them, do you?" Clive's attempt at an apology falls flat.

"I only meant that after what happened-." Caroline does not finish.

"You have to let it go Caroline. It's done, in the past. You can't keep doing this. You can't keep being suspicious of everyone

Madelaine talks to. It isn't helping either of you. You have to give Madelaine a chance to put it behind her."

He shakes his head morosely, pained at his wife's thought and the memory.

"No." Clive says heavily. "No, I do not think that boy had anything to do with either Madelaine's or Zoe's disappearances. He's just a bloody kid. I don't think he did anything to make Madelaine take off, or Zoe either. We know why they did. Madelaine went looking for that dog of hers and Zoe went looking for Madelaine."

He sighs heavily, considering whether or not to say his next words.

"If we have to blame anyone, we have to blame ourselves," he says. "None of this would have happened if we didn't get her that dog. As if a dog was somehow going to make things better. We shouldn't have dragged her out camping. She didn't want to come. This trip has been nothing but miserable since we planned it, with the girls fighting and Madelaine moping-." He doesn't finish the last thought about Caroline; her clinginess and over-protectiveness towards Madelaine, their own strained relationship, and how unhappy she has been.

He feels like he is the reason for her unhappiness. He failed them.

"I'm going to bed," Caroline says coldly.

Clive can hear the pain behind the cold angry tone. It digs his own pain a little deeper.

Caroline gets up and crawls into the tent, leaving Clive sitting alone in the darkness before the low fire.

He stays there, feeling unwelcome in the tent and in his own bed.

Clive sits there in the dark, feeling the chill quiet solitude. He looks up at the dark sky and back at the fire that gives off so little light.

"Where are you?" he whispers heavily.

He can't hold it back anymore and breaks into soul-wracking sobs.

The hair on Mocha's hackles rises up like gooseflesh raises the hairs on your arms. Her ears go back and her lips pull up to show her sharp little teeth. A low rumble vibrates through her chest.

Mocha growls, looking up at Hornsby, the hair on her back rising more.

Madelaine looks up at him with teary eyes, afraid he is going to take Mocha away.

"Did Hornsby bring Mocha?" she wonders. "Did he kidnap Mocha for me or did she find me on her own?" The questions whirl around in her head. She needs to find out. She is afraid to ask, afraid of what the answer might be.

"Come," Hornsby rasps, "it is time."

"T-time for what?" Madelaine sobs through her tears.

"Little sister is found," Hornsby says.

He motions Madelaine to follow and turns, shuffling off unhurriedly down the hall.

"Zoe?" Madelaine tries to blink through her tears. "Zoe is found? By who? Did my parents find her or did Hornsby? He couldn't have found her already. He wasn't gone long enough. Unless, Zoe was very close or," she pauses the thought, afraid to let herself think it, "unless we are much closer to the campground than he said."

A flush rises up her neck.

"Of course Hornsby lied to me," she thinks. "He kidnapped me."

Another thought comes on the heels of the realization that Zoe was found, that Mocha is here. That it is time.

"Time for what? Am I going home now too? Is Hornsby letting me go after all?" Madelaine feels like she will burst with all the questions spinning in her head.

She realizes Hornsby has gone some distance down the hall. Her head snaps up, staring after him.

"Zoe. Mocha, we have to find out what's happening with Zoe."

She jumps to her feet.

The excitement has Mocha hopping up and growling towards the retreating figure of the old man down the hall.

Madelaine jogs after Hornsby, Mocha pattering after her.

She follows him through a maze of hallways. Mocha follows along, stiff legged and her tail and ears down showing her distress. She keeps giving him distrustful looks.

They arrive at another room. Hornsby stops at the door and opens it. He looks down, almost apologetically, or perhaps in embarrassment, Madelaine isn't sure which.

He motions Madelaine to go in.

She looks at him then at the open door, suddenly terrified of what she might find on the other side.

"If he kidnapped me, he could have kidnapped Zoe too," she thinks. "What if she put up a fight? Are Mom and Dad okay, or are they dead?"

Her chest is so tight she feels like she will never be able to draw another breath. It's painful. She can't swallow and the knowledge suddenly makes swallowing imperative.

Panic fills her.

Mocha's low growl releases her from the paralysis.

Stumbling, her feet uncertain of what to do, Madelaine steps forward into the doorway and stops.

There, laying on a table like a corpse in an old movie, is the motionless body of her little sister. She cannot see Zoe's face. It is there, but her mind refuses to see it. Seeing it is believing; knowing that Zoe is there, not moving, silent.

"Is she breathing? Is she dead?" she thinks numbly.

Horror fills Madelaine in a wash of dread and agony that feels like it will tear her apart.

"Zoe!" she cries. "What have you done to her?"

She rushes forward without thinking, pawing and grabbing at Zoe, shaking her and terrified that she is dead.

"Zoe! Zoe! Open your eyes," she sobs. "Please don't be dead. Zoe!"

The whole world is crushing her now, squeezing her so hard she cannot breathe.

Madelaine closes her eyes tight, fighting the agony building inside her like a pressure that must explode to relieve itself soon.

Mocha had come into the room and is standing there looking up at Madelaine with sad eyes. She whimpers, smelling her pain. She smells something else too.

Standing on her back legs, Mocha tries to stretch up, trying to put her front feet on the table. She can't reach. She sniffs and tries to lick at Zoe's hand. It is out of her reach too. Mocha looks at Madelaine, letting out another soft whimper.

Hornsby steps into the doorway and approaches.

Mocha drops down, giving him a low growl.

The old man reaches one withered hand towards Madelaine as if to lay it on her shoulder to comfort her.

Mocha stiffens, her growl intensifying.

It breaks Madelaine back to the horrible reality of being imprisoned in this place, her kidnapper only feet away. The same old man who brought Zoe here.

Madelaine turns and glares at Hornsby.

The anger and pain filling her eyes makes him drop his hand uselessly at his side.

"She's dead," Madelaine accuses him. "Zoe is dead and you killed her!"

"No." Hornsby shakes his head.

"Then who else? Who else killed her?"

"M-Madelaine?" The voice is weak, soft, and coming from behind her.

Madelaine turns in stunned surprise, staring at Zoe.

Zoe blinks at her, alive.

It takes a moment to sink in; then Madelaine pounces at her, crying over her.

"Zoe, you're alive! You're alive!"

"Little Sister is fine," Hornsby rasps.

Zoe rubs her tired eyes. They are red from tears and exhaustion.

Madelaine hugs Zoe as hard as she did Mocha. She is flooded with relief that Zoe is okay.

"You're squishing me," Zoe complains and Madelaine pulls herself away with a weak smile.

Madelaine starts checking Zoe over, fussing and making sure she has no injuries.

Zoe tries to fend her off.

"I'm fine Madelaine."

Madelaine blinks at Zoe. Her breath catches in her chest and fear fills her. She has to know, but she is terrified of what the truth may be.

"Zoe, is- do you know if Mom and Dad are alive?"

Zoe nods. "They were sleeping. I snuck out to find you."

Tears fill Madelaine's eyes. Tears of relief, pain, and heartbreak.

19   Madelaine and Zoe

Madelaine looks up at Hornsby, her eyes and expression desperately pleading.

"Please," she begs, "you have to let us go."

Zoe realizes Hornsby is there. Her eyes widen with fear and she instinctively pulls back, staring at him.

"Can not," Hornsby says.

"But, my sister," Madelaine says. "Our parents, they can't lose us both! Please Hornsby. We just want to go home."

The agony she knows her parents must be feeling right now fills her up. The pain is unbearable and she feels she will explode with it.

"Little Kitten stays," Hornsby says, pointing at Madelaine.

"Little Sister goes home," He says, pointing at Zoe.

A surge of fear rushes through Zoe and she grips Madelaine as tight as she can, holding on desperately.

"He can't!" she thinks. "I only just found her! I'm here to bring Madelaine back home! I can't lose her again!"

"No!" Zoe cries. "You can't keep my sister!"

She tightens her hold on Madelaine even harder.

Madelaine bites back the words that almost spill out of her mouth, words that would beg her captor to not take Zoe back, to keep her here where she knows she is safe and not left somewhere in the forest.

"Don't lie to yourself Madelaine," she thinks. "You really just don't want to be here alone."

She clings to Zoe as hard as Zoe is clinging to her, her head filling with the pain of loss. She feels it acutely, the loss of her chance of freedom and the loss of her sister again. She feels a little loss of herself for the selfish urge to keep Zoe here with her, imprisoned together so that she does not have to be alone.

"Hornsby needs Little Kitten. Little Sister Hornsby does not. Little Sister goes home to parents," Hornsby says, pointing at Zoe.

"You need her?" Zoe says shrilly. "I need her. We need her! What do you need her for?"

The girls look at each other, terrified.

"No!" they wail together, clinging to each other.

As desperately as Madelaine wants Zoe to go back and be safe with her parents, she just as desperately does not want to stay here alone, a prisoner of this crazy old man.

"I'm so sorry," Madelaine sobs into Zoe's hair. "I'm so sorry for all of this. It's my fault. I don't know why or how, but somehow it's all my fault."

"No," Zoe sobs into Madelaine's shoulder. "I'm sorry. I'm sorry for being such a pest and a little sister. If I didn't make you mad, if I didn't make us fight so much-."

"No," Madelaine says. She pulls away from Zoe so she can look her in the eyes.

All of the strange events of the past days catch up to Madelaine with a maddening dizzying rush and she suddenly feels faint and nauseous. The room and everyone in it are spinning wildly and she feels weak and an icy sweat break out.

Time is rushing backwards in her mind. Zoe waking up, seeing her and thinking she is dead, finding Mocha, the bright room with the windows. The awe of the discovery of the grand hallway rushes backwards, muted and dull. The surprisingly delicious meal. The fear of stepping out of the dark room into the cluttered one with the strange man waiting for her.

Waiting endlessly in the dark, alone and terrified and filled with the ravenous agony of insatiable thirst and the empty pain of hunger.

Crawling into her sleeping bag, desolate at the loss of Mocha, sick with worry and reaching under her pillow.

Finding the smooth stone under her pillow and rubbing it between her fingers, finding small comfort in its smoothness but enough to finally fall asleep. Wishing in those moments before sleep took her, oh so desperately wishing she were somewhere else. Wishing she were out somewhere in the woods, but not wandering the woods with the bears and wolves and other wild animals, but someplace they can't get to.

Wishing desperately to find Mocha there.

The impossibility of it all opens a crack in her mind, a crack of impossible possibilities. It opens her to a belief in imagination that she outgrew and forgot, thinking it stupid and childish.

The stone.

"This is my fault," Madelaine sobs. "It is all my fault. I found the stone. It was pretty and strange looking. I-I pretended it had to be a wishing stone, but I didn't really believe. I was playing, being stupid and childish. I kissed it and held it tight and made a wish. But I wished for real."

Zoe looks at Madelaine tearfully.

"You wished on a stone?"

Madelaine nods.

"W-was it round and black and smooth with red swirls?" Zoe chokes out.

Madelaine nods again.

"Wh-what did you wish for?" Zoe sobs.

"I wished to marry a prince," Madelaine wails. She feels utterly stupid and ridiculous saying it out loud. "And then I wished I was somewhere away from the campsite, not just in the forest, and that I would find Mocha."

Zoe cries harder. She starts to laugh through her tears. In all the fear and pain the whole thing strikes her as absurd.

Madelaine looks at her in confusion, about to ask what can possibly be funny.

Then it hits her too. She, the girl who has always ridiculed princess stories over the girls' helplessness and need to be saved by and marry a prince, wished for the very thing she made fun of. She never believed in make believe, never played it. She always thought herself too practical for that. Make believe was silly.

"I wished on a stone, a stupid little stone. And now I'm talking like it's real. I'm as crazy as old Hornsby."

Zoe, younger and more prone to believing in the impossible, in magic like the wishing stone she blamed herself for wishing Mocha away on, blinks back at her. Her breath catches as she speaks, dreading Madelaine's response.

"I-I found one too," Zoe chokes through her tears, looking at Madelaine with quiet desperation, needing her to understand.

"A stone? What was it like?"

"Small and round and smooth, a little flat. Dark with swirls."

"That's my stone!" Madelaine cries. "You took my stone."

"No, I found it by that big old tree with the branches that go everywhere."

"That's where I found it. But it was in my pocket."

Madelaine thinks.

"Zoe, we found the same stone, you and me, in the same place."

"Wishing stones," Zoe whispers.

"Wh-what did you wish for?" Madelaine sobs.

"I was just playing around. I didn't really believe." Zoe pauses.

"I can't tell Madelaine all of it," she thinks. She continues.

"I wished that you were a vampire," Zoe cries. "I-I was mad at you and I thought it would be cool to have a vampire sister."

Madelaine stares at Zoe in shock. She almost laughs even as she cries.

"Hornsby and his insane idea of making me a vampire," she thinks. "But there is no prince in my future."

Zoe stares back at her and realizes what they have done, even if Madelaine does not see it yet.

They both laugh and cry together at the same time at the absurdity of it.

"It's all nonsense, just make believe," Madelaine says. "Who would think something as silly as a wishing stone could be real?"

"Yeah," Zoe says through her tears. Her sobs sound more like hiccups now. "Vampires aren't real. I was only playing."

"But they are real," Madelaine says, pointing to Hornsby.

For a moment they both almost forgot he is there.

Zoe is confused.

"What are you talking about?" she asks.

"He said he's going to turn me into a vampire," Madelaine whispers, feeling that saying the words out loud might somehow offend the old man keeping her captive. She doesn't want to anger him. Not now when she needs to protect her sister.

Zoe turns to stare at Hornsby in shock.

Madelaine looks down at Zoe, seeing the horror in her younger sister's eyes when Zoe turns back to meet her eyes.

She nods and an understanding passes between them. Madelaine thinks Hornsby is going to kill her.

Zoe blinks back the tears, struggling to believe this is really happening.

Hornsby nods, finally responding to Madelaine's words.

"They are real. Your vamp pyre."

Zoe looks at Hornsby in shock again and back to Madelaine, who nods.

Resting her forehead against Zoe's, Madelaine whispers in her ear.

"I am pretty sure he is going to kill me."

Hornsby steps forward. He reaches and takes Madelaine by the arm, pulling her away gently but firmly.

Madelaine turns to him, startled.

She despises his touch on her arm and tries to pull free.

Zoe stares after her, her tears suddenly gone, blinking at the ugly realization of what her sister said.

"No!" Madelaine cries, fighting Hornsby harder, trying to pull away, to stay with Zoe.

Mocha jumps at Hornsby, growling and barking, threatening him with her sharp little teeth.

Zoe can only watch in stunned shock as Hornsby drags Madelaine out of the room, Mocha snarling and biting at his long robe.

She finally tears herself out of her paralysis after they vanish through the doorway, half falling as she rolls off the table; she flies across the room at the door.

Hornsby is closing the door as she starts to move, the open gap narrowing as her closes the distance. It thuds shut just as she reaches it, her hands already reaching to grasp it and tear it open.

She pulls at the door, but it doesn't budge. Zoe stares at it in disbelief.

"No. No no no. No!"

She throws herself at the door, attacking it and screaming.

"No! I want my sister! Madelaine!"

She lets out a blood curdling shriek. Even through the heavy door the scream echoes through the cavernous hallways and rooms of the ancient stone castle in the forest.

Mocha doesn't know what to do. She races back to stand staring helplessly at the door with Zoe screaming and banging against it on the other side.

She turns back the way Madelaine is being taken uncertainly, not knowing who or what to attack, who to fight, which girl to try to save. Smaller younger Zoe who smells stronger of fear; or her cherished Madelaine?

"What are you going to do with her?" Madelaine screams, fighting to break loose from Hornsby's surprisingly strong grip; a grip she never imagined this gnarled ancient man capable of.

"Back to Little Kitten's mother," Hornsby says gruffly, in as gentle a voice as he can.

Madelaine stares back towards the room with Zoe as he continues dragging her down the hall. She sobs desolately.

She is sure this is the last time she will ever see Zoe again.

Mocha whimpers, still torn between staying with Zoe and wanting to go back to Madelaine.

"I'm sorry Zoe!" Madelaine cries loudly, her words echoing through the halls, "I'm sorry and I forgive you! Remember, I'll always love you!"

Zoe calls back but it is muffled. Madelaine can't make out her words.

Madelaine turns on Hornsby, hitting him with her fists, tears streaming down her cheeks.

"You monster!" she cries. "You are a horrible monster! Don't you hurt Zoe!"

Hearing Madelaine's frantic cries, Mocha abandons trying to save Zoe. She turns and scampers back down the hall, rushing back to save Madelaine.

20   Madelaine and Mocha Reunited

Hornsby releases Madelaine when her grief takes over and she stops fighting. Madelaine falls limply to the floor, sobbing.

Mocha runs to her, wriggling into Madelaine's lap.

She wraps her arms around the little dog.

"Mocha," Madelaine sobs, "What will we do?"

Hornsby stands by, letting her cry it out.

When her sobs finally begin to turn to hiccupping breaths and then stop, Hornsby approaches her.

He pats her on the shoulder with one wrinkled hand.

"Little Dog can stay," he says in his rough voice. "Little Dog gives comfort to Little Kitten."

Madelaine hugs Mocha closer, filled with a sudden surge of nausea and fear. She forgot all about the possibility the old man might take Mocha away too. Now that she realizes it is very possible, the thought terrifies her. She would be here all alone.

"I don't want Mocha to be held a prisoner in this horrible place with me," Madelaine thinks, the idea sending a fresh wave of pain and desperation through her.

The words are on her lips. Please send Mocha back to Mom and Dad with Zoe. Please let Mocha and Zoe both go. Please don't keep either one here. I will do anything, anything you want. Please let both Mocha and Zoe go home.

Madelaine is being crushed under the weight of her sorrow and loss. As much as she desperately wants Zoe and Mocha to be free, the thought of being all alone here is unbearable.

"I can't do it," she thinks miserably. "I can't bring myself to beg Hornsby to send Mocha home with Zoe. I can't survive if I have to be here alone. I am so selfish. I am such a horrible selfish person."

Feeling like the most wretchedly horrible person in the world, Madelaine again almost begs Hornsby to send Mocha home with her sister. She can't bring herself to say the words. She squeezes Mocha tighter without realizing it.

Mocha squirms in Madelaine's grip.

Realizing she is squeezing the poor dog, Madelaine lets her go.

Mocha jumps up, trying to lick the tears on Madelaine's face away.

Madelaine pushes Mocha's face away, rubbing the tears off herself.

"Come. Hornsby shows Little Kitten room for sleep," Hornsby says. "Little Kitten is tired."

He motions at Madelaine to get up and follow him.

Madelaine obeys weakly. "What else can I do?" she thinks hopelessly.

Getting slowly to her feet, feeling the weight of the world and everything horrible in it dragging her down, Madelaine is half up when Mocha bolts and runs off.

The little dog dodges around Hornsby, her nails clicking on the floor as she scampers off.

"Mocha!" Madelaine cries, turning and unable to reach the little dog fast enough. She falls back to the floor lunging at the dog. "Mocha, come back!" She stares after her, wanting to chase her but not daring to with Hornsby between her and the dog.

Mocha's feet pitter-patter as she scampers off and disappears down the hall.

"Mocha, no!" Madelaine calls after her.

"Do not worry Little Kitten," Hornsby says. "No place for Little Dog to go."

"But she got in," Madelaine thinks. "Hornsby was as surprised to find Mocha inside as I was," she tries to convince herself. "I saw his surprise. I bet he doesn't know how she could have got in."

Hornsby motions again for her to follow and starts shuffling away.

Madelaine stands up and follows Hornsby. She keeps looking back down the hall and listening for the sound of Mocha's paws and nails on the stone floor.

She turns up the next hall behind Hornsby, pausing and looking back again with a worried frown. She stares down the hall anxiously, hoping so see Mocha. There is no sign of the dog.

"Mocha won't know where we went," she thinks.

Madelaine is worried about Mocha, but she has to follow Hornsby. She doesn't think he will wait or let her not go wherever it is he is taking her. The feeling of aloneness is suffocating her with the worry she won't see Mocha again and worse, what will happen when they get wherever they are going.

Madelaine studies Castle Blachedone as Hornsby leads her on down the hall and then down another. Like the other hallways, the ceilings in these halls are high. The few rooms she has been in have lower ceilings, much more like most buildings would have, but she doubts the vampires would have a reason to go in those rooms.

"Vampires," she almost laughs at herself out loud. "He can't really think they are real. But, I think maybe he does."

She decides the thought doesn't sound so dumb. She nods at herself and her own intuitive thinking.

"Good idea," she thinks. "Go along with his crazy vampire nonsense. Pretend you are buying into it. If he thinks you believe he might start to trust you, then you might get the chance to escape."

Madelaine speeds up her pace to catch up and walk beside Hornsby.

"Are the vampires very tall?" Madelaine asks, pointing up at the high ceilings.

"Tall," Hornsby says. "Not that tall."

His answer only confuses Madelaine. "Are they tall or not?" she thinks. She pictures impossibly tall skinny figures dressed in black capes towering over her.

"They are probably at least twice as tall as a grown man," she thinks.

"Are they mean?" Madelaine asks. "I mean, do they hurt people?"

Hornsby chuckles. "Depends Little Kitten," he says.

"Depends on what?"

"Are you food or friend?" Hornsby chuckles at his own joke. He knows the humans' belief that vampires prey on them in the night, feeding on their blood to drain them dry.

Madelaine does not think it is funny at all. She crinkles her forehead in disapproval and makes a face of displeasure.

They turn into one of the arches leading to another hallway. This hallway is as wide and tall as the other.

"This place is huge," Madelaine thinks. She tries to remember which way they came. "As soon as I am alone and have a chance, I am going to try to escape. I will search for a way out. I don't know how Mocha got in, but if the she got in, then there has to be a way out."

Madelaine's thoughts pause with a realization and a surge of panic rushes through her.

"Mocha is small. What if I'm too big to fit? No, don't give up. Think. There has to be a way. If Mocha fit to get in, then at least she can get out. I hope. At the very least, I can tie a note to Mocha's collar and send her back to Mom and Dad. But what if she doesn't know what to do? What if she just sits there waiting for me? What if she gets lost? What if she gets eaten by some animal?"

The idea of sending Mocha out alone into the forest terrifies her.

"It could be my only chance," she thinks miserably. "But Mocha ran off. What if she doesn't come back? I can't escape and leave Mocha behind. And if only Mocha can get out, well that won't work without Mocha."

The further they go, the more she worries Mocha won't find her in this huge place.

"Why did you have to run off Mocha?" Madelaine thinks.

Hornsby stops before a closed door. He opens it and shuffles into the room, stopping inside the doorway and behind a partially closed thick dark curtain that can be drawn closed to hide the door. Madelaine follows unhappily, going past him to stand in the curtain opening staring into the room.

Madelaine looks around. It is a bedroom, but it looks more like the stone walled chambers of movies from the days of knights and kings and queens riding around on horseback.

The ceilings are not as high as the hallway, but are still higher than normal. The floor and walls are continuous unbroken stone like the rest of the place.

"Bed chamber for Little Kitten." Hornsby's motion with his hand encompasses the room.

Madelaine looks at him in surprise, swallowing her uncertainty. She can't push away the misery and feels even worse now. A sick feeling of horror and loss washes through her, making her legs almost buckle under her. The room is the last nail in her coffin.

"You don't give a bedroom to someone you are going to let go." The thought fills her with a cold hollowness. The world seems to be expanding and rushing away, growing larger with that hollowness as she shrivels up to become smaller.

Madelaine studies the elegant room. She has never had so much space or such a beautiful bedroom in her life.

Sadness sinks in deeper again.

"I have to share my bedroom at home with my sister," she thinks. "I'm never going to see Zoe again if she gets to go home. It doesn't matter how large or beautiful the room is, it isn't home and I'm a prisoner."

She sighs unhappily.

"Now I know what the saying about being a bird trapped in a gilded cage means," Madelaine whispers, her voice rough with unshed tears.

She misses Zoe and her mom and dad already. The idea of spending the next years here alone trapped with only her kidnapper and maybe Mocha for company fills her with a mind-numbing sadness.

"That is, if he isn't going to kill me soon," she thinks.

"Enter," Hornsby says.

A dull sickness fills her stomach.

"It's a bedroom," Madelaine thinks. She can feel Hornsby's presence, the physical space he takes up, and it is a distressing oily sick feeling.

"Please don't follow me in," she thinks.

A surge of nausea washes through her with an icy cold sweat. Madelaine suddenly feels weak and dizzy.

She looks at Hornsby, her face sickly and pale.

He motions her to go on and enter the room.

Willing her legs to hold her, she takes that first step and then another, entering what she suspects is either her new prison or the room where very bad things are going to happen.

Madelaine walks slowly through the room, exploring but seeing it through the stifling dark misery filling her.

Hornsby watches her with his old rheumy eyes that seem to see everything.

A large bed occupies the whole room in her perception. Posts rise towards the ceiling from the bed corners and a canopy of luxurious fabric is draped over and across the posts, hanging down the corners to almost touch the floor. The bed has curtains that can be closed. Not like the ugly curtains hanging from the ceiling of a hospital bed, but rich curtains draping from the canopy over the bed. When she pulls her attention off the bed to look at the rest of the room, she notices a bulky dresser in the room, and a table with chairs. There are even two small couches with tables.

The light in the room is the soft yellow flickering glow of oil lamps and candles. There is no sign here either that electricity exists in this place.

Everything is large. Large and empty like the hollow loss filling her heart.

Madelaine looks at the empty table and chairs.

"Will I have to eat here, alone, or will I will be allowed out of this room?" she wonders. "Is this room my new prison? At least it isn't dark and tiny like the other room was."

There are two large bookcases with very old looking books. Madelaine wanders to them, tracing her finger along the spines of the books on one shelf.

She thinks about Hornsby's words.

"Little Kitten will be vamp ire." They echo hollowly in her mind like the faintest chill in her cavernous prison.

"I'll choke myself on one of these books if they are about vampires," she thinks. "I have no idea what I will be able to do for fun. If I can't at least read a good story I will go crazy in this place. Vampire stories are not good stories, especially not with a crazy person who plans to kill you because he thinks they're real." She almost laughs at herself. "Fun. You are a kidnapping victim, dummy. There is nothing fun in that."

Madelaine wanders aimlessly away from the bookcases.

"Even with the books I'm going to go crazy with boredom," she thinks. "Ugh, these books are so old. And even with these dumb old books, how many books is Hornsby willing to find for me to read?"

The thought of being trapped here for possibly the rest of her life with only these same old books to read over and over sends Madelaine falling to a new depth of despair.

The room also has a window. It is a small relief.

"At least I will have daylight and will be able to look outside," she mutters miserably.

In his motionless silence she almost forgot Hornsby is still there.

Madelaine catches herself before she says the next out loud. "Maybe I can even escape out the window," she thinks, glancing quickly at Hornsby. "I will have to see later, when I'm alone."

"Little Kitten sleep. Eat later," Hornsby says as he turns to leave.

Madelaine starts, looking at him in frightened shock.

"Wait, Hornsby," she says urgently.

He pauses, looking at her.

She hesitates uncertainly and has to force herself to say it.

"Where do I-, you know?"

There is an awkward silence. At least it is awkward for Madelaine. Her heart is racing in her chest.

"Don't make me say it," she thinks.

He shakes his head. "Where what?"

Madelaine swallows and her voice trembles.

"You know-," her voice lowers with embarrassment, "go to the bathroom."

Hornsby does not respond for so long she wonders if he understood. Finally he speaks as she is about to repeat it.

He points towards the bed and a red flush raises in Madelaine's cheeks. His words bring a slow relief.

"Chamber pot," he says, jabbing one long withered bony finger towards the bed. "Under."

"I thought he was telling me to pee in the bed," Madelaine thinks, feeling foolish. It quickly turns to confusion. "What is a chamber pot?"

She moves nervously to the bed, looks at it, and looks at Hornsby.

He motions again. "Chamber pot. Under."

Bending down, Madelaine pulls up the blanket to reveal what looks like a large ceramic bowl. Reaching under, she pulls it out. The bowl is delicate with intricate flowers tracing in a looping pattern around it, both in form and carefully painting. It has two handles.

She turns and stares at Hornsby.

"Am I supposed to-? Like the bucket?"

The thought horrifies her and a crimson blush rises up her neck and cheeks.

Hornsby nods. "Pee in the bucket."

"I can't pee in this," Madelaine complains. "I need a real bathroom."

"Chamber pot." Hornsby motions again.

While Madelaine is trying to digest this, he turns to leave again, leaving Madelaine alone in the room, closing the door behind him.

"Wait!" Madelaine calls in a panic at being left alone, putting the ceramic pot down and rushing to the door as Hornsby is swinging it shut.

She is too late. The door closes with an echoing thud as she reaches it.

Madelaine leans against the door and closes her eyes, trying to stop the tears threatening to come.

"I'm locked in," she whimpers.

She sinks to the floor and sits there on the cold hard stone floor, leaning against the door. She feels filled to the point of bursting with sadness and despair.

Mocha's feet pitter-patter as she scampers off down the hallway. She runs with an urgency only she knows the reason for.

When she raced out of the room, Madelaine called her back and Mocha knew she should obey. She almost did turn around and run back. The urge to obey was so strong.

But this is important. Mocha does not know why it is important; she just feels that it is.

She runs through the halls back the way she came, towards where she fell to the floor after crawling through the air shaft.

Mocha stops before she gets there. She sniffs and snuffles. She is looking for something. She smelled it before when she was looking for Madelaine, but didn't have time to investigate it then.

The little dog runs, sniffing and searching.

There! She finds the smell and loses it again. But it is close.

Mocha snuffles and sniffs around more, searching for the scent until she finds what she is looking for. It is a small dark object.

She picks it up in her mouth and races back through the maze of halls, following her own scent to where she left Madelaine.

Mocha gets there and stops, looking around eagerly, her tail wagging.

Her tail and ears droop. Madelaine is gone.

Mocha looks around and whimpers. She trembles with fear. She has to find Madelaine again.

She sniffs around and finds the smell trail and follows it. Mocha follows the scent down the hall and down another hall and another until she comes to a barrier.

The smell of the bad thing is everywhere, but Madelaine has only been in a few rooms. Mocha can sense Madelaine's presence on the other side. She can smell her fear and sorrow.

Mocha whimpers.

She scratches and digs at the barrier, trying to dig her way through.

Madelaine doesn't know how long she sat there against her new prison door.

Suddenly there is a scrabbling noise on the other side of the door.

She scurries away from the door, frightened, staring at the door and wondering what is on the other side.

"Hornsby would have opened the door," she whispers fearfully. "Does a place like this have rats? Maybe it's rats."

Then she thinks she hears a whimper with the scrabbling noise.

"What's that?" Madelaine whispers.

Mocha barks, digging and scratching at the heavy door.

Her ears perk up. She thinks she hears something on the other side of the door.

Madelaine hears a muffled bark from the other side of the door.

"Mocha!" she gasps. "Mocha came back! She found me! But it's locked."

Mocha scrabbles on the other side of the door again, barking again for the door to open.

"I have to try," Madelaine decides. "Please let him have forgotten to lock it."

She gets up and grasps the strange looking door handle. Jiggling and trying to pull it different ways, it takes Madelaine a few tries to figure out how to open it. Her mind is shut down with sorrow and fear and she can't seem to think.

Mocha barks again, louder.

Madelaine feels the latch release and stifles a cry. She pulls on the handle. The door is heavy and thick, but it opens.

"It's not locked," she says in surprise.

The barrier moves, swinging away from Mocha on its heavy hinges. She looks up at it and renews her digging at the door.

Mocha squeezes and squirms through the narrow opening, trying to get through it before it is wide enough to fit her, finding Madelaine on the other side.

Madelaine barely pulls the door open wide enough for Mocha to squirm through when the furry little body squeezes through and leaps at her. Mocha's tail is wagging furiously.

Mocha yips eagerly, running to her.

"Mocha!" Madelaine cries happily, scooping up the dog and hugging her.

Mocha squirms happily in Madelaine's arms, yipping happily.

The little dog drops something.

Madelaine almost misses it.

She puts Mocha down, looking at the object Mocha dropped.

Madelaine picks it up and stares at it, standing up in shock.

Caroline is sitting in the darkness of the campsite staring vacantly at the cold fire pit. The remnants of a long dead fire still sit dark and sooty. Dusk has passed and night settled in. The insects have gone quiet and even the nocturnal animals seem to be honoring her need to be alone.

A vehicle stops in front of the campsite and the door opens with a dull squeal, closing a moment later with the clunk of someone trying to close it quietly.

She doesn't bother to turn around.

Footsteps crunch in the gravel and come into the campsite as the vehicle drives away.

Caroline hears the scuff of the shoes come to a stop behind her.

"You're still up," Clive says. His voice is rough with stress and exhaustion.

"Have you eaten anything?" Caroline asks, knowing he probably did not.

"I wasn't hungry."

"You should eat something."

"How about you?" Clive asks.

He comes forward and stops right behind her. He reaches a hand out to touch her shoulder and stops before making contact.

Caroline feels his presence and stiffens.

"Don't touch me," she thinks, wishing she could ward off his touch.

Clive notices her stiffen. Feeling the rejection and knowing the small touch to try to console her is unwanted; he lets his hand fall to his side.

He needs it too, a small gesture of human contact to console him.

"I'm fine," Caroline lies. Her voice is distant, reflecting the void engulfing the space between them.

Defeated, Clive retreats to the tent. He feels hollow and lost inside as he changes for bed and slips into the cool sleeping bag.

"She blames me," he thinks. "For all of it; Madelaine, the girls getting lost. She hates me."

He closes his eyes, his rough breathing slowing as he tries to make himself fall asleep.

Outside the tent, Caroline cocoons herself in her dark misery. She sits in the chair staring at the dead fire in the cool night air.

She hears the crunch of footsteps on the road. Someone is walking past, away from the campsite.

21   The Wishing Stone

Mocha wags her tail and looks up at Madelaine. She watches Madelaine study the little object, turning it over in her hands.

It smells like Zoe, so Mocha is sure Madelaine would like to have it. She thought it would remind Madelaine of Zoe and make her feel better.

Madelaine turns the little object over and over, staring at it in disbelief.

It is a stone, small and round and a little bit flat. The stone is black with red veins swirled through it.

"The wishing stone," Madelaine gasps. "How? I left it in the tent. It should still be there."

Then she remembers Zoe. Zoe said she found one too.

"This must be Zoe's."

Madelaine turns it over, examining it again and marveling at how it seems to be an exact match for the one she found.

Her thoughts turn back to those awful fateful moments that led to her being here, held captive in this isolated stone prison.

At first, her mind goes to the reason for this trip. She doesn't want to think about that. The reason her parents decided they had to take her and Zoe and get away from everything and spend quality time together as a family. She almost snorts at the thought of quality time.

"As if any of it was 'quality' from the start. I guess quality doesn't necessarily mean good quality."

The distraction of focusing on the quality of the time doesn't work. Her mind stubbornly goes back to the cause of the trip. The reason they got her Mocha, a guilt present.

She pushes the memory away before it can take shape in her mind and fill her with fresh pain.

"No, I am not going to think about that."

Madelaine pushes her thoughts instead to their arrival at the campground and what happened then.

"That's the real reason I got kidnapped," she thinks.

Days earlier: on the day of their arrival

Madelaine stared out the car window at the endlessly passing trees and fields, trying to drown out Zoe's nonstop chatter. She held her book up as if reading, ducked low in her seat behind the book while staring moodily out the window.

For Madelaine the car ride was an endless torture and misery. She mostly spent it hiding behind her book watching nothing but trees and fields through the window to the steady drone of the tires on pavement. They had the radio for a while at least, but then they couldn't pick up any stations her parents liked so they turned it off.

Her butt and legs were sore and stiff from sitting for so long without moving.

"Stupid camping," she thought angrily. "Why did they have to make us all go? I didn't want to go. Now I'm going to be stuck in the middle of nowhere with no phone. Stupid forest. I hate camping. I'm probably going to get ticks and bug bites all over. I'm probably going to get Lyme disease, whatever that is. Why did they insist on this stupid trip? I want to be at home."

Madelaine turned her eyes back to the book, trying again to concentrate on the words printed on the page. The words danced and blurred in and out of focus, defying her. Next to her in the back seat Zoe was still prattling on about who knows what. Madelaine has been trying very hard to ignore her.

"Ugh, Zoe, stop talking," she thought, her irritation flaring.

"Madelaine, what do you think?" Zoe persisted, her voice starting to sound angry at her sister's continued ignoring her.

Madelaine shrugged. "Whatever."

"You weren't even listening," Zoe complained. "I asked you what you think about that song."

"It's fine," Madelaine said moodily, wrinkling her nose in irritation.

Zoe gave her a cold stare, knowing Madelaine had no idea what she was talking about. She shrugged it off and decided to sing the song anyway.

Madelaine tried again to read her book.

"I wish Zoe would stop trying to talk to me," she thought, sitting stiff and angry next to the irritant sitting beside her. The seat was too small. The car was too small. Zoe was much too close and it was grating on her nerves.

Zoe started singing and Madelaine stiffened, working to control her temper. She had the urge to lash out and hit Zoe to make her stop.

"That is even more annoying," Madelaine thought. "Does she have to sing? Why can't she just sit quietly? Better yet go to sleep."

With her hand tucked between her and the door where no one could see it, Madelaine dug her nails painfully into the side of her thigh. The sharp pain was not enough to pull her out of the urge to leap onto Zoe, force her hands over her mouth to gag her, and scream at her to shut up.

Madelaine sensed motion at her feet and it sent a new wave of annoyance through her. She felt the pressure of Mocha leaning on her feet and wanted to shove her off. Even the dog touching her was too much to bear in her heightened state of annoyance.

"Don't start again," she thought.

Mocha nudged her with her nose again. She has been restless for much of the trip. Squirming and nosing at her for constant pets and trying to climb into her lap. When she let her in her lap, Mocha was soon jumping back down to the floor.

Madelaine felt like she was going to explode with the stress and frustration of the drive.

Mocha's nudging became more persistent, her insistence more firm.

Sensing Madelaine's stress, Mocha nudged her again. She wanted to make her feel better. She started climbing into the seat between Madelaine and Zoe and Madelaine shoved her back down to the floor.

Determined to help her feel better, Mocha tried again. She nudged Madelaine's hand holding the book harder with her nose, trying to make room to climb in her lap. Usually Madelaine wanted her in her lap, especially when she was upset.

Mocha's persistence in pushing on her book and trying to crawl into her lap was the final push sending Madelaine over the edge of control. Anger flared in her and she shoved Mocha back down to the floor more roughly than she intended, yelling angrily at her.

"Get off me Mocha! Get away from me!"

Mocha cringed under the harsh tone, only hurt emotionally by the rough shove. With a sorrowful look up at Madelaine, she slumped on the floor and curled up with an unhappy sigh.

Zoe looked startled at Madelaine, glancing down at Mocha. "Poor Mocha," she mumbled.

Madelaine flashed her an irritated look.

"Madelaine!" Caroline snapped, her own irritation stretched thin with the long drive after the hours spent fighting with everyone to get them packed and the car loaded.

Clive gripped the steering wheel tighter, clenching his jaw and saying nothing. This trip was supposed to give them time together to reconnect as a family. So far he regretted even trying. Everyone was miserable and the trip already unpleasant.

Madelaine stared moodily out the window watching the trees and fields go by in an endless stream. The world was moving by much too slowly. She felt sorry for yelling at Mocha, but was too angry to try to make it up.

After Madelaine's angry outburst, Zoe gave up on trying to entertain anyone, including herself. She leaned toward her door, putting space between her and Madelaine, and stared out the window unhappily.

Clive and Caroline both sat staring ahead in irritated silence. The tension in the car was too thick to not feel it.

Mocha laid there on the floor for a long while, refusing to look at anyone, and finally went to sleep.

After hours of awkward driving, Clive spotted the sign he was waiting for and finally spoke. His voice was forced light-heartedness, trying to ease the tension.

"We are almost there. I can't wait to get out and stretch my legs."

Madelaine rolled her eyes in irritation.

After what felt like an eternity, proving her father's words false, the car slowed and turned up another road.

Clive drove more slowly up the winding road, trees pressing in on the road on both sides, and past a sign announcing the campground.

By the time they got to the campground it felt like they drove for days instead of hours. Even the drive through the campground was too long, compounded by Clive's need to drive around aimlessly lost until he found the ranger's office to check in.

Parking the car, he got out.

"Wait here. I'll just be a minute."

Zoe perked up a little, staring out impatiently and eager to finally escape the confines of the car.

Madelaine stared out moodily, wishing she was in her bedroom at home.

A boy around Madelaine's age whizzed by on a mountain bike, observing the car with the unhappy faces staring out, and continued on his way unnoticed.

It took more than a minute. Finally Clive stepped out of the ranger's office and returned to the car, an unfolded park map held loosely in his hand flapping in the breeze.

He let Caroline take it when he got in the car.

"It won't be long now. We just have a short way to go to find our campsite."

The drive to find the campsite took too long for both Zoe and Madelaine. Clive finally found the site and parked the car.

"Here we are." He got out, stretching hard, his muscles stiff from the long drive.

Zoe jumped out, practically dancing in her eagerness to escape the cramped car and move around.

Caroline climbed out wearily, studying the campsite and deciding how best to use the space.

After sitting moodily for a while, Madelaine finally opened her door and got out.

Realizing Madelaine finally moved; Mocha raised her head. Her ears perked at the sight of the open door, her nose twitching at the bouquet of unfamiliar scents. She instantly forgot her unhappiness at being yelled at.

Mocha leapt from the car, perky and alert now. She raced circles around everyone and the car the moment her feet touched the ground, tail wagging so hard her butt wiggled, letting out a few excited barks.

Madelaine walked around unhappily, feeling stiff and sore and very tired from the long drive.

Mocha raced around her and Madelaine had the urge to yell at her to stop. She stopped herself.

"Mom and Dad will only get mad at me," she thought moodily. She glared at their backs, her anger at them flaring hotter. "They could have at least let me bring my phone to listen to music and play games on, but no. They said no electronics allowed."

Bored, Zoe looked at her parents bustling around, Mocha getting under everyone's feet, and Madelaine who kept ignoring her.

"Madelaine, come check this out," Zoe interrupted her thoughts.

Madelaine tried to ignore her. She turned away from Zoe as if she didn't hear her.

Caroline and Clive were arguing while they unpacked the car.

"Madelaine, Zoe, come help!" Clive snapped at the girls.

Mocha was still racing around, dodging everyone's feet.

"Madelaine," Zoe complained, "stop ignoring me. What dad?" She turned on Clive with an annoyed face and turned away, ignoring his demand for help to avoid doing any work.

"Madelaine, come on, play with me."

Madelaine reached down and found a stick quickly; waggling it for Mocha to see and throwing it, hoping it would make Zoe leave her alone.

"I'm busy playing with Mocha." Her tone was irritated and dismissive.

Mocha raced off after the stick, dodging around Clive and Caroline and almost tripping them.

Madelaine's head pulsed with the sharp pain of her growing headache. The headache that started coming on in the car only continued to get worse with each annoyance.

"Mocha, get! Madelaine do something with your dog," Clive complained, almost tripping over Mocha again as she raced around, dodging his feet while he carried the large tent bag.

"Madelaine tie this dog up! She's tripping everyone," Caroline said sternly, dodging the dog while carrying sleeping bags.

"She's not going to run off," Madelaine sniffled defensively.

"I don't care," Clive said, "tie her up."

"It's the forest, she might get lost," Caroline warned her.

Mocha raced past Madelaine, annoying her further. But she still didn't want to tie her up.

The busy activity continued with Zoe watching unhappily, Mocha racing around everyone, and Clive and Caroline angrily setting up the campsite. Madelaine moodily wandered around the site, wishing she was at home.

"Madelaine only cares about her dog," Zoe thought. "She doesn't even like me at all. And Mom and Dad are too busy and cranky."

Hurt and angry, she walked off with tears burning her eyes and sat alone. After a while she got up and wandered to the edge of the campsite. She stood there aimlessly for a while, looking back at her family and then up and down the road.

With a shrug, she wandered out and up the road.

"I'm not going to go far," Zoe thought, "just up a campsite or two and back."

She did that, glancing back into their site. Nothing changed. Everyone was still busy and arguing.

Zoe went past the campsite, going a couple sites the other way. Turning around again, Zoe returned, looked in again, and kept going up the road past it.

Kicking at the dirt and stones in the road, Zoe wasn't paying attention to where she was going.

A chipmunk poked its head out of the bush at her, darted into the middle of the road, and sat on its haunches grooming its head and staring at her.

Deciding this person had no food to give it; the chipmunk abandoned its grooming and darted across to vanish in the bushes on the other side of the road.

Zoe watched the spectacle curiously. She considered trying to lure the animal out, but had nothing to use. She walked on.

A white butterfly with black veins and tips of the front wings fluttered into view, dancing around her weightlessly in the air, and fluttered on up the road. With a smile, Zoe followed the butterfly. She had nothing else to do.

"Where will you take me?" she asked.

As if in answer, the butterfly danced around her head and fluttered on ahead again.

Zoe's grin widened and she followed.

The campsite was half set up when Caroline paused, looking around.

"Where is Zoe?"

Clive stopped and looked up with a questioning expression.

Caroline was still looking around. "Zoe? Zoe!" she called, then listened. There was no answer.

Clive looked around for the missing girl then turned to Madelaine.

"Where is your sister?"

Madelaine shrugged. "I guess she left the campsite."

Caroline looked alarmed.

"We only just got here. We haven't discussed limits with the girls, how far they are allowed to roam. Zoe doesn't know the area."

"I'm sure she didn't go far," Clive said, walking out the driveway to look up and down the road. There was no sign of her.

"She could get lost," Caroline insisted.

Clive's shoulders slumped. "I'll go look for her. This better not take long. I want to get this campsite set up so we can relax."

He left and Caroline returned to sorting through their stuff, deciding where to put it.

"I saw a park on the way in," Madelaine said. "I could go check it."

Caroline looked at her in alarm. She wanted to say no. Her first impulse was to keep Madelaine close. But worry over her younger daughter being lost in a strange campground also weighed on her. She frowned.

Despite her misgivings, she decided.

"It's not far, is it?"

"It's pretty close. Dad went the other way."

"Stay on the road and make sure you keep track of which way you went. I don't want you going too far or getting lost."

"Yes," Madelaine thought with a rush of defiant victory. "I can get out of this campsite and away from them all. I'll pretend I'm looking for Zoe and come back after all the work is done. I don't want to be here at this stupid campground. I mean I will look for her, but I'm not going to kill myself doing it. Who knows, I might even find her."

"I know that look," she thought, looking back at her mom. "Mom will change her mind in about a minute."

Relieved to have something to do other than standing around looking at the leaves, Madelaine quickly left the site before her mother could change her mind.

Mocha happily trailed after Madelaine as she hurried out of the site and up the road.

Madelaine was right. Shortly after she left, Caroline's misgivings got the better of her. She went to the entrance and looked up the road for Madelaine to call her back.

She was nowhere to be seen.

With a flutter of anxiety over both her daughters now gone who knows where in a strange campground, she returned unhappily to sorting out their belongings.

"It's amazing how much stuff one small family can pack and fit in a car for one short trip."

Clive was walking angrily down the road, looking into campsites and up roads and paths as he crossed them. The longer his search took, the angrier he was getting.

"I wanted to get the campsite set up," he complained.

The fluttering butterfly led Zoe down a little path that opened up to a green space. The bushes filling in around it were lush and the grass long with spindly shoots with seeds waving in the breeze with the rest of the grass. Wildflowers dotted the grass, dancing with it in the breeze as if bobbing on a green sea of grass.

Zoe followed the dancing butterfly to a tree in the clearing. The tree was large with a trunk fat enough to be a group of trees and branches that spread out as if trying to fill the little clearing.

The butterfly bobbed and danced in the air, finally landing on the tree.

Zoe stopped under the tree and looked up at the butterfly just out of her reach.

"I wish you would come down."

After a moment the butterfly danced into the air again, fluttering around Zoe. She turned with it, watching it. The butterfly fluttered and landed in the grass near the base of the tree. The grass was much shorter here, the shade slowing down its growth.

She sat in the grass, watching the butterfly.

The insect moved and something in the grass where it was caught her attention.

"What is that you are showing me?"

She leaned forward, reaching, and picked it up. Zoe turned it over in her hand, inspecting it.

It was a stone; small and round and smooth, and a little flat. The stone was dark with interesting red swirls running through it.

"I've never seen a stone line this before. I wonder what kind it is."

She studied it harder.

"It's pretty."

The little butterfly darted around her face, forcing her to wave it off, and making her drop the stone.

"Oh no, the stone."

Zoe searched around, looking for the stone. She gave the butterfly a stern look and resumed her search. After a few minutes she found it. Picking it up, she inspected it again.

Holding it carefully in her palm, she rubbed it with her finger.

"It's even smoother than it looks. This must be a very special stone."

Zoe's imagination took off, playing through the possibilities.

"Why is this stone so special?"

Sadness crept in. She still felt hurt by her family's behavior. Her anger at them burned hotter with the memory.

"A stone I could make wishes on would be pretty special. I could wish everyone would be nicer to me. That they liked me."

She frowned at the stone, wrapping her fingers around its silky smoothness. It felt warm in her hand.

"The sun must have warmed it," she decided.

"Maybe it is a wishing stone. If I had a wishing stone, I would wish-."

The butterfly bounced off her face, making Zoe swat it away again. It would not stop and it was making her annoyed.

"Stop it!" She waved it off again.

Zoe thought about her parents, who seemed to be angry all the time. They were even angrier after the drive. She thought about Madelaine. Madelaine, who used to be nice to her sometimes, but never seemed to be anymore.

"She's always annoyed with me now. Madelaine wants nothing to do with me; nothing to do with anything but her dog. She hates me now that she has that stupid dog."

Zoe closed her eyes and gripped the stone tight in her fist.

"I wish Mocha would go away," she wished angrily as hard as she could. "I wish Madelaine never got a puppy. I don't know why she gets a dog all for herself. Mom and Dad said it was because of something that happened, but nobody would say what. They were all quiet and cryptic when I asked. When I asked Madelaine, she only shrugged and walked away. They treat me like I'm a baby.

Whatever the big secret is, it's not fair that she got her own dog and I didn't. Madelaine sometimes rubs it in, making it worse. If Madelaine never got Mocha, then she would have nobody to play with on this camping trip but me.

Without Mocha, maybe Madelaine would talk to me again. She never wants anything to do with me anymore."

Tears rolled down her cheeks.

"Go away Mocha. Go away Mocha. Go away Mocha." Zoe whispered it over and over, squeezing her eyes closed and the stone tight, and wished hard.

Not having Mocha didn't feel like enough punishment for Madelaine. She needed something stronger. Something unbelievable. Something ridiculous.

Another thought came to her.

"I-I wish," she choked the words out. Zoe stopped and swallowed. A fierce feeling of revenge pushed her tears away. She smiled. It was not a happy smile. The smile was filled with pain and sadness and a little cold vengeance.

"I wish Madelaine was a vampire."

A small flush of satisfaction made Zoe feel a little bit better. Pretending often made her feel better; even though Zoe knew it was not real and could never come true.

"It would be kind of cool to have a vampire for a sister," she decided with a pained smirk.

Zoe looked around. The butterfly had abandoned her and she was all alone in the little clearing. The wind picked up a little and sent a chill through her that was too cold for the air.

Not feeling any better, she got up and looked at the stone again before shoving it in her pocket.

She left the clearing, following what she thought was the same path out.

Madelaine was walking down the road. Mocha followed at her heels sniffing enthusiastically at everything. Every now and then the dog raced off up ahead only to turn and come charging back to run around Madelaine as if trying to urge her to hurry up.

"That Zoe is always such a pain," Madelaine complained. "Always bugging, always having to have everyone's attention. Just because she wasn't getting it she takes off and makes us have to go looking for her."

The feeling she was being watched came over Madelaine. She had the urge to look behind her. She made a conscious effort not to look.

"I bet Mom is following me. She never gives me any space. It's driving me crazy."

The thought threatened the small feeling of freedom leaving the campsite alone gave her. She sped up, hoping to put more distance between herself and the campsite.

"If Mom does come looking for me I don't want her to find me. Not yet. She'll drag me back and make me sit there where she can keep an eye on me."

The idea irritated her.

"Watching me like a baby. No. Like some damaged kid she has to watch all the time. Like I'm going to do something dumb and hurt myself."

She huffed at the thought.

"I'm not going to do anything. I want to be left alone. Nobody ever leaves me alone."

A dark feeling started creeping up on Madelaine and she pushed it away, refusing to accept the thought, the ugly memory.

She sped up her pace again, slowing only when she was sure she went far enough that her mother wasn't likely to find her.

"At least Zoe taking off gave me a chance to be alone. I'm amazed Mom even let me go."

A little guilt tickled at her.

"Mom was pretty worried about Zoe," she admitted.

Madelaine renewed her resolve to find Zoe, letting go the urge to find a quiet place to hang out and not look for her.

"Zoe!" Madelaine called, cupping her hands to her mouth to make the sound carry. "ZOOEEEYYYY!"

"Why does she always do these things?"

She hiked through overgrown paths and walked around bays, ducking into some campsites to check hidden corners, every now and then calling Zoe.

After a while, Madelaine's irritation got the better of her and she abandoned the search.

"Ugh, I'm never going to find her. Where is she? Zoe obviously doesn't want to be found. She's probably found a park or something and is playing there."

Guilt tickled at her again.

"I did see a park on the drive in. I didn't lie about that. Zoe probably saw it too. I should be looking there. But, after the long car ride I really just want to be alone for a little while."

Madelaine was about to go find the park when she spotted a white and black Pine White butterfly sitting on the leafy branch of one of the bushes on the side of the road. The bushes were thick, making a seemingly impenetrable wall that the road cut through.

Madelaine paused to watch it.

"Butterfly. That's right up her alley. Zoe is always getting butterflied. She probably would have followed it if she saw one."

The butterfly danced off the branch, bobbed weightlessly in the air, and meandered along the road.

Madelaine wrinkled her nose at it and shrugged. She followed the butterfly.

"She could have followed it. If she did, maybe I'll find her. If I find Zoe, Mom and Dad might not be so mad at me all the time. Maybe they'll finally give me a little slack. Maybe Mom will give me a little space, a little trust."

The butterfly bounced along, changing course towards the entrance to a path.

Just as Madelaine entered the path behind it, the insect bounced up and over the bushes and out of sight where she could not follow.

Already on the path, Madelaine kept going. Mocha raced off ahead.

"It's as good a route as any to find one little sister who could be anywhere."

The path led to a small clearing with a large sprawling tree and no Zoe. The long grass swayed in the wind like a sea of green with scattered wildflowers floating in its midst.

"That looks like a tree Zoe definitely would climb."

Madelaine approached the tree and looked up into its canopy of branches. The trunk was as large as many trees growing together.

Mocha was snuffling and sniffing everywhere, her tail a flag sticking up from the long grass whenever she bounced. She came to sniff around the tree and stopped to look up too. She barked.

The little dog moved around the tree, sniffing and snuffling hard at its base with a determination Madelaine never saw in her before.

"Was she here? Was Zoe here? Is that what you smell?"

Her ever-present unhappiness started to fill Madelaine up again. She sat down and leaned against the tree. She looked around the clearing.

"It's so peaceful here. I could stay here. Everyone would probably be better off without me around anyway."

Tears burned at her eyes. It has been a long drive and an exhausting stressful day. It was starting to catch up with her.

Madelaine put her hands down absently on the ground to brace herself while she leaned forward to look around the tree for Mocha.

She felt something hard and smooth in the grass under her hand. Madelaine pulled her hand back impulsively in case it was something she didn't want to touch.

She leaned forward, looking in the grass for whatever it was, and spotted the stone. She picked it up and turned it over in her hand, examining it.

The stone was round and smooth. She rubbed her finger along its smooth surface to see if it felt as smooth as it looked. It was smoother than it appeared and had almost a luxurious warmth to it, a trick of its smooth surface. She studied it again, tracing the red swirls through the black stone as best she could.

"This is the strangest looking stone I have ever seen. I wonder if someone left it here. It's so smooth, like someone polished it."

Madelaine looked around.

"If anyone lost it, they are probably long gone. It's just a stone anyway."

She studied the stone again.

"I wonder what kind of stone it is."

"I know, it's a wishing stone," she decided with a playful smirk. "What should I wish for?"

Madelaine thought hard. She thought about the miserable drive, her parents fighting, and her irritating sister Zoe. She looked at Mocha, who was still sniffing hard around the base of the tree.

With a sick feeling in her stomach, Madelaine started thinking about other, darker, thoughts.

"No," she pushed those thoughts away.

"What will make my life better?" She smiled, nostalgically thinking about the princess movies she secretly loved when she was little, although she always insisted she hated them. Even when the princesses' lives were at their worst, even when they were not really a princess at all, their prince found them. Wherever they were, he rescued them and took them away. She always wished they would be stronger, self-sufficient and able to save themselves instead of wailing and pining for their prince to save them. But they always married and lived happily ever after despite their weakness and helplessness.

She frowned. "Where is my happily ever after?"

Feeling a little silly with her childish game, she glanced around to make sure there was still no one around to see. Madelaine kissed the stone and held it tight in her hands.

"I wish I would marry a prince. For real. A real prince."

Madelaine thought again about her wish.

"Only I don't want to be one of those princesses who are completely helpless. Why are they always so hopeless anyway? Why can't the princess be strong and brave? Why can't she be independent? Why can't the prince just find her and love her for her strength without having to rescue her?"

She gripped the stone tighter.

"I wish I could marry a prince and be the kind of princess who has to save herself; me and Mocha and the prince together."

Madelaine giggled. "I'm so dumb."

She got up, shoved the stone in her pocket, and looked around for Mocha. Not seeing the little dog, she felt a surge of panic.

"Mocha? Mocha."

Mocha came snuffling around the tree and looked up at her, wagging her tail.

Relief washed through Madelaine.

"For a minute there I thought I lost you. Come on Mocha, we are supposed to be looking for Zoe."

She left the little clearing, Mocha trailing behind.

Now:

Madelaine comes back to the present, the memory leaving her with a chill that gives her the urge to shiver.

"We found Zoe. She never said anything about finding a stone. Then Dad decided we had to go for that stupid hike because of Zoe taking off. That's when we lost you, Mocha."

She looks down at Mocha.

"I wished on a stupid prince. I guess it's going to be just me and you, Mocha; and Hornsby. He's not a prince, is he? He's just some crazy old man who kidnapped me."

"Zoe," Madelaine whispers. "She must have had the stone when she came looking for me. She must have dropped it when

Hornsby brought her into Castle Blachedone. This must be the stone Zoe found."

She stares at the stone in awe.

"It looks exactly the same. Is it mine? Or are there two stones exactly the same?"

Madelaine drops down and grabs Mocha in her arms, hugging the little dog and burying her face in her fur.

"Oh Mocha," she sobs into the dog's fur, "thank you Mocha, thank you. At least I have something to remember Zoe by."

Madelaine sits back and looks at the stone again.

"Thinking it's a wishing stone is dumb. Thinking it somehow has any kind of magic powers is dumb. But how do you explain what happened? Zoe and I both wished things that came true."

She looks at Mocha.

"Zoe wished you gone and I lost you. She wished I would be a vampire and-."

She swallows.

"I wished I would marry a prince and I was kidnapped by some crazy guy who thinks vampires are real and that he is going to turn me into one."

She looks at Mocha.

"I wished I was a princess who had to save herself. That it would be just you, Mocha, and me, and the prince. Mocha, I wished myself into this mess. Zoe and I did."

Madelaine chuckles. It is not a humorous sound, but one of fear and desperation. She is desperate to believe there can be help. She can't help but feel some hope that the wishes coming true means something, even as she knows deep inside that it is impossible.

"Do you know what this means Mocha?" she says uncertainly. "Can I wish us free? If it's real, can I wish our escape? I know it sounds dumb, but I don't think I can afford to ignore any possibility to get out of here."

Madelaine thinks for a moment.

"Oh, but we will have to be very careful," she says. "I have a feeling this wishing stone is very tricky. After all, I wished to marry a prince and ended up kidnapped by some weird old man, am being held prisoner, and I'm pretty sure he is going to kill me because he thinks he can turn me into a vampire."

"Oh," Madelaine realizes. "Zoe wished me to become a vampire. Silly little Zoe."

She ruffles Mocha's fur, looking down at her sadly, her belief and her hope slipping. She continues with the wistful game.

"I wonder if it might take two wishes together to get us out. Is that how it works? Two stones the same and two wishes to make them work? But how will we ever find out? How will Zoe know to look for the other wishing stone and make a wish? How will we get her to make the right wish at the right time?"

She looks down sadly.

"How do I know Hornsby will really take her back to Mom and Dad?"

Mocha wags her tail, staring up at Madelaine as if she can understand her.

"Oh Mocha," Madelaine sighs, "I really do wish you understood what I am saying."

Mocha perks her ears and licks her hand.

"Only I can help us. I have to save us Mocha. No one knows this place exists and I don't know if Hornsby told the truth about taking Zoe back to Mom and Dad. If he takes her back she can tell and that's a risk he probably won't take."

She sniffles, wiping away a tear.

"Zoe could still be a prisoner here. We will have to search for her before we get out in case she's still here."

She pushes away the other, darker, thought. The thought that Hornsby may kill Zoe because he does not need or want her.

Madelaine thinks hard about what she can do.

"Mocha, if I can tie a note to your collar and get you to go find Mom and Dad at the campsite, then they can read the note and know to come looking for this place. Maybe I can include a special message to Zoe about the wishing stone too, just in case she's there, something to give her hope. But how do I get you out?"

She remembers the window.

"What if we both can escape together out the window?"

Madelaine gets to her feet and rushes across the room to the window. She leans over and looks. It is an impossible sheer drop. She can't see a bottom. The forest spreads out forever below in a sea of green. From this vantage point Castle Blachedone seems to be built behind the rock face of a sheer cliff.

All of Madelaine's hopes are crushed as her world comes crashing down on her with a sinking swimming feeling. She feels like she is going to drown in it.

"No." She tries to cling to that one shred of hope. "It can't be that bad. There has to be a way. Some slope to the cliff, hand holds, foot holds, something."

She leans as far out as she dares, looking straight down.

What little hope she had flies out that horrid open window into the vast forest stretching out below her.

"This is no good. The fall will kill us. There is no way I can climb down that alone. And I can't leave you here Mocha."

Madelaine sinks down to the floor and sits there desolate, leaning against the wall and letting the tears come.

"They will never find me." The thought almost shatters her.

Mocha whimpers and scoots next to her, looking up at her with sad eyes and licking her hand, trying to console her.

Madelaine lifts her hand, opening her palm, and looks at the stone.

Her mind takes a dive into the impossible. It is all she has.

"We still have this."

She looks down at Mocha.

"It's our only hope now. But what do we do with it? How do we make the right wish? It tricked us once and now I'm here."

She thinks hard.

"We need to make a list of wishes and figure out the best, and the best way to word it."

Madelaine gets up and goes to the door. She had left it slightly open. She pulls the heavy door open more, wide enough for her to squeeze out.

"Come on Mocha; let's find that other room with the window. I saw paper and stuff to write with there. And maybe we can find how you got in, or maybe get you out one of those windows. That is, if I can't get out that window myself too."

Madelaine races out of the room and down the hall with Mocha scampering beside her. She pauses uncertainly when she comes to another hall, not sure which way to go. She tries her best to remember how she got to her new prison, makes a decision, and turns left, breaking into a run again.

"We will have to think very carefully on what wishes to make," Madelaine says breathlessly as she runs. "We don't want these tricky wishing stones getting us into worse trouble."

They find the room with the windows and shelves of books with little trouble. It is more by accident than by Madelaine's sense of direction and memory of the route.

Madelaine rushes through the first room, almost running to the window to see if she can escape that way. She stops in the doorway between the two rooms, her heart sinking. It is no good.

She remembers it is like the bed chamber, the window opens to nothing but open sky. She races to the window and quickly leans out over the windowsill to look down, confirming her memory.

She is seized immediately with vertigo, feeling like the whole world has fallen away and that she too is falling. Madelaine grips the windowsill hard and pulls herself back, leaning over more carefully this time as she looks again.

Looking down makes her dizzy. The ground is impossibly far away and the window cut out from the side of a cliff with sheer flat rock wall above and below. She looks to the left and right and sees nothing but more flat cliff wall. Below is a sea of green forest spreading out as far as she can see.

For a moment she imagines Castle Blachedone is really one big round mountain of sheer cliffs, like a fat wheel lying flat on the ground, with no exits. Common sense tells her the two rooms must have the windows cut out of the same mountain cliff wall.

"Those are the only two rooms I saw that have windows."

She turns away from the window with an unhappy groan.

"Now what Mocha?" Then she remembers her note idea and her earlier thoughts.

She looks down at the little dog.

Mocha looks back up at her, wagging her tail slowly.

"If you got in Mocha, then there has to be a way for you to get back out. How did you get in? Never mind. We will figure that out. First, we need paper and a pen and some string or something."

Madelaine turns her attention to searching the desk and tables.

She finds paper and some sort of feathered pen. The paper is unusual, off-white and thicker than normal paper, without the perfect shape and smoothness of factory-made paper. It is smaller than a normal page too, more like the size of a paperback book. There are also papers rolled up and tied with coarse string.

Madelaine searches, unable to find the string, and finally takes some off the tied scrolls.

She thinks long and hard before starting her note. She has to get this right.

She looks at the pen, turning it over and scribbling on a piece of paper. It leaves no marks behind.

"How do you make this thing write?"

She tries shaking it and scribbling again. Still no mark is left on the paper.

Madelaine frowns at the pen. Then she notices what looks like a jar of ink or paint and remembers seeing something like this in cartoons.

Carefully prying the lid off, Madelaine manages to open it without spilling it. She dips the pointed tip of the quill pen in the ink and tries to write, but the ink globs all over the paper. She tries again and the pen just scratches, mostly dry, on the paper, leaving a faint trail of splotchy marks.

Madelaine grits her teeth in frustration.

"How do you make this work? This is no good!" She moans. "If I can't write a note, how can Mom and Dad and Zoe read it?"

She tries repeatedly and each time is the same.

"How do they do this?" Madelaine whines. Frustrated tears burn at her eyes.

Then she has a thought. Madelaine remembers when she and Zoe learned about pencil rubbings. For months they pretended to be spies passing secret messages back and forth.

"Maybe Zoe will remember," Madelaine says.

Madelaine piles paper together to make a pad. Careful not to cut through the paper, she uses the sharp feather pen tip to scratch out her message. She studies her work carefully, seeing the indented lines of her message in the paper.

"Now, if Zoe remembers, she might think to rub the side of a crayon or pencil tip across this to reveal the message."

Madelaine is proud of her cleverness.

She carefully folds and ties the note to Mocha's collar. Standing up, she looks down at the little dog.

"We have to find out how you got in. But how?"

Madelaine puffs out a big sigh.

"If only you could talk. If only you could understand me. If you could show me how you got in, then maybe we can get you out so you can take the note to Mom and Dad and Zoe."

Mocha stares up at Madelaine. She tilts her head as though listening intently, her tail still wagging slowly.

Madelaine sighs again, looking down at the floor sadly. This time it is the slow soft sigh of someone who is giving up.

"I feel like I should give up. It's hopeless. This place is too big and I will never find how Mocha got in."

Mocha whimpers at Madelaine, sensing her unhappiness. She steps forward and nudges her leg with her nose.

Madelaine looks down at the dog.

"Outside Mocha. We need to find outside."

A thought occurs to her and she almost smiles.

"Mocha, do you have to pee?"

The dog dances her front feet and ducks her head at her the way she does when she needs out.

"Mocha outside," Madelaine commands. "Outside Mocha. Go pee."

Mocha races for the door, stops, and looks back at Madelaine. She yips one high bark.

"That's right girl. Go pee. Outside."

Mocha dances her front feet where she stands. She yips again, turns to the door, and takes two more steps, and then stops to look back at Madelaine again.

"You want me to show you, don't you?" Madelaine says unhappily. "It's not going to work. Mocha wants me to show her the door when I need her to show me the way out."

Not feeling like moving at all, Madelaine gets up slowly. She follows the little dog.

Mocha rushes out ahead of her and down the hallway.

"Where are you going, Mocha? Please let this work."

Madelaine follows her up another hallway that Madelaine had not been up before. The dog races back when she loses her and scampers ahead again. Madelaine breaks into a run to keep up.

At last, Mocha stops and stares up at a statue near the wall.

"What?" Madelaine asks.

Mocha yips, runs in a small circle, dancing on her front feet, and looks up again.

Madelaine looks up where the dog is staring. She doesn't see it right way, but when she is about to give up she sees it; a hole in the ceiling.

She looks down and sees for the first time the mud on the floor, left from Mocha's entrance.

"Is this how you got in?" Madelaine gasps.

Mocha runs to her with her tail wagging hard. She turns back, standing in the midst of the dirt, staring up at the hole in the ceiling. She lets out a bark.

Madelaine stares up at the hole. Her face falls into devastation, her eyes reddening and becoming watery, and tears threaten to flow.

She stands there, staring at the hole.

"I would have to stand on a giant's shoulders to reach that or find a very tall ladder. The hole is too high up for me to reach," she chokes out.

"Mocha!" Madelaine wails. "Neither of us can get out. I can't even use you to get a note to anyone."

She thinks of poor Mocha falling that distance.

"Oh, poor Mocha," she sobs, hugging the little dog. "I can't believe you fell that far without getting hurt."

Mocha's ears and tail droop. Madelaine is so sad. Mocha does not know what to do.

Madelaine opens her palm where she still holds the wishing stone and looks at it.

"I guess it's just you and me and the wishing stone, Mocha," Madelaine says, sniffling through her tears. "I will have to think extra long and hard on how to wish us out of here, if it even works. Zoe and I both made wishes that got me here. What if it takes both wishing stones? How will Zoe know to make a wish too? How will she know what to wish?"

Madelaine hugs Mocha tighter.

"Yes Mocha, I know the idea that magic stones will somehow free me is stupid, and it's time to stop playing childish games, but it's the only tiny hope I have left to cling to now."

She sobs.

"It looks like we might be here for a very long time Mocha," she says sadly.

The earthy stink of something that should have rotten way never to return permeates the air. Mocha stiffens and a low growl rumbles in her throat.

Madelaine turns and looks up dully at a sound behind her.

Hornsby is standing there and he looks angry.

22   Return to Darkness

"Girl, come," Hornsby rasps, motioning Madelaine to follow. His gruff voice sends a chill through her.

She gets up obediently.
"Are you taking me back to the bedroom?"
"No."
 "He is angry," she thinks. "He calls me Little Kitten when he is in a better mood. He's nicer to me then too."
She follows him through the maze of halls with no idea where they are or where they are going.
Mocha follows at a distance, head low and hackles raised, looking at Hornsby with distrust.
Madelaine recognizes the room the moment they step through the doorway of the small cluttered room. She stops in the doorway, feeling sick. Her eyes lock on the open door of the small dark room she first woke up in.
Her eyes burn with tears.
"No," she moans miserably, her voice cracking.
Hornsby stops in front of that hateful door, looking back at her.
"Girl, come."
"No Hornsby, please," Madelaine begs. Tears fall to wet her cheeks. "I'm sorry I left the room. I won't do it again. Please, don't put me back in the dark."
His expression changes the barest amount, his lips tightening and his eyes hardening.
"Girl, go in." He motions to the open door of the dark room.
Madelaine takes an instinctive step backwards, itching to run, and he takes a step towards her, filling her nose with his unpleasant earthy smell. She feels threatened and trapped.
"He smells kind of like old compost, like he is half dead," she thinks, the odor cloying but not overpowering.
A low growl comes from Mocha at Hornsby's movement towards Madelaine.

"There is no way out, nowhere to go," Madelaine thinks wretchedly.

Mocha stands uncertainly watching them both, tail tucked between her legs.

Feeling her already dark world crashing in on her, Madelaine takes those unsteady steps forward. She has to will her feet to move with each step. A chill fills her and she starts trembling.

The old man between her and the door is everything that is bad in the world; her nightmares and her sorrow.

She stays as far from him as she can, obediently stepping back inside her dark prison.

Hornsby grasps the door and starts swinging it shut.

Madelaine panics, filled with terror of being locked in there again; in the dark alone.

Her eyes focus on Mocha. The little dog is staring at her from across the room.

"No Hornsby, please!" she cries.

Madelaine lunges for the door as it swings shut.

"Mocha!"

Mocha bolts for Madelaine, just making it through the narrowing space of the closing door. She jumps at Madelaine and Madelaine catches her in her arms as the door thuds closed.

Madelaine stands there staring at the utter blackness that was a doorway, swallowed up by the fear and pain and loss of that small taste of freedom that is now gone.

The latch locking sounds loud in the silence of that dark room.

Dropping Mocha to the floor, Madelaine rushes forward, crashing into the door in the dark, pounding her fists on it and kicking it.

"Hornsby! Please Hornsby, please! Don't do this! Don't leave me here like this, in the dark! Hornsby, please!" She screams it over and over.

Finally, her hands and feet in pain from kicking and pounding the door and exhausted from the effort, Madelaine stumbles blindly back to the far corner of the little room and sinks to the floor.

"No Hornsby, please," she whispers, her voice rough and hoarse from screaming.

Mocha skulks to her, climbing in her lap and laying there huddled and shivering while Madelaine sobs softly over and over.

"No Hornsby, please."

Caroline is sitting in the folding chair in front of the empty fire. The darkness fills her soul as much as it does the night sky.

"Both my girls are gone, maybe forever. I know the odds. They try to keep it from me. It's a large forest, and Madelaine doesn't even have a jacket or shoes. If they haven't found any sign of them yet, they probably won't find them. Not alive.

Ranger Davis Morgan and the other park rangers found nothing. Not a single sign of either girl. Not even the dog."

She closes her eyes against the pain filling her, opening them again to her empty desolation.

"No, that's not right. They did find Zoe's trail, but then lost it. How could they lose it?"

Knowing they were that close to finding Zoe feels like losing her all over again. Her heart aches with the loss of her girls and fear of not knowing what happened to them.

"Are they still alive? Are they injured somewhere?"

She stares at the empty fire pit, staring at nothing, feeling nothing but the emptiness of a sorrow so deep it has no bottom, no end.

They all left her alone all day. Everyone, while they were out searching the forest for the girls.

"Someone has to be here in case the girls come back," she whispers to herself, trying to give reason to her having to stay behind and failing. The same reason that keeps being repeated to her until she wants to scream at them all to stop. She cannot justify it to herself, no matter what. She feels she is letting Madelaine and Zoe down by not helping look for them, like she is somehow abandoning them.

"Mocha even, in case she comes back, someone has to be here."

Caroline both hates them all for leaving her here alone, Clive, the rangers, and the other searchers, and is relieved by it. She cannot take one more expression of pity, one look, one single word.

Exhausted, Clive had crawled into the tent when he came back from searching for the girls. He had been out searching with the others all day and well into the night, leaving Caroline alone in her misery at the campsite.

She can feel him in the tent behind her. His presence feels cloying, unwanted. Unwelcome.

Despite the late hour he returned, Caroline still feels anger and resentment towards him that he could even think to give up searching. She knows it is for the best. They need to come back and get some rest so they can keep searching. She knows that it is too dark to continue. But he still stopped searching for her girls.

Clive lies there in the tent, unable to sleep, listening to the night sounds and feeling Caroline's presence outside like an unwelcoming physical force.

"I need so badly to go to her," he thinks, "to hold her and tell her everything is going to be okay. I need it as much for me as for her. I need someone to be strong for me right now and tell me everything is going to be okay."

Clive lets the empty hollowness of loss fill him. He is so full of loss and sorrow that he cannot stand it. He needs someone to hold him and tell him they will find Madelaine and Zoe safe and sound, that his girls are okay.

He thinks about Caroline.

"She is so distant. She blames me for the girls getting lost. Of course she does, I blame me. I should have been a better father, a better husband."

He swallows in the dark, trying to not make a sound. He can't stop the tears that come, the clenching of his throat, and the pressure behind his eyes.

"I don't know if we can survive this. I am terrified our marriage will not survive this, that I will lose Caroline too."

Caroline feels a presence behind her. A sudden chill. She does not want to turn around.

"There is nothing there," she tells herself silently.

"Mommy?"

The voice is so small.

Slowly, Caroline turns, afraid. "What if I'm imagining it?" she thinks. "What if it's a dream?"

Standing there looking so small and tired is Zoe.

She blinks, unable to believe it.

"Zoe," she breathes.

23   Madelaine's Fate

Madelaine's eyes are swollen from crying and sore from trying to peer through the absolute blackness of her prison cell. She is huddled in the corner, wrapped in the blanket and gripping Mocha as if she might be torn from her arms at any moment in the darkness. She is still wearing only the nightgown she wore the night she was stolen from the tent where she slept with her family. She doesn't remember when she stopped trying to wish on that stone.

She could not remember seeing the blanket and lantern when Hornsby locked her back in the tiny room. When Madelaine finally crawled away from the wall she was huddled against to look for the blanket, she found it with relief. She knocked over the lantern groping for the blanket, spilling its oil on the floor and blanket.

The lantern now sits on the floor, useless, in a puddle of oil. She has nothing to light it with. Even if she did, she would be too scared to light a match or lighter, afraid she might set herself on fire with the spilled oil.

The room smells foul, overriding the oil soaked into the blanket. Both Madelaine and Mocha had to use the bathroom in the long hours they have been locked in. Madelaine managed to find the bucket in the corner and used it. The little dog tried valiantly to hold it, being trained only to do her business outside. Unable to hold it any more, she first peed then released her bowels in the little room. Mocha sulked and moped afterwards, expecting to be scolded and seeming embarrassed about the situation.

"I wish I was dead," Madelaine thinks miserably. "If I'm dead I won't have to be here anymore, hungry and thirsty and scared in the dark." It is the only thought she can muster now, over and over.

Mocha squirms in Madelaine's grip. She needs to move after staying motionless for Madelaine for so many hours. She is anxious with the need to run around and burn off the energy filling her.

The little dog freezes. Her head snaps to stare towards the door she cannot see in the darkness.

A shiver trembles through her, alerting Madelaine that something is wrong.

Madelaine grips Mocha tighter, a surge of panic rushing through her. She stares at where she thinks the door is.

"What it is Mocha? Did you hear something?" she whispers. Her voice is a dry croak, her throat and tongue dry and swollen. Her body has been screaming with thirst for hours. She had to repeatedly stop the thirsty dog from trying to drink the spilled oil, then later felt the craving to drink it herself, her body desperate with thirst.

A low growl comes from Mocha.

Madelaine stiffens more.

"He's back, isn't he?" She is filled with both fear and relief.

The latch unlocking is loud in the silence, startling her with a new rush of panic although she half expected it. She also half feared that door would never be opened again and she and Mocha would die in the dark in this tiny room.

With a dull thud and the squeal of its hinges, the door swings open to reveal the familiar form of Hornsby in his long robe, head as always invisible beneath the deep hood.

The light from the open door reveals the lantern and its spilled oil, and a dirty and disheveled wild eyed girl huddled in a blanket in the corner gripping her dog, the small dog's lips pulled up to reveal sharp little teeth.

Mocha gives a warning bark.

Hornsby's gnarled hand holds the door.

"Come, Little Kitten," he rasps.

It takes Madelaine a moment to think and realize, and another moment to digest the command.

The old man waits patiently while Madelaine tries to command her muscles to move. Still gripping Mocha, Madelaine gets stiffly to her feet, hunched over, and shuffles towards the door as if she were the old man. She squints her eyes against the unaccustomed to light.

Hornsby swings the door wide open and steps back, giving her room when she reaches the doorway.

Madelaine entertains the thought that he is as afraid of her as she is of him. Like her and spiders. The thought is fleeting and gone.

Madelaine licks her cracked lips, trying to make them move, to talk.

"Eat," Hornsby says, motioning towards the same little table she ate at before.

"How many days ago was that?" Madelaine wonders. She looks at Hornsby and looks away. She doesn't want to look at him. She is angry at him for locking her back in that little room. She is terrified of him, that he is going to kill her. Or worse, leave her to die in that little room.

Madelaine stumbles to the little table, falling into the seat weakly. She looks at the food, the goblet of water. Her stomach churns sickly. As desperate for food and water as she is, she can't make herself eat.

"Eat Little Kitten," Hornsby says.

Tears stream down Madelaine's face. She didn't think she was capable. She felt too dry. Too dehydrated.

Madelaine looks at Mocha, who is shivering in her lap and staring intently at the food.

She reaches a shaking hand and picks up a piece, giving it to Mocha.

Mocha almost snaps her fingers in her eagerness over the food. She gobbles it so fast her teeth don't touch it.

Madelaine is reaching for another when Hornsby grunts. She looks at him and he points to a plate and bowl on the floor. He did not forget about Mocha.

She puts Mocha on the floor and the little dog is hungrily devouring the food and lapping the water, emptying both before Madelaine turns back to her plate.

Her stomach still churning sourly, Madelaine picks at her food. She almost throws up when she guzzles the water.

"You left me in there," Madelaine says, her voice still a weak croak.

"Little Kitten must do what Hornsby tells her."

"I left the room. That's all. Did that deserve to be locked in there and left to die?"

"Little Kitten did not die."

"I could. Next time. You left me in there too long. You didn't come back. You didn't feed me or give me water."

Hornsby motions to her plate with a gnarled finger. He did feed her.

"Why? Why did you put me back in there?"

Hornsby shakes his head.

"Hornsby. Little Kitten make Hornsby angry. Do not do that again. Hornsby-," he pokes at his head, "bad temper." He shrugs.

"Where is Zoe? What did you do with my sister?" Madelaine asks. "Is she in a dark little room too?"

He shakes his head.

"Little Sister gone."

Madelaine's eyes widen and her mouth drops open. Her face twists with pain.

"You killed her?"

"Gone home. Little Sister with Momma."

Madelaine is trembling. She blinks back the tears, feeling dizzy with disbelief.

"You- you sent her home?" she chokes. "I want to go home too. Please Hornsby, I want to go home."

Hornsby looks at her for a long moment.

"Little Kitten stay. Be vamp pyre."

Madelaine's chin quivers.

"I don't want to be a vampire. I want to go home. I don't want to die. Don't kill me Hornsby, please."

"Come Little Kitten."

"Where?" Madelaine's lip trembles.

"Room."

She looks at the dark little room, panicked.

Hornsby turns and starts walking, but he does not go to the door of her little prison. He goes to the other door. He stops there and looks back.

"Little Kitten. Come."

Madelaine gets shakily to her feet and follows him.

"Are you taking me to the other room?"

"Yes, bed chamber. Little Kitten sleep. Then vamp pyre."

She almost stumbles, staring at him.

"You- you are going to kill me now?" she chokes the words out with fresh tears.

Hornsby waves her words off.

"When?" Madelaine chokes.

"Moons. Many moons."

Madelaine swallows, trying to understand.

"He's going to keep me a prisoner here for months?"

A shimmer of hope grows deep inside her.

"That could give me time to find a way out," she thinks, "or for Mom and Dad to find me."

24   Zoe is Back

Caroline stares at Zoe, a ghostly specter standing in the dark at the edge of her sight in the darkness. She is terrified that any movement, any sound, and the vision will vanish. That she will wake from this dream and Zoe will not be there.

Her Zoe, who they have been looking for, searching the campground and forest, afraid she is injured, dead, or lost forever in the forest, is back.

Just like that.

"Zoe?" she whispers.

"Mommy," Zoe says again, her voice as tiny as that first tentative sound.

Zoe takes a step towards her and crumples on the ground.

Caroline is out of her chair before she realizes it and scooping Zoe up, kneeling and gripping her tight.

"Clive!" Caroline shrieks.

The fear and strain in her voice has Clive in motion before she stops screaming his name. Leaping from the tent he is looking around for some threat, his mind conjuring a bear or some other animal in the campsite.

"It's Zoe!"

Caroline's voice has his attention on them immediately. His mind is numb. He stares at his wife clutching their youngest child. Zoe isn't moving.

Without thought, he lunges at them, pulling Zoe away from her mother's arms and turning away with her. He is frantically checking her. Is she breathing? Is she alive? Hurt?

Caroline stares at him mutely, shoved out of the way and feeling abandoned in her own desperate need to know Zoe is okay. She blinks back the tears and swallows.

"She's breathing," she says quietly. Clive doesn't hear her.

Zoe's eyes blink open, looking exhausted.

"Are you okay?" Clive asks. "Zoe, are you hurt? Can you talk?"

Zoe shakes her head.

Caroline wants to rush in there, to hold her daughter and reassure herself that she's okay. She can only wait on the outside looking in, feeling like she would only be pushed away again. It's what everyone has done to her since Madelaine disappeared.

"Are you hurt Zoe?" Clive asks again. "Where are you hurt?"

"I'm not hurt," Zoe says, trying to sit up. She has to squirm and push him away to get enough room.

"Where were you?" Clive asks. "How did you get back?"

She looks at him then at her mom.

"I was with Madelaine," she says.

They both stare at her in numb shock.

"You were with her?" Caroline looks around, hoping desperately to see Madelaine. "Where is she? Where is Madelaine?"

"With the man," Zoe says.

Clive and Caroline look at each other with matching shock.

"What man?" Clive asks. Their focus is now intently on Zoe.

"Out there." Zoe points away from the campsite.

"Did he find you? Rescue you? Where is Madelaine? Why isn't she with you?"

"He found me and took me to Madelaine."

"So where is she?" Caroline's voice goes up an octave with stress.

"Out there. I don't know." Tears shimmer in Zoe's eyes. "He's keeping her."

Clive stiffens. Caroline grabs his arm, squeezing hard. He looks at her.

"We have to contact the ranger and the police," Clive says.

Caroline nods.

"What man is this?" Clive asks Zoe carefully.

"An old man," Zoe says.

"I'm very tired," Zoe says. She looks dead on her feet with exhaustion.

"Come, lie down while we wait for the ranger," Caroline says.

Caroline takes her into the tent, tucking her into her sleeping bag. She doesn't want to leave Zoe, but she has to. The thought is burning inside her head, threatening to devour her with its terrible heat. "What if Zoe vanishes again when she's out of my sight?"

Zoe's eyes flutter closed and her breathing slows.

Caroline gets up to leave, but Zoe's quiet voice stops her at the door.

"It's going to be okay, Mommy. Mocha is with Madelaine."

Caroline looks back at her, but Zoe's eyes are closed as if she is asleep.

She leaves the tent and does not see Clive at first. He walked to the entrance of the campsite to talk on the phone out of Zoe's hearing.

Caroline rushes to him, staring at him as he talks on the phone. He hangs up and looks at her with a pained expression of loss and remorse. Caroline's own expression reflects that and is filled with fear.

"You told him about the man?"

"Yes," Clive says heavily. He sounds defeated, lost.

"Clive," what if he's back?" Caroline stares up at him, horror stricken. "What if he's out and he took her again?"

"It's not possible," Clive says, trying to reassure her. "He's locked away for a very long time. She is just lost in the forest."

He looks into her eyes.

"Davis doesn't think there was a man. If anyone found either of the girls, he wouldn't return one and not the other. Davis said he's heard the same thing before, someone who was lost talking about the old man in the forest. He said there is no old man; that it's probably a tree or rock formation they imagined was a man. The mind plays tricks when you are under great stress."

His own words are not reassuring to him. Caroline has planted the seed of doubt in his mind. What if he was somehow released, or escaped?

"Lost in the forest," he thinks. "What has become of us that the thought of our daughter only being lost in the forest, where every minute out there she is in danger, is a relief?"

His eyes cloud.

"What became of us is we survived our daughter falling to the depravity of a sick monster and got back what is left of her to try to piece together," he thinks.

"We'll be fine," Clive says. "We will find her again and she will be safe."

Caroline looks up at him, her heart breaking and her eyes filled with fear and doubt.

"Do you think she could have run away again?"

"To go find him and be with him? After what he did? No. Not our Madelaine."

"But, she did once, after-." Caroline breaks off in a choked sob.

"Madelaine was messed up. After what he did to her, she wasn't thinking right. She's had hours of counselling, therapy. She isn't the same now. She wouldn't."

A flicker of doubt dances in Clive's mind. "Would she?"

"She isn't the same as she was before," Caroline says softly, her voice full of the anguish of a mother unable to protect her baby. "She will never be the same."

Clive moves closer, putting his hands on her shoulders. They slide down her arms, wrapping around her. She leans against him. For the first time since Madelaine disappeared from the tent, she lets Clive hold her.

They stand there taking what strength they can from each other.

"We will find her," Clive says. "We won't give up until we do."

Madelaine is leaning on the open window of the bed chamber staring out at the sea of trees below. The night sky is peaceful, filled with pinpricks of light and a large sallow moon.

No breeze disturbs the still air.

Behind her Mocha makes a sneezing sound; her way of getting attention.

Madelaine turns and looks down at the little dog. Her eyes hold a deep unhappiness.

Mocha chuffs at her. A little bark.

"You want to walk the halls," Madelaine says. Her voice matches her eyes, quietly sad.

Mocha shakes her head.

"Okay, let's go."

They walk to the bed chamber door. Just as Madelaine is reaching for the handle, Mocha's body posture stiffens and she bares her teeth with a low growl. She can smell the putrid stench of wrongness and withheld decay through the door.

Madelaine looks down at her and opens the door, looking up at the age-wrinkled face.

"Hi Hornsby."

END

Zoe to the Rescue

Book 2: The Wishing Stone Series

1   Zoe is Back

Caroline stares at Zoe in the blackness engulfing the campsite, a ghostly specter standing in the dark at the edge of her sight in the darkness. She is terrified that any movement, any sound, and the vision will vanish. That she will wake from this dream and Zoe will not be there.

Her Zoe, who they have been looking for, searching the campground and forest, afraid she is injured, dead, or lost forever in the forest, is back.

Just like that.

"Zoe?" she whispers.

"Mommy," Zoe says again, her voice as tiny as that first tentative sound.

Zoe takes a step towards her and crumples on the ground.

Caroline is out of her chair by the fire pit before she realizes it and scooping Zoe up, kneeling and gripping her tight.

"Clive!" Caroline shrieks. "Clive! It's Zoe!"

The fear and strain in her voice has Clive in motion before she stops screaming his name. He scrambles out of the sleeping bag at the first sound of Caroline's voice crying out his name. He fumbles with the zipper, tearing the fabric in his rush to escape the tent, tripping on the zipper and stumbling out of the tent

He looks around for some threat, his mind conjuring a bear or some other animal in the campsite.

"What! Caroline!"

He staggers a few steps from the tent and freezes, his exhaustion playing tricks on him.

"For a moment I thought I heard Caroline say Zoe is here," he thinks, his mind racing and muddled at once. He rubs his face wearily. "I thought I saw her hugging Zoe."

"It's Zoe!" Caroline cries out again.

Caroline's voice has his attention on them immediately. His mind is numb. He stares at his on the ground wife clutching their youngest child. Zoe isn't moving.

Clive's eyes widen in disbelief and he stumbles forward, so exhausted he can barely walk, eyes blurred and head heavy and stuffed with cotton. He is filled with the stiffly draining after effects of grueling days of stress and fear, searching for his lost daughters. It buzzes through him, just as it has since Madelaine vanished, making it impossible to do more than doze in and out of sleep and keeping him up at night.

Clive rubs his eyes, trying to shake the sleep off.

"Caroline?" His voice is confused, worried.

She turns to him, still clinging desperately to Zoe.

Wordlessly, Zoe clings to her as if afraid something will come from the trees and snatch her away. Her face is etched with exhaustion, stress, and fear; her eyes closed as though she cannot wake.

"Clive, Zoe came back." Caroline's voice is almost pleading.

Clive feels the world crash in on him. All the distant muffled sounds of the forest at night suddenly pound in his ears; the crackling of a campfire somewhere and the whispered strained words of the people sitting around it, also stressed and unable to sleep after the past days.

He hears the rustle of something in the bushes.

Caroline's face, wet with tears and aged with the strain of her sorrow, comes whooshing into focus, clear and large. The hope in her eyes. She is staring at him with such hope that it breaks his heart.

And Zoe. "Zoe, can it be real? Is she really there?" he thinks, afraid to trust his eyes, to hope for the improbable.

"Zoe," he manages and rushes forward, needing to touch her, to feel her for himself so that he can know it is true.

Without thought, he lunges at them, pulling Zoe away from her mother's arms and turning away with her. He is frantically checking her.

"Is she breathing? Is she alive? Hurt?" he thinks frantically.

Caroline stares at him mutely, shoved out of the way and feeling abandoned in her own desperate need to know Zoe is okay. She blinks back the tears and swallows.

"She's breathing," she says quietly. Clive doesn't hear her.

Zoe's eyes blink open, looking exhausted.

"Daddy," Zoe says so quietly only he hears, her voice still very small.

"Are you okay?" Clive asks. "Zoe, are you hurt? Can you talk?"

Zoe shakes her head.

"Where were you?" Clive asks. "How did you get back?"

She looks at him then at her mom and back at him.

"I was with Madelaine," she says.

They both stare at her in numb shock.

"You were with her?" Caroline looks around, hoping desperately to see Madelaine. "Where is she? Where is Madelaine?"

"With the man," Zoe says.

Clive and Caroline look at each other with matching shock.

"What man?" Clive asks. Their focus is now intently on Zoe.

"Out there." Zoe points away from the campsite.

"Did he find you? Rescue you? Where is Madelaine? Why isn't she with you?"

"He found me and took me to Madelaine."

"So where is she?" Caroline's voice goes up an octave with stress.

"Out there." Tears shimmer in Zoe's eyes. "She's dead Daddy. Madelaine is dead. The man killed her."

She throws her arms around him gripping him tightly around the neck. Clive holds her tight, barely believing she is really there while Zoe keeps repeating those same words over and over.

"She's dead Daddy. Madelaine is dead. The man killed her."

Clive wakes up with a start, sitting bolt upright in bed, his heart pounding and his body drenched with sweat.

One thought pounds through him with his racing heart. Zoe is gone.

It takes a painfully long time for where he is to register. He is in a tent, in a sleeping bag by himself.

The soft sound of sleep breathing is the only sound besides his own rustling movement.

Blinking in the darkness, Clive looks around, feeling panic surging. He sees them. Caroline, in her own sleeping bag now separate from his, huddled up against Zoe in hers. He can see both their heads. They are both still there.

He can't help it. He looks at Madelaine's sleeping bag, as empty as the hollow hole inside him.

He swallows, trying not to cry.

"Don't cry. Be strong for them," he thinks, fighting the pain growing inside him.

Other books by Vivian Munnoch:

<u>Latchkey Kids Series:</u>

The Latchkey Kids

What would you do if you came home from school alone and heard noises in the basement?

Five kids, twelve and thirteen years old and on their own before and after school, each faces their own struggle. A broken home, illness, crushes, bullying, depression, absent parents, suicidal thoughts, broken friendships, and fears of being only a kid and home alone.

Madison, Andrew, Kylie, Anna, and Dylan are brought together by circumstances that feel overwhelmingly out of their control. The temptation of exploring an old abandoned brick building, loneliness, and fleeing an attempted abduction, each is drawn to the old abandoned building for different reasons.

There, they will fight for their lives, where the monsters in the basement nest.

The Latchkey Kids: The Disappearance of Willie Gordon

Spring break is over and, still in shock from the events of the night of the fire; the kids are forced back into everyday life as if nothing happened. But it did happen. And it is happening again.

While the kids try to come to terms with what happened the night of the fire at the abandoned factory, nothing in their lives seems to have changed when everything feels like it did.

A broken home, illness, crushes, bullying, depression, absent parents, suicidal thoughts, they all continue as before.

Amber Shaw returns to school and the Mean Team is broken up, but will it last?

Everything is back to normal. Right?

And then Willie Gordon vanishes.

While new jealousies burn, problems kept secret are revealed and Joshua joins the group after his sister committed suicide, the group feels they are the only ones who can find Willie. Nobody believes them the monsters are real.

The kids have to face the monsters again, in the basements where they nest.

<u>Wishing Stone Series:</u>

Madelaine & Mocha

It started with a walk in the woods.

Madelaine and her family are on a boring, no electronics and thank you very much for ruining my life, camping trip that changes Madelaine and her life forever.

First, her little dog Mocha is lost in the forest. Then Madelaine vanishes from their tent without a trace in the night. Everyone assumes she snuck out to look for Mocha.

Madelaine wakes in the dark, dressed only in her nightgown, with no idea how she got where she is, locked in a small room.

While searchers comb the forest looking for her, Madelaine is trying to figure out how to escape and return to her family. But they will never look in the right place.

Only her little dog Mocha knows what really happened to Madelaine.

About the Author

Vivian Munnoch is a Canadian author, a member of the Manitoba Writers' Guild, the Horror Writers Association, and Authors of Manitoba.

Vivian grew up with a love of the darker side; sneaking down to the basement at night to watch the old horror B movies, devouring books by horror authors, and has always had a passion for books and the idea of creating stories and worlds a person can get lost in since reading that first novel.

This love of storytelling has this author working writing and editing into a busy life that includes a full time job, family, and doing the little things to help the writing community including offering encouragement to others in the online writing community and volunteering time helping with the Manitoba Writers' Guild Facebook presence, proofreading for the HWA newsletter, and visiting schools for I Love to Read month.

Vivian Munnoch currently lives in Winnipeg with two rescue dogs, spouse, and kids.

Follow Vivian Munnoch:
Facebook:
https://www.facebook.com/VivianMunnoch.author/
Twitter: @VivianMunnoch
Wordpress: https://vivianmunnoch.wordpress.com/

Madelaine & Mocha

The Wishing Stone Series Book 1

Madelaine thought things could not possibly get worse when her parents dragged her out on a boring, no electronics and thank you very much for ruining my life, camping trip.

Then Mocha, her American Cocker Spaniel and currently her only reason for getting through each day, is lost in the forest. Their attempts to find the dog are futile and Madelaine is devastated.

A local boy, Geoffrey, joins Madelaine in her search, promising to not give up and showing her the beauty of the forest.

Then, Madelaine's family wakes up to find her gone, vanished from the tent in the night wearing only her nightgown.

Madelaine wakes in the dark, locked in a small room with no idea how she got there.

The prisoner of a strange old man, Madelaine begs for escape, even in death. But she knew death once. Almost. It was not the blissful drifting off asleep she imagined it would be. It was agonizing and ugly.

The old man's reason for kidnapping her is nothing she could have ever imagined. Madelaine keeps her hope up by wishing on a stone. Playing wishing games will not be enough to free her and escape her fate.